D0171457

PRAISE FOR DONNA GRANT'S
BESTSELLING ROMANCE NOVELS

"Time travel, ancient legends, and seductive romance are seamlessly interwoven into one captivating package."
    —*Publishers Weekly* on Midnight's Master

"Dark, sexy, magical. When I want to indulge in a sizzling fantasy adventure, I read Donna Grant."
    —Allison Brennan, *New York Times* bestseller

5 Stars! Top Pick! "An absolute must read! From beginning to end, it's an incredible ride."
    —*Night Owl Reviews*

"It's good vs. evil Druid in the next installment of Grant's Dark Warrior series. The stakes get higher as discerning one's true loyalties become harder. Grant's compelling characters and continued presence of previous protagonists are key reasons why these books are so gripping. Another exciting and thrilling chapter!"
    —*RT Book Reviews* on Midnight's Lover

"Donna Grant has given the paranormal genre a burst of fresh air..."
    —*San Francisco Book Review*

DON'T MISS THESE OTHER SPELLBINDING
NOVELS BY DONNA GRANT

CONTEMPORARY PARANORMAL

REAPER SERIES

Dark Alpha's Claim

Dark Alpha's Embrace

Dark Alpha's Demand

Dark Alpha's Lover

Tall Dark Deadly Alpha Bundle

Dark Alpha's Night

Dark Alpha's Awakening (2019)

DARK KINGS

Dark Heat (3 novella compilation)

Darkest Flame

Fire Rising

Burning Desire

Hot Blooded

Night's Blaze

Soul Scorched

Dragon King (novella)

Passion Ignites

Smoldering Hunger

Smoke and Fire

Dragon Fever (novella)

Firestorm

Blaze

Dragon Burn

Constantine: A History (short story)

Heat

Torched

Dragon Night (novella)

Dragonfire

Dragon Claimed (January 2019)

Ignite (April 2019)

DARK WARRIORS

Midnight's Master

Midnight's Lover

Midnight's Seduction

Midnight's Warrior

Midnight's Kiss

Midnight's Captive

Midnight's Temptation

Midnight's Promise

Midnight's Surrender (novella)

Dark Warrior Box Set

Forbidden Highlander

Wicked Highlander

Untamed Highlander

Shadow Highlander

Darkest Highlander

Dark Sword Box Set

ROGUES OF SCOTLAND

The Craving

The Hunger

The Tempted

The Seduced

Rogues of Scotland Box Set

THE SHIELDS

A Dark Guardian

A Kind of Magic

A Dark Seduction

A Forbidden Temptation

A Warrior's Heart

DRUIDS GLEN

Highland Mist

Highland Nights

Highland Dawn

Highland Fires

Highland Magic

SISTERS OF MAGIC

Shadow Magic

Echoes of Magic

Dangerous Magic

Sisters of Magic Boxed Set

THE ROYAL CHRONICLES NOVELLA SERIES

Prince of Desire

Prince of Seduction

Prince of Love

Prince of Passion

Royal Chronicles Box Set

MILITARY ROMANCE / ROMANTIC SUSPENSE

SONS OF TEXAS

The Hero

The Protector

The Legend

EVERBOUND

THE KINDRED

DONNA GRANT

This is a work of fiction. All of the characters, organizations, and events portrayed in this novel are either products of the author's imagination or are used fictitiously.

EVERBOUND
© 2018 by DL Grant, LLC
Excerpt from *Thieves* copyright © Lexi Blake
Cover Design © 2018 by Charity Hendry

ISBN 10: 1635765528
ISBN 13: 9781635765526
Available in ebook and print editions

All rights reserved, including the right to reproduce or transmit this book, or a portion thereof, in any form or by any means, electronic or mechanical, without permission in writing from the author. This book may not be resold or uploaded for distribution to others. Thank you for respecting the hard work of this author.

www.DonnaGrant.com
www.MotherofDragonsBooks.com

The bite of winter was cruel and exacting. Helena didn't pay any heed to the snowfall as she put one foot in front of the other. She kept moving from one place to the next, always checking to see if any witches from the Coven were about.

She'd run across two in the weeks since the Staff of the Eternal had been found. Helena hadn't hesitated to dispatch both witches. It was bad enough that the Coven had the staff, but more worrying was the fact that all three elders were dead.

And Sybbyl had taken over.

Helena paused next to the river she followed and looked at the path ahead. There was a forest, which would allow her to find a spot to rest. Nightfall was a few hours away, but she was tired of sleeping out in the open, and so exhausted she didn't think she could remain on her feet much longer. The idea of having the cover of trees was too good to pass up.

With a tug on the hood of her cloak to keep out the snow, she continued onward. It would be so easy to use magic to conceal herself, but all that would do was signal Sybbyl as to where she was.

Helena knew she would have to battle Sybbyl. As soon as the witch claimed the staff, Helena had reconciled that fact. But she would get to pick the time and place.

Twice she'd faced the Coven. The third—and final—time would most likely end in her death. Helena didn't face anyone unless the odds were in her favor.

And she was going to make certain of that fact when it came to Sybbyl.

The snow began to fall so thickly that she could barely see her hand in front of her face by the time she reached the forest. The trees and their numerous branches helped to shield her from the onslaught of snow.

Helena took refuge in the gnarled limbs of an ancient oak. She huddled in her cloak, hungry, cold, and alone. Part of her wanted to find the witch hunters.

They had helped her escape the Coven's clutches once. She'd repaid that debt by saving one of them. They had asked her to join them in their fight. A few years ago, she wouldn't have hesitated. Yet now, she found it nearly impossible to trust anyone.

She weighed her distrust with the facts. The Coven elders had been formidable when the three stood together, and Helena never could have bested them if she faced them alone.

However, now there was only Sybbyl. Yet that didn't make Helena's job easier. Sybbyl had killed the last elder, then took the Staff of the Eternal. That in itself made Helena hesitate to confront the witch alone.

But someone had to.

If not, the Coven would continue to grow in power. Their goal was to find the scattered bones of the First Witch and reassemble her. The Coven had lost out on the Blood Skull. Thankfully, the Hunters had that safely in their possession.

With each group having one item from the First Witch, it nearly put them on equal footing. Somewhat. The witches still had magic. Though Helena had witnessed firsthand the skill of the Hunters.

They had taken out many Coven witches. But not enough. Not nearly enough.

The Coven sought out witches, giving them the option to join their ranks or die. Helena had chosen death when the Hunter appeared in the Witch's Grove and freed her.

Many, many other witches had also preferred death over joining the Coven. But the vast majority joined the Coven because they didn't want to die.

While Helena wanted to fight the Coven, she knew she couldn't do it by herself. And no witch would join her, for they mistrusted as deeply as she did, fearing that it was a ploy by the Coven to get them out of hiding.

That left Helena only two options. Continue on her own.

Or find the Hunters.

She dropped her forehead to her knees. Her eyes closed as she let her memories take her back to happier times. Of a time when life had been simpler, a time when she hadn't feared anything or anyone.

The jingle of a bridle snapped her head up. She blinked, only vaguely realizing that while she had been deep in her memories, she had fallen asleep. She had no idea how long she slept. It was still light out, but the heavy clouds and thick trees made it difficult to tell where the sun was in the sky.

She leaned back against the trunk of the tree and listened for another sound. For endless moments, there was nothing. Just the silence of a winter wood. She was beginning to think she'd imagined the jangle when she heard a horse blow out a breath.

Cautiously, Helena peered around the tree and saw two men setting up camp about a hundred yards from her. She sighed in frustration and turned away. Now, she'd have to hear them talking all night.

She closed her eyes again and tried to sleep, but despite her eyes hurting from lack of rest, she couldn't. It wasn't long before the crackle of a fire reached her. Helena was able to ignore the thought of the warmth right until she smelled something cooking.

Her mouth watered, and her stomach grumbled just thinking about food. The last thing she had eaten was a piece of stale bread she'd stolen the night before. The fact that she could solve her problems with magic but didn't dare for fear of alerting the Coven made it even more difficult to bear.

The hours stretched by as the sun set and darkness fell over the land like a thick blanket. And the snow continued to fall. The men laughed and talked and ate as if they didn't have a care in the world.

Helena dozed, but every little sound the men made woke her. She was attempting to find a more comfortable position when a woman's voice reached her. She stilled, trying to hear the conversation.

When she couldn't stand it any longer, Helena leaned around the tree to take a look. Her blood went cold when she saw the yellow-orange magic moving from the witch's palm towards the men.

One lay unmoving, but the other was handing over all his possessions while gazing at the witch as if she were an angel come down from Heaven.

There was no way Helena could sit there and allow the witch to get away with such behavior. It didn't matter if the woman was part of the Coven or not. Just because she had magic did not mean she could use it in such a fashion.

Helena rose and walked around the tree. As she did, she felt the rush of her magic run through her body. Her strides were long, her gaze locked on the witch.

As soon as Helena was close enough, she let the purple coils of her magic fly from one palm. Before they could strike, the witch leaned out of the way. The woman forgot the men as she shifted her attention to Helena.

"Do you have any idea who I am?" the witch demanded.

Helena lowered the hood of her cloak. "Not a whit."

"I'm part of the Coven. You will bow before me. Now."

There was a smile on Helena's face as she said, "Make me."

The witch peeled back her lips. The yellow-orange magic flew straight at Helena. With a wave of her hand, Helena blocked one blast, but the other slashed her across her upper left arm.

Helena ignored the pain as she lunged over one of the men and sent more coils of power toward the witch. And, once more, they were evaded.

When Helena was struck once again with the magic, she clenched her teeth and focused everything she had on the witch. This time, when her blast went for the woman, it sank into the witch's skin. She began to thrash and scream as she was burned from the inside out.

The witch turned to ash before she hit the ground. Helena then faced the men to find both of them watching her with fear in their eyes. She grabbed what remained of their meal and stalked off.

She had to get far away. The Coven tracked any witch not of their group who used magic. They would come for her, so she had to put as much distance between herself and the men as she could. Helena bit into the cold meat of the rabbit as she lifted her skirts in her other hand and trudged through the snow. She glanced behind her to find the newly fallen powder covering her tracks.

Helena didn't pause until the sun crested the horizon. The snowfall had finally halted, and the food in her belly helped to keep her on her feet. But what little energy she had was fast being depleted. She needed sleep. Even if it were just a few minutes.

She spotted a cave and headed toward it. Anything that got her out of the weather was a plus. Her teeth chattered uncontrollably by the time she stumbled inside the shelter. Though she desperately wanted a fire, she didn't have the wherewithal to find dry wood. And using magic was out of the question.

She huddled in a ball and tried to find warmth as her eyes slid closed of their own volition.

2

So much had changed.

And yet, so much stayed the same.

Jarin held his staff and squatted down as he studied the ground of a well-used road. His faithful falcon, Andi, gave a cry overhead. He didn't need to look to the trees on his left to know that his wolf, Valdr, stood waiting and watching.

As a Varroki warrior, Jarin's life was spent alone as he tracked down Coven members. Unlike his counterparts, he chose to have the animals with him.

The Varroki were descended from the First Witch, a Viking. Jarin's people had found one of the northernmost isles off the Scottish coast and made it theirs, combining their Viking heritage with that of the Celts. It was an unusual mix of cultures, but one that made his people strong.

For generations, they were responsible for keeping the Coven from gaining too much power. It wasn't an easy task, yet it was one he relished. He'd been born for this position. He was an excellent tracker and a powerful warlock. The exact combination needed for a Varroki warrior.

He hadn't even been put off by the fact that all warriors were celibate. It was the way of his people. And his position wasn't the only one that required such dedication.

Such strict rules had put the Varroki in a tenuous position with rapidly dwindling numbers, however. It was their new Lady—the one chosen to rule his people—who discovered that she had the ability to make changes.

And she did it without hesitation. Now, the rules for Jarin's position, along with any others that previously required celibacy, were reversed. He honestly didn't care one way or another. He had a job to do, and he was going to do it.

His searching gaze found what he was looking for. He leaned over and traced his finger along the imprint of a shoe. It was small—likely, a woman's. It was the only one he saw in the muck and mud of the road.

Jarin got to his feet and looked ahead. He'd been tracking Sybbyl since the witch had disappeared with the Staff of the Eternal. She used magic to move, which made it difficult to follow her.

But not impossible.

He moved into the forest with Valdr, using his staff as a walking stick, though it was much more than that. The wolf came up beside him, rubbing his head against Jarin's leg. He patted the animal absently.

"Where are you going?" he whispered, trying to figure out where Sybbyl was headed.

So far, the new Coven leader had zigzagged all over England. She would stay at a spot for half a day at most and then leave. It meant that Jarin was constantly moving. And continually one step behind her.

That's not how he liked to hunt. He needed to figure out where Sybbyl was going—and why. With the staff, she could do untold damage. But, oddly, she hadn't used it on others.

"Yet," he said.

His thoughts took him to the last time he'd seen Sybbyl. He'd been fighting alongside a nobleman named Carac, and his group of knights to help free one of the Hunters from Sybbyl's hold.

Everything had been in Sybbyl's favor. She hadn't counted on Jarin, though, and it helped to swing the tide of things away from her. But just when he believed they would save the Hunter *and* get the staff, Sybbyl managed to get her hands on it.

He should've reported back to Malene, the Lady of the Varroki, with all that he knew. It was his duty to keep her apprised of things. There was magic within Malene that was fiercer than anything he'd seen in the previous Ladies before her. Malene was different in many ways.

And she might just be what the Varroki needed to not only survive but also thrive.

If they could stop the Coven.

Jarin glanced down at Valdr and grinned. "Ready to run?"

The wolf panted, making it appear as if he were smiling. Jarin took off at a steady jog, while Valdr loped beside him. Above them, Andi followed.

After fifteen minutes, Jarin slowed when his instincts warned him there was something he needed to see. He stopped and looked at the road. The falcon dove into the trees and landed on a limb above him. The three of them remained silent as a cart drove past.

The horse threw up its head, snorting and dancing as it smelled Valdr. Jarin didn't need to tell the wolf to remain beside him. The animal knew.

Once the cart finally moved past, Jarin walked alone out onto the road. The snowfall from the day before left the ground icy. Frozen mud was great at collecting and holding tracks, but the amount of travel on the road stopped him from seeing whatever it was he'd sensed.

He glanced back the way he'd come before looking ahead. The road branched off to several locations. Sybbyl hadn't followed any roads before. So why now?

His gaze returned to the trees. There were Witch's Groves deep within the forests. It was a place witches went to perform ceremonies, but since it was sacred and kept anyone out that wasn't a witch, it was also a safe haven, of sorts, for them.

He made his way back to his animals. Something told him to remain right where he was. He felt no magic, had no inclination of what kept him there, but he stayed nonetheless.

Jarin sent Valdr off to hunt. Andi came and went as she pleased, but she stayed with him this time. He found a comfortable spot between the roots of a tree and sat, placing his staff beside him on the ground, his gaze moving from the road to the forest and back again.

Hours passed. The moon rose, and with it came Valdr. The wolf lay down beside him, resting his large head on Jarin's leg. Jarin sank his hands into Valdr's thick fur to pet the wolf.

Jarin was about to reach into his bag for some food when he felt it. *Magic.* Coven magic. He jumped to his feet, Valdr already facing the direction of the power in the air. Jarin never questioned how the animal sensed these things, and the wolf wasn't the only one. Andi did, as well.

The falcon spread her wings and flapped them once, her head swiveling to Jarin.

"Go," he urged her.

She jumped into the air and disappeared into the night. Jarin turned toward the magic when he was hit with another dose of it. Except this surge wasn't from a Coven witch.

He grabbed his staff and took off toward the witches. Valdr ran ahead of him, leaping over fallen trees and boulders.

The cold air Jarin sucked in as he ran filled his lungs, making them ache. But he didn't stop.

Nearly forty minutes later, he came upon the men sitting around a fire, seemingly unaware of the snow. Both of their faces were ashen with fear, and neither spoke. They kept looking at a spot on the other side of the fire. Jarin could just make out the pile of ash.

He walked out of the darkness, holding a hand toward Valdr to keep him out of sight. The men's heads jerked toward him. They scrambled to their feet.

Jarin studied them a moment. "What happened here?"

"Nothing," one replied.

The other swallowed, his gaze lowering to the ground.

Jarin pointed to the ash with his staff. "That is ash from a witch. Which of you will tell me what happened?"

"They were witches?" the second asked in a hoarse whisper.

"William," the first man chided.

But William ignored his friend when Jarin nodded his answer. The man licked his lips. "She came upon us out of nowhere. She made it so I couldn't move, but I saw everything. She had h-him."

"Stop," the other man said and turned away.

"The second woman came up from behind us," William continued. "She went straight for the first one, and the two fought. The newcomer killed the other with purple things that sank into the woman. It looked as if she burned up from the inside."

Jarin bowed his head at the men. "You were fortunate this night."

"She's hurt," the first man said, his back still to Jarin. "The second woman. She's hurt."

Jarin looked at the snow-covered ground that showed no

tracks. He spotted Valdr sniffing a tree. "Which way did she go?"

Both men pointed behind and to the left of Jarin. Without another word, he headed in that direction. Instantly, Valdr was by his side. The wolf had a scent, and he was pursuing it. It wasn't the first time the wolf had helped Jarin track someone, and no doubt it wouldn't be the last.

The duo moved swiftly over the land, with Andi calling out often from above. When dawn arrived, Jarin paused long enough to drink deeply from a stream. Valdr was next to him, lapping at the water, his gaze on the opposite bank, scanning for anything.

Jarin gave a nod to the wolf when he finished refreshing himself. They started off again. After two hours, Valdr suddenly stopped, his ears pricked forward, his gaze directly ahead.

Jarin put his hand on the animal and waited for Valdr to decide when to continue. There was much Jarin could do with magic, but animals saw and smelled the world differently. He trusted both Valdr and Andi with his life.

Finally, the wolf moved forward. He was cautious, stealthy, and Jarin made sure to act accordingly. When he caught sight of the rock formation, he realized that the witch must have gone there to tend to her wounds.

Valdr led the way to the opening of a cave. It was dark inside, no fire, and no embers. Jarin thought perhaps the witch had moved on, but the wolf's attention remained on something in the shelter.

Jarin walked forward. In five steps, he'd cleared the opening. It took a moment for his eyes to adjust. When they did, he saw Valdr lying next to a form huddled into a ball, shivering uncontrollably.

He inched closer as the wolf lay his head on the ground

and blinked. Jarin couldn't see much of anything about who the witch was with the way her dark brown cloak was pulled over her head.

That's when Jarin realized that the wolf was using his body heat to warm her. Whoever she was, she hadn't used any magic for a fire. If he didn't know she'd fought a Coven member, he might think that she didn't know how to use magic.

But the simple fact was...she did. And that meant she knew the Coven could track it, so she hadn't chanced using more.

He sighed and leaned his staff against the cave wall as he lowered himself to the ground. The Coven was unable to track Varroki magic as yet, so he didn't hesitate to start a fire.

It took hours before the woman stopped shivering. Even then, Valdr wouldn't leave her side. Andi was perched on a rock right at the entrance of the cave, and the falcon stared at the woman for a long time.

Jarin stretched out his legs and crossed his ankles. He'd known when he felt the Coven magic that it wasn't strong enough to be Sybbyl's, but he'd gone anyway. It was his duty to stop any Coven member. He hadn't expected to find a second witch.

Though he wasn't sure what he was going to do with her when she woke. The Varroki were secretive. They didn't make a habit of letting anyone—especially witches—know who they were. Sybbyl discerned that fact quickly in their battle.

Perhaps he should leave the witch. He and Valdr had warmed her. It was time to get back to tracking Sybbyl. It would take Jarin days to return to where he'd been and pick up her trail again.

His gaze slid to the wolf, who was sleeping with his body curled around the witch. Jarin had never seen Valdr react to anyone other than him in such a manner.

He climbed to his feet and grabbed his staff. But Valdr didn't rise. The wolf opened his yellow eyes and blinked at Jarin. His intention was clear. The wolf wasn't leaving the witch.

Jarin replaced his staff and lowered himself to the ground again. He wanted the witch to wake so he could discover whatever it was that Valdr had already sorted out.

There was the sound of a soft sigh as the witch finally moved. Her legs straightened, and her arm moved enough that Jarin thought he might see her face until he spotted the hood pulled up.

Jarin felt the bottom of her cloak that had a long way to go before drying out. He spotted the dirt and the frayed hem of the garment, and that's when it hit him.

The witch was running from the Coven. She'd had the wherewithal to fight one of its members, but she was smart enough to run instead of facing others that would inevitably come for her.

Jarin recalled the men saying that she was wounded. He reached for his staff, holding it over her while he sent magic through it with a spell to heal her. He set it aside once more when he was finished and eyed her.

He propped himself up with one hand. "Who are you?"

3

The moment Helena opened her eyes, she knew she wasn't alone. Just as that realization went through her, she discovered that she was no longer cold. Nor did she feel pain from her injury.

She shifted her head so she could see from beneath the hood of her cloak. Her eyes landed on a man who squatted beside her, staring at her with what looked like cold detachment in his pale blue eyes. Her eyes drifted to his shoulder-length blond hair that had the top half pulled away from his face.

He was startlingly handsome. His nearly white eyes were impossible to look away from once they had you in their hold. Then there was his square chin and jaw seemingly carved from granite that couldn't be hidden by his blond beard.

Sitting calmly on his arm was a peregrine falcon, who tilted its head to the side, studying her. And sitting beside her, watching her with unblinking large, yellow eyes, was a massive wolf with tawny brown fur.

Without a word, the man rose and walked to some rocks where he placed the bird. He spoke quietly to it, lovingly stroking the blue-gray feathers. Helena eyed the wolf, who remained next to her. Though he had given no indication of wanting to harm her, he was a wild animal. She inched up into a seated position and spotted the fire.

The man grabbed a staff she hadn't noticed and looked over his shoulder at the wolf. An unspoken message passed between human and animal, and then the man walked out of the cave.

No words, no look in her direction. Nothing.

Helena raised her brows, wondering if her mind might be breaking.

A moment later, the wolf rose and shook. When the large animal lay down again, he leaned against her before resting his head on his paws.

Whoever the stranger was, he'd had plenty of time to kill her. There was no telling how long he'd been there while she had slept. Exhaustion had taken her, and she hadn't been strong enough to fight it.

If the man hadn't harmed her, that meant he wanted something. Her first instinct was to run, but she was tired of it. Fighting the Coven witch had felt good. Right, even. It was what she should be doing.

She'd run because she had yet to be in a position where she felt as if she could win against a group of the Coven. Or worse, Sybbyl.

In a flurry of slate feathers, the falcon flew from the cave, leaving her alone with the wolf. Helena hesitantly rested her hand on the animal. When he didn't growl or move away, she began to slowly run her hands through his thick fur, marveling at the softness and the varied colors from black, brown and cream to white.

"Where's your pack?" she asked the wolf.

She yawned and shifted to a more comfortable position. With the warmth of the fire and the animal, there was an illusion of safety that had her becoming drowsy again.

It had been so long since she'd slept for longer than an hour or two, that now it was all her body wanted. That, and food. She wrinkled her nose at the idea of leaving the warmth of the cave to look for something to eat. That would have to wait. Right now, she was losing the battle against keeping her eyes open.

Helena yawned again. Her mind wandered, but it wasn't long before it returned to the handsome, silent stranger. Who was he? Where had he gone? When would he return?

And did she want him to?

More questions filled her mind as she drifted off to sleep.

The rumbling of her stomach pulled her awake. The smell of something roasting over the fire filled her nostrils, making her mouth water. She opened her eyes and saw four quail skewered on a spit. Apparently, she had slept through the stranger returning.

Her fingers curled, expecting to feel fur, but it was the wool of her cloak instead. She looked down to find the wolf gone.

"He went to eat."

Her head jerked toward the voice. The stranger sat in a shadowed corner, far from the fire. Though she couldn't see his face, she felt his gaze.

"He is quite taken with you," the man stated.

His voice was as smooth as velvet, the timbre deep and alarmingly sexy with the hint of an accent she couldn't quite place. She didn't want to like it.

Helena looked at the food before her gaze swung to the

cave entrance, gauging to see if she could make it before the man caught her.

"Leave," he said as if reading her thoughts.

Despite her unease, her eyes slid back to him. Helena had been toyed with before. This man knew nothing about her, and while he had animals who could kill her, she had magic—something he didn't know anything about.

"I have no intention of keeping you prisoner. You can leave at any time."

Oh, how she wanted to believe him. A part of her was tempted to see if she could leave without being stopped. But another part—the part that had been on the run for weeks, barely sleeping and rarely eating—wished to remain.

Her toes were no longer frozen and painful to move. She could feel her fingers and nose again. There was food waiting. Only a fool would walk away from it all.

The silence stretched endlessly. The man didn't speak again, and Helena didn't know what to say. She stared into the flickering flames, watching them devour the wood. He...well, she didn't know what he was doing. And she didn't care.

That was a lie. Helena had a thousand questions, but none fell off her tongue.

What seemed an eternity later, the stranger rose and walked to the fire. He took a thin stick from the spit that held two birds and brought it to her. She looked up at him, meeting his unusual gaze before she accepted the offering. He took the other two birds with him as he resumed his position in the shadows.

Despite the heat of the meat that burned her fingers and tongue, Helena tore off a piece and closed her eyes as she chewed. She forgot about the man, the wolf, and the falcon as she greedily devoured the first quail so quickly she didn't look up from it. She'd just started on the second when the wolf returned.

She was oddly offended when the animal didn't come to her. He maneuvered himself to sit between her and the man. When the wolf's eyes moved in her direction, she smiled at him. He was a savage creature that could—and likely, would —eat humans. But, oddly, she didn't feel afraid of him. Because he had slept beside her, warming her? Maybe. There was something almost...calming about the beast.

"It is not common to see a man with a wolf," she said to the stranger.

There was a sound that came from the shadows that resembled a snort. "There is nothing common about Valdr or me."

"Valdr," she said and grinned when the wolf's ears swiveled to her.

"It is Nordic. It means ruler and mighty one."

"It suits him," she replied as she took a bite of meat. Then she tossed some to Valdr. Helena lifted her gaze to the man. "What about the falcon?"

There was a pause. "Andi. It means spirit in Norse."

Helena swallowed and pulled another piece of meat from the bird. She tore off a section and tossed it to Valdr. "And your name?"

"I was wondering when you would get to that. I am Jarin."

"My name is Helena."

"Ah. I see."

She frowned. "Just what do you see?"

"We have mutual friends. The Hunters."

Helena froze, her stomach falling to her feet in stunned disbelief. "How do you know of them?"

"I helped Braith and Leoma. I also aided Carac and Ravyn against Sybbyl. You assisted Carac and his men. You should have stayed to help us. Perhaps then Sybbyl would not have ended up with the staff."

Anger churned within her. "I stood against the Coven before. I lost everything by doing it."

"So, you'll keep running from them?"

"Until I know I can win."

Jarin snorted loudly this time. "Then you will be running forever. The Coven grows stronger each day."

"How do you know so much?" she demanded.

He sat forward, the shadows melting away as the light of the fire illuminated his face. "Because I am one of you."

"Impossible," she replied. But the longer she looked at him, the more she considered the possibility.

The smile that tilted Jarin's lips was anything but friendly. "I am a Varroki."

For the second time that night, she stared at him in astonishment. "They are a myth."

"I promise you, we are anything but. We have been fighting the Coven for generations. Always before, we were able to keep them in check, but not this time."

Her appetite gone, Helena set aside the rest of the quail and rose to her feet. She walked toward the entrance and placed her hand on the stones, trying to come to terms with what she just learned. The rock was cold beneath her palm, evidence that the wall was too far from the fire to benefit from the flames.

"You killed a Coven witch," Jarin said.

She shrugged. "I've killed many, but it does no good."

"Leoma saved you. The Coven had captured you and wanted you to join them."

"I do not need you to retell the story. I was there."

"Perhaps you do."

He was close behind her now, just a step or two at her

back. She hadn't even heard him move. He was quick and as quiet as the grave.

Helena shook her head. "The Hunter gave me a second chance. I returned the favor by helping Carac."

"It's going to take all of us to bring down the Coven."

She whirled around to him. "Why? You said yourself that the Varroki have been fighting the Coven for generations. This will continue to happen again and again and again."

"So you just want to give up and let them win?"

Helena swallowed the angry retort and the hated tears that filled her eyes. "I will *never* stop fighting them."

"Neither will I, nor will any of the Varroki. And I suspect the Hunters are with us on this."

"What do you want of me?"

"Join me."

She blinked, taken aback by his request. "The legends I heard of the Varroki say that you are twice as powerful as any of us. You do not need me."

"Perhaps not. I'm a warrior for the Varroki. I have always been on my own, tracking and fighting members of the Coven. My success is measured by the number of Coven members who are no longer breathing. I make a dent, as do other Varroki. The Hunters make some headway, as well. And you do some damage, but few witches are willing to rise up against the Coven."

"You think by joining forces we can have more of an impact?"

"I do not think it. I know it. I have been part of it twice now. Even Malene, who leads the Varroki, agrees with me."

Helena had to admit that what Jarin said made sense. There was also the fact that she would no longer be alone. Having someone with her to help watch her back would relieve a great deal of stress from her.

Then there was the Varroki himself. Jarin was intense. It was in the way he looked at her with his pale blue eyes, but also in the way he spoke and in his bearing. The kind of man that always got his target and rarely failed.

He was a warlock used to getting what he wanted. And right now, his sights were set on the Coven. She would be a fool not to join him.

"All right," she said with a nod.

One side of his mouth lifted in a grin. It was crooked, the look in his eyes full of satisfaction, and the sudden heart-stopping transformation on his already handsome face made her breath catch. She couldn't remember the last time she had been around someone so gorgeous that it made it hard for her to concentrate.

"You need more rest," Jarin said and pivoted on his heel.

Apparently, that was the end of the conversation. Helena watched as he returned to the shadows. She looked at the wolf, who stared lovingly at the warlock.

The chill from outside finally reached her. She wrapped her arms around herself and made her way back to the fire. After lowering herself to the ground, she reached for the second quail and ate some more.

"What was your plan?" Jarin asked into the silence.

Helena shrugged. "To survive. The Coven knows when a witch uses magic. They come for them immediately."

"That explains why you did not start a fire."

She glanced at him. "My actions make it look as if I fear to face them."

"Only a fool would claim not to be distressed by such a meeting."

"I have stood my ground against them twice before. I was caught the second time. That's when Leoma came."

There was a long pause. "And the first time?"

She couldn't think about it. If she did, she would sink into the mire of hopelessness and depression that had taken her before. She'd barely clawed her way out the first time. After everything, she didn't know if she had the strength to do it again.

4

The magic hummed from the trees, the flowers, from the very ground she knelt upon. And Sybbyl couldn't get enough.

Her entire make-up had been altered. She didn't question it, merely accepted it. Because this was her destiny. She had seen it in a dream when she was but a small girl. For years, she had made her way from one task to another, each one bringing her closer to her dream of leading the Coven.

And now, here she was.

Finally.

She held the staff while hovering the palm of her other hand over the ground as she closed her eyes. Sybbyl pushed her magic down into the soil, calling every Coven witch to her.

"It's time," she whispered.

After the summons had been sent, she opened her eyes and looked at the staff. The First Witch had been the strongest, most powerful of them all. Some claimed she only did good, but Sybbyl had heard other tales that stated otherwise.

It didn't matter what the First Witch did or didn't do. Now that Sybbyl had one of the bones, she would be nearly untouchable. It was a dark mark against the Coven that the Hunters had lost the Blood Skull because it didn't matter if the Coven gathered every bone from the First Witch. Without the skull, their goal of resurrecting the woman would never happen.

That had been the mission of the elders. Sybbyl had agreed with it, but now that she was in charge and holding the Staff of the Eternal, she saw another path. One that didn't involve the other parts of the First Witch.

She wanted the Blood Skull simply because it galled her that the Hunters had managed to attain it. If she had been there, Sybbyl knew she would've been able to seduce Braith, ensuring that when he got the skull, he would have brought it to her.

But she would deal with Braith and the Hunters in due course. When she and the Coven swept through each village, it would merely be a matter of time before she ran across a Hunter.

A sizzle of power ran through the staff and straight into her hand. She smiled, breathless from the sensation of it. No wonder the bones of the First Witch had been scattered and hidden. People killed for such power.

She had killed for it. And would again.

Sybbyl looked around at the Witch's Grove. It was large, as well as one of the oldest in England. This would become her new home.

She smiled as she climbed to her feet using the staff. The old trees were gnarled, their limbs intertwining with each other to form a wall. Within the trees lived the Gira. The nymphs were indiscernible from the trees themselves, which is what made them so dangerous.

But they were allies with the witches. The Gira could live freely in the Witch's Groves and take any unwary person who was brave enough to venture inside without any consequences.

And Sybbyl knew that the Hunters willingly entered the Groves. Perhaps she could use that to her advantage. The Hunters believed they could get in and out without falling prey to the Gira.

Or anything else.

That was going to change.

Then there was the warlock. Sybbyl very much wanted him. But not to kill him. Since the beginning of time, men had held women prisoners, using their bodies however and whenever they wanted.

Now, it was her turn, and she had her sights set on the warlock. Sybbyl would keep him for herself, taking her pleasure until her belly swelled with child.

Maybe, just maybe, during all of it, she could convince the warlock to join the Coven. She would never share her rule with him, but together, they could be a formidable force.

Sybbyl turned in a circle. The beginning of everything started now. With her. In this ancient Witch's Grove. She lifted the staff and pounded it into the ground.

Tendrils of black smoke shot up from the earth where the staff sat and wrapped around her, enveloping her so tightly that she could hardly breathe. But she wasn't afraid. This was the magic of the First Witch, power she now commanded.

The smoke swirled around her several times before it dispersed in all directions. The wisps grew larger, thicker the farther from her they moved. Soon, the entire Grove was filled with them.

She tilted her head to the side and watched it all while slowly understanding that she was altered. A glance down showed that her gown was now the color of midnight.

Her head felt heavy, and she realized something was sitting atop her hair. She tentatively reached up and touched it. Carefully, she lifted the weighty object to examine it. Her face split into a broad smile when her gaze landed on the black crown with dozens of spikes of different lengths.

It wasn't set with jewels but with a lattice-work of onyx crystal that shimmered even in the semi-darkness of the Grove. Sybbyl replaced the crown. It set upon her head as if it had always been there, just waiting to reveal itself. The crown was one of many things she'd been destined for.

Her gaze moved to the staff. If she had known what the leg bone of the First Witch would give her, she would've sought it out years ago. Now that it was in her hands, she would never let it go.

The whispers began softly, growing louder and filling the quiet of the Grove. Sybbyl looked toward the tree line and the Gira who gathered. She turned her head first one way, then the other, taking in the number of nymphs who watched her with a mixture of glee and fear.

Suddenly, her body pulsed with an uncontrollable need. She gasped, bending over as her sex clenched. Sybbyl fell to her knees as her gaze moved to the Gira. Somehow, they were doing this to her.

Their whispers.

Words she couldn't quite make out reached her. But her body understood them. The louder their whispers came, the more her body ached for the release that swelled uncontrollably within her.

One Gira stepped away from the others. As the tall Gira moved closer, Sybbyl couldn't take her eyes from her. Sybbyl had never looked too closely at the nymphs before. There were both males and females, utterly naked with branches and leaves for hair and skin like bark.

Sybbyl grasped the staff tightly in one hand while the other pressed against her aching sex. The female slowly knelt down before Sybbyl, her dark gaze locked on the staff.

Sybbyl fought against the tide of desire with determination and then magic. In retaliation, the Gira's whispers increased. Sybbyl's mouth opened on a silent moan as desire coursed like fire through her blood.

The nymph focused on Sybbyl's face then. Her dark gaze lowered to Sybbyl's breasts, lingering there and causing them to swell, her nipples erect and hard.

A small smile pulled at the Gira's thin lips as if she knew exactly what Sybbyl was going through. Sybbyl wanted to hate the nymphs for such power, but it felt so good.

"We serve you."

It took a moment for Sybbyl to realize that the Gira had spoken. Sybbyl blinked, but no words came to form a reply. In the back of her mind, she knew she could stop all of this. But she didn't want to.

With a crescendo of voices, the orgasm took her unexpectedly. Sybbyl was rocked by the force of it. When it finally faded, and her breathing smoothed out once more, she lifted her head to look at the female.

The Gira smiled. "We serve you."

With that, the nymph rose and returned to the others.

Sybbyl didn't trust her legs. She remained on her knees and sat back on her haunches. Of all the things she knew about the Gira, she had never heard of anything like this happening. It rattled her. And it excited her.

The lot of them had sworn themselves to her without Sybbyl having to do or say anything. Few realized just what the Gira could do because they remained hidden.

The witches had always had a symbiotic relationship of

sorts with them. Perhaps it was time for Sybbyl to move things in a new direction—with the Gira folded into the Coven.

They were creatures of magic, after all.

The whispers tapered off to silence. As one, the Gira bowed their heads before retreating back into the shadows of the forest.

Sybbyl glanced at the staff. The only reason the Gira treated her this way was because she held a bone from the First Witch. They knew how powerful the first of the witches had been. Did they fear the staff? Or recognize the authority Sybbyl now wielded?

It didn't matter. The Gira would guard the Grove, and Sybbyl's magic would alert her to anyone who entered. If they got past the nymphs, then she would deal with them.

Sybbyl climbed to her feet. She was about to take a step when she glanced down. The dim light of a Witch's Grove made it difficult for anything to grow on the ground. It was bare earth covered with years of decaying leaves and the bones of those who died.

Sybbyl noticed that the leaves had been moved to form something. She walked around the illustration to see that it looked like a face. The smile that stretched her lips was one of pure joy because she knew the woman. Helena.

The witch had escaped from the coven twice. There wouldn't be a third time when Sybbyl found her. But she didn't understand why the Gira had shown her this.

"Why is Helena important?" she asked, hoping a nymph would reply.

But only silence met her question. Sybbyl blew out a breath, undeterred. The Gira must know something, and it was time Sybbyl figured out what that was.

She put the staff before her and grasped it with both

hands. "Show me the other bones of the First Witch," she demanded.

The magic that went through her was so strong that it caused her to sway on her feet before she caught her balance. The flashes of places went through her head so quickly, she couldn't figure out where each of them was.

It was time to come up with another way of getting what she wanted. "What part of the First Witch is closest to me besides the staff?"

There was a moment of nothing, and then an image of Helena filled her head. Was it mere coincidence that the Gira had drawn her face with leaves and then the staff showed the same witch? Surely not.

"Does she have one of the bones?" Sybbyl asked.

"*The Heart.*"

The two words filled her mind, spoken by another voice. Sybbyl frowned, not understanding. "No organs survived."

"*The Heart.*"

With all the power she now held, she should be able to get the answers she needed. Sybbyl took a deep breath and tried again. "What is Helena?"

"*The Heart.*"

Sybbyl opened her mouth to ask another question when it dawned on her. She laughed as the pieces fell into place. "Helena is a descendant of the First Witch. She *is* the Heart."

The staff warmed in her hands. Now, she had a target. Because if she could have Helena in the Coven, then she would control two parts of the First Witch.

Sybbyl jerked her head to the side when she felt someone enter the Grove. Within moments, the first Coven witch she'd summoned arrived. It would take time for the others to reach her, but Sybbyl wasn't worried about Helena.

The witch was on borrowed time. No doubt she was hiding, but there was no place she could go that Sybbyl couldn't find her. Not now. Not when she had the staff.

"Welcome, sister," Sybbyl said to the witch, who stared at her with wide eyes.

5

The witch intrigued him. That was a rarity for Jarin. Most times, he was able to figure out a person after studying them for a short time. Sometimes, he didn't even need to converse with them.

But Helena was different. Whatever the Coven had done to her the first time had left profound, deep scars. He wanted to know what happened, to discover what the Coven had done, but he didn't press her further.

She kept her pain and suffering in private. All he had to do was look into her stunning green eyes to see the weight of what she carried.

While she gazed silently into the flames that seemed to dance specifically for her, he found himself staring at her. Much as he'd done since the moment he was finally able to see her face.

She was strikingly beautiful. Breathtaking, actually. With long, deep red tresses fashioned in a thick braid, and creamy, pale skin. Her oval face was perfection, with a defiant tilt of her chin that made him grin inwardly. Large, green eyes speared him with a glance, and full lips that made his balls tighten warred for his attention.

"What is your plan?" she asked without looking up.

He propped a foot on the ground and rested his arm atop his knee. "I am going to continue my hunt for Sybbyl. Any Coven witches that cross my path will be taken out."

Helena was silent for a long stretch. Then she lifted her head and swung her gaze to him. "You are not worried about the Coven picking up your magic?"

"They are unable to sense it."

"But if they *could* find you from using it? Would you do it, knowing that others could surround you?"

The way her gaze held his made him realize that was exactly how they'd found her before. "I doubt it."

"Liar," she said, but there was no heat in her words. "You have fought them, but you do not fear them. You believe your magic is superior."

He shook his head. "I believe good will triumph over evil."

"And if you ever find yourself held by the Coven and forced to either join them or die? Which will you choose?" she asked, her head tilted to the side.

There was no decision for him. "Death."

At this, her brows rose high on her forehead. "What of your people? They would be down a warrior. Would you give up so easily instead of fighting?"

"You gave me but two options."

Helena smiled as she scratched her neck. "So I did."

"If there was a third option of fighting them, that is what I would do."

"Will other Varroki join us?"

He hadn't considered that. Warriors always fought alone, but he had changed things the first time by helping Leoma and Braith. Would his fellow Varroki feel the same? He knew he could count on Malene, and possibly her commander, Armir.

"I see," Helena said.

"I did not reply."

"Your silence said it all."

Jarin blew out a breath. "I was thinking. I believe I would get aid, aye."

"I will not. Not from the other witches."

"What of the Hunters?"

A small frown formed as she shrugged. "I'm not sure."

"They would come. All we would need to do is ask."

Helena drew up her legs to rest her chin on her knees. She wrapped her arms around her legs, bringing her cloak with her as if using it like armor. "All the stories I heard of the Varroki... It makes me sad that all this time, I believed you to be nothing more than myth. Why keep yourselves secret?"

"There are many reasons."

"You fear others trying to usurp your power or take your magic?"

He watched as Andi glided into the cave and resumed her spot on the rock. "I am sure that is how it began. We have lived for so long as we are currently, that change is not welcome."

"Could you take me to your people?"

Her question surprised him. "Is it protection you seek?"

"No," she said with a sad smile. "The Coven will never stop looking for me no matter where I go."

"They would not find you with the Varroki."

Helena looked back to the fire. "I would like to see a society of witches and warlocks who live together without being forced, who survive by doing something other than evil as the Coven does."

"You do not believe witches can live together?"

She laughed, the sound going straight to his cock. "There are few witches who live together except for the Coven. The rest of us are spread out. Sometimes, there might be another near, but we keep our distance. Mostly out of fear. We do not want the others to know we have magic and be burned or hanged."

"You could always get free of those people."

"And have another group chasing me?" She shrugged. "I do not find that appealing."

It seemed there was much Jarin had taken for granted. He had never worried about the people he lived with discovering that he had magic because all of them did, as well. Even when he left Blackglade, he didn't care if anyone saw him doing magic because he knew he could get away.

Helena and so many others didn't have that choice. Perhaps it was time that he mentioned that to Malene. The Lady of the Varroki had the authority to open the gates to anyone who sought refuge.

Yet that was unlikely to happen until the Coven was dealt with. Though they could never fully wipe the Coven out. There would always be those who did malicious things. Just as there would always be those, like him, who sought to stop them.

It was a balance that had to be kept at all times. The good could not triumph over evil for too long, nor could evil demolish good.

"Tell me what it is like to be a Varroki," she urged.

He let her change the subject. "I do not live at Blackglade. Warriors leave and only return a few times a year to report to the Lady."

"So you live as I do for the most part?" she asked, cutting her eyes to him.

Jarin shrugged and motioned to the cave. "I bed down for

the night most times at places like this. A few occasions, I stop at an inn, but those instances are rare."

"Because of Valdr and Andi."

He gave a nod. "I search for any Coven member, moving from one to the next."

"So you have no home."

Jarin blinked, taken aback by her words. He had never thought about it. In truth, Blackglade was his home. It was the place he'd been born, but he was there so rarely that it couldn't be called his home anymore.

"I spoke out of turn," Helena hastily said. "My apologies."

"You did no harm."

She wrinkled her nose. "I beg to differ."

"I just had not thought about my life in such a way."

"If it makes you feel better, I do not have a home either."

There was much that he and the witch had in common, but he knew that she was the type who needed a place to call her own. "You will not always be running."

"I once believed that. Now, I am not so sure. The Coven is strong."

"So are you."

Eyes as green as a fern met his. Helena smiled. "Thank you."

He stretched out his leg and shifted to get more comfortable. Valdr was snoring softly as the crackle of the fire filled the silence. Jarin's continued solitude made it difficult for him to interact with others. Carrying on a conversation was almost painful for him.

Oddly, he didn't find that with Helena.

Perhaps it was because he saw the hope she desperately clung to and the inner strength that kept her going. Or it could be the pain that wrapped around her like her cloak. All he knew was that he liked talking to her.

Her eyes moved to him, catching him staring at her. Their gazes held as he searched his mind for a question. But she beat him to it.

"Do you have family?"

Jarin gave a nod. "I was the middle child of five."

"They live in...Blackglade is it?"

"Aye."

"Do you see them at all?"

He glanced at the ground. "As I am hardly ever there, nay."

"But you could. If you wanted to."

"I suppose."

"Perhaps you would not know what to say to them," she said and turned her head to the fire.

Jarin drank in her profile. "Do you have family?"

"I did once. They are all gone now."

He frowned as he tried to think of some way to reply. "The Varroki have dwindled in size because we seldom venture from Blackglade or let others in."

Helena's eyes slid to him. "Warriors like you could find withes and bring them to Blackglade. Or marry yourselves."

"Up until recently, that was not permitted."

Her brow furrowed. "Marriage was not permitted?"

"Warriors were required to be celibate."

Her eyes rounded in surprise. "So you have never..." She trailed off, but her meaning was clear.

He shrugged, hiding his smile.

"Never?" she asked, shocked.

"We are also asked to do whatever it takes to curb the Coven."

She lifted her head, grinning as she tucked her legs beneath her. "So, you have."

"I do whatever is necessary to catch my quarry."

Her grin was conspiratorial. "That is one way of getting around the rule."

"The Lady of the Varroki has reversed such laws so that we can grow as a people again."

"It sounds as if you like...what did you say her name was? Malene?"

"I do. She had no wish to be Lady, but she has taken on the role better than we hoped."

Helena shifted toward him. "Who does not wish to be in power? I would not turn down such a role."

"Malene had no magic. She was chosen and given the blue radiance in her left hand that proclaimed her as our Lady."

"I'm confused. She had no magic? Who chose her?"

Jarin shrugged. "Whoever or whatever chooses each of them. Armir, or whoever is commander at the time, goes in search of the Chosen."

"You make it sound as if it happens often."

"Sadly, more often than not. Like other Ladies before her, Malene was taken from her family and brought to Blackglade."

Helena nodded, understanding. "So she is not a Varroki."

"Nay. However, there were laws that required the Lady to be celibate, as well."

"Please tell me she reversed that."

Jarin grinned. "She did. She is very intelligent. And while she fights the bonds that tie her to the Varroki, she has learned to use them in order to do what she feels is right."

"The others before her did not?"

"They rarely lasted longer than five years."

Helena gawked at him. "Are they mistreated?"

"Not at all. They are given everything."

"Can they leave?"

"Nay. They have a duty, as each of us does. Malene is the only one who seems to have accepted that fate. The fact that the radiance is now in both of her hands speaks of a prophecy that says the Varroki will be ushered into a new era."

Helena contemplated his words. "I would very much like to meet her."

"I think she would like you. You both have fire within you. A strength that you do not know is there until you are backed into a corner."

Green eyes softened before she slowly looked away.

6

There were so many mysteries about life that Helena would never understand. At a time when she felt the most alone, the most frightened, Jarin was suddenly there.

He was quiet and reserved, his strength and power evident in the way he held himself—and looked at the world. At first, she had been uncomfortable with his silence, but when she realized that she didn't need to fill it with words, she quickly discovered how easy it was to be in his presence.

That allowed her to be comfortable enough to ask questions. And she was shocked by the answers. She really wanted to go to Blackglade and meet the Varroki, especially Malene.

Just hours before, she'd acknowledged that she would pick the time and place to confront the Coven. She also accepted the fact that it would likely mean her death.

Now, with just a few words, Jarin gave her hope. Hope that, despite the odds against her, she just might be able to defeat the Coven.

She glanced toward the Varroki warrior and found his eyes closed. The cave was warm with no prying eyes searching for her. Her belly was full, and her body more rested than it had been in weeks. Still, her eyes began to droop, seeking the oblivion of slumber.

Helena yawned and pulled her braid over her shoulder. Once she loosened the leather binding, she slid her fingers through the plait to loosen it. She shook out her hair and dropped her head back, massaging her scalp.

She would love a bath, preferably in water that wasn't freezing. And a clean gown. But there were other things to be concerned with at the moment.

With another yawn, she curled up on her side, using her arm as a pillow, and embraced the void that was sleep.

There were no dreams, no nightmares, and no worries that plagued her. Just a restfulness that she hadn't experienced in many years. She sank deeper into slumber.

It was the pressure against her back that prevented her from rolling over that woke her. It pulled her from the dreamless state to discover that Valdr was lying behind her.

That made her smile. She blinked open her eyes, expecting to see the fire, but there was nothing but scorched earth and ash there now.

Helena pushed up on her elbow and looked around. Jarin was nowhere to be found. Valdr lifted his head and blinked at her before he rose and trotted to the cave entrance. There was no denying the sunlight that spilled into the opening. She got to her feet and followed the wolf.

A world of white met her. She shivered, wrapping her cloak tighter around her as she gazed at the sparkling wonder that covered everything. Already, she missed the cozy warmth of the cave.

Her gaze spotted the tawny fur of the wolf as he walked through the deep snow. She turned to go back into the cave when she found Jarin leaning against the side of the entrance, watching her.

"You startled me," she said breathlessly.

"You sleep like the dead."

Helena glanced away. "It happens when I am tired."

"You mean exhausted," he corrected. "How long did you go without rest?"

She shrugged and shook her head. "Days. Weeks. I lost track. I slept when I could."

"If I removed that cloak, I bet I would find you skin and bones beneath your gown."

Now uncomfortable, she turned away to face the snow once more. "I only lost a little weight. A few weeks rationing food will not kill a person."

He grunted in response. "Ready?"

So, they were leaving. Helena knew it would happen. Morning had come much swifter than she anticipated. It was difficult to leave a place where she was fed, safe, and warm, but there was no other choice. She had to do this. For herself and for the family she lost.

"Lead the way."

"Do you need another day?" he asked.

Helena shook her head. "It would be easy to hide here."

"You were not hiding."

"Aye, I was," she said with a bark of laughter.

Jarin stared at her a long, silent moment before he moved closer. She cut her eyes to the side but didn't face him. He stood beside her. Then, slowly, he lifted a lock of her hair before letting it slip through his fingers.

That simple touch made her acutely aware of him. His presence, the heat of his nearness, and his strength. The entire world melted away until there was only him.

And he hadn't even touched her. Not really. Just her hair.

Finally, she looked at him. There was something in his eyes that she didn't recognize. Something that bordered on...hunger. She had always hated her hair. It made her stand out, the color a deep red, not a pretty, lighter shade.

Jarin said nothing more as he moved past her and began walking. She hurried to follow. It wasn't long before Valdr was loping between them. Every once in a while, Andi's cry reached them from high above.

The warlock walked swiftly. Helena had to hike up her skirts and double her steps just to keep up. Twice, she caught him looking at her over his shoulder. When he got too far ahead, he would pause and wait for her to catch up. She hated that she was slowing him down.

The food she'd consumed the night before had done wonders to restore her, but it wasn't long before her stomach rumbled again, and her body grew weak. She was determined to make it until noon. Then she would ask Jarin to stop so she could eat. What she would eat was another matter entirely. But first, she had to make it to midday.

The higher the sun rose, the harder it became to put one foot in front of the other. She kept her gaze on the ground, making sure she didn't trip over anything. Because if she went down, Helena knew she wouldn't get up anytime soon.

She was concentrating so hard on keeping one foot in front of the other that it took her a moment to realize that Jarin had his hand on her arm while trying to stop her.

She swung her head to him with a frown. "Did you say something?"

"Aye," he bit out, a muscle jumping in his jaw. "You should have told me you needed to rest. Sit."

She was so tired, she didn't even care about the abrasive tone of his order. She lowered herself to the fallen tree he had already dusted the snow from the surface of before she comprehended how easily she followed his command. But she didn't have the energy to think about that.

Her gaze lifted to land on Jarin's retreating back. Valdr remained with her, so at least she knew the warlock wasn't leaving her. She wanted to ask where he was going, but her eyes wouldn't stay open. When she nearly fell off the log dozing off, she lay on the tree and closed her eyes—just for a moment.

All she needed was to rest for a few moments and then she could focus again.

Helena didn't know what made her eyes fly open. Embarrassment stole over her when she realized she had slept deeply once more. She pushed herself up with her arms and licked her lips at the sight of the rabbits roasting over the fire.

If the Coven had found her, she would be captured or dead right now because she would've been sleeping instead of ready to defend herself.

"Next time, tell me," Jarin stated as he came from behind her and walked to the fire.

She glanced at him, grateful that he hadn't left her. "I suppose I was more worn out than I realized."

He motioned to the meat. "It is nearly done."

"I do not want to hold you back, which is exactly what I am doing. You could have covered twice as much ground this morning without me."

His pale blue eyes lifted to her. "We agreed to work together. I should have realized you were not up to travel yet."

She opened her mouth to talk when he spoke over her.

"Adrenaline and fear kept you moving these past weeks regardless of your hunger or exhaustion. You can survive on that for only so long before your body gives out. Food will replenish you."

"I am not weak." Helena didn't know why she felt the need

to say that. He hadn't mentioned anything about it, but she wanted him to know that she could continue, that she would keep up.

He frowned, his brow furrowing deeply. "Not once have I thought that. Your survival shows great strength. The fact that you need more sleep and food is not weakness. It is a fact after what you have endured."

She looked away and fidgeted with the edge of her cloak. "Stop being so nice."

"I will not let it happen again."

Was that a smile she heard in his words? She wished she had been looking at him. She would love to see a grin on his face and watch how it transformed him.

Valdr placed his head on her lap. Without thinking, she petted him. The wolf was a part of Jarin's family, whether he realized it or not. Same with Andi.

"They do not fight the Coven with you, do they?" she asked.

Jarin paused in stoking the fire with a stick to look up at her. He glanced at Valdr before he shook his head. "A few times, but I try to keep them out of it. I know the Coven would happily kill them because it would hurt me."

"Do not ever let them near Sybbyl," she warned. "She is crafty. She will realize the animals' importance to you and go after them."

"Is that what happened to you?"

"Something like that."

He rose and checked the meat before he pulled it from the fire and came to sit with her on the tree. "Eat your fill. If you need more, then I'll find more."

She accepted the meat and blew on it to cool it off. "Where are we headed?"

"South."

"You know where Sybbyl is?"

He gave a shake of his head, his gaze looking out over the land. "We are going to find the Hunters. I know an approximate location."

"Is that time we have?"

"It is time we will make," he stated before glancing at her.

She tore off a piece of meat. After several more bites, she held it out for Jarin to take some. He pulled off a chunk and gave the rest back to her. Helena devoured the rabbit in little time. She didn't even share any with Valdr this time.

Jarin handed her a waterskin, and she drank her fill then sighed and wiped the back of her hand over her mouth, once more feeling refreshed.

Helena looked up at the sky, happy to see it was blue again instead of gray. The sun shone brightly, making the snow appear as if it sparkled with diamonds.

When Valdr moved away, she got to her feet and raised a brow at Jarin. He grabbed his staff and said something. She spotted the tip of the staff glowing white when the fire went out.

"Do you need the staff to do magic?" she asked.

"Nay."

No other explanation. Helena smiled and fell into step beside Jarin. He walked considerably slower this time. She used far less energy trying to keep up, which made the walk more enjoyable. Although, when she thought about running across any Coven members, it wiped the grin from her face.

She also wasn't too sure about the Hunters. They had saved her, but she was a witch. She knew very little about the Hunters. However, Jarin seemed to trust them.

Should she be concerned at how easily—and willingly— she trusted *him*? He was a warlock, which meant he was in the same boat she was. So, if the Hunters wanted to come for her, they would have to do the same for him.

The four of them traveled for three days, frequently stopping so Jarin could put food in her hands every chance he could. Helena had never eaten so much. When night came, she fell into a deep, dreamless slumber from the exertion.

By the end of the third day, she was so drained, she was fantasizing about sleep. Then Jarin suddenly stopped walking.

Helena looked around as Valdr sat, ears perked forward. "What is it?" she asked.

"Wait," Jarin urged.

A moment later, a woman came from behind a tree, an arrow notched and aimed at them. The lower half of her face was covered by material, and her hood was up so that only her eyes were visible. But the outline of her womanly curves was evident beneath her clothes. "What do you want?" she demanded.

"To speak to Leoma or Braith. I am Jarin of the Varroki."

The woman slowly lowered her bow as her gaze raked over him. She shoved the hood of her cloak back to reveal blond hair.

She then tugged down the wrapping on her lower face and nodded. "We were told you might come."

Helena lifted her chin when the Hunter's amber gaze landed on her. "I am Helena."

"I've heard of you, as well. I'm Synne. Guess you two better follow me," she said and put the arrow back in her quiver as she pivoted and walked away.

Helena eyed the woman's pants. The Hunters tended to prefer them, and she was leaning in that direction, as well. It would make maneuvering in battle much easier.

7

The moment Jarin was within the confines of the Hunters' sanctuary, he understood why they were so careful about keeping the location secret. There was magic being used to shield it. However, the founder of the group, Edra, used wards and herbs mixed in with her magic to make it nearly impossible for it to be located by the Coven—or anyone for that matter.

The combination prevented the Coven from detecting the magic, and it kept the Hunters and all those who sought sanctuary there safe.

Jarin brought up the rear with his animals behind Helena, who followed Synne through an archway of ruins before making their way down the stairs. The old abbey had been converted into a home. No longer derelict and crumbling, it now stood tall and grand.

Despite Helena's brave face, he could tell that she still needed rest. She claimed she had been on the run only a few weeks, but he would guess it was much longer than that.

Most likely from the moment Leoma freed her from the Coven.

That was a significantly longer period of time than she let on. His admiration for the witch grew. He could only imagine what she had endured and suffered. Helena wasn't one to complain, so he might never know specifics. But he could guess.

It took someone with a strong soul to still be standing. The fact that Helena wasn't just standing but also wanted to fight said much about her.

He tried to make himself believe that was the only reason he couldn't keep his eyes from her, but it was a lie. Her deep red tresses called to him like a beacon, and once he was ensnared by her beautiful green eyes, all he could think about was getting close to her.

Touching her. *Feeling* her.

"Welcome."

Jarin was jerked from his licentious thoughts. He turned to find a witch with long, wavy, blond hair and smiling, blue eyes. He knew without being told that this was Edra. "Thank you for allowing us here."

"You must be Jarin," Edra said. "Between Malene, Leoma, Braith, Ravyn, and Carac, I feel as if I already know you."

Out of the corner of his eye, Jarin saw Helena lean against one of the many trees surrounding the abbey. He didn't wish to draw attention to her exhaustion, so he didn't mention anything. But he shifted so that he could better see her.

The Hunter who brought them also eyed Helena before exchanging a look with Edra.

The witch turned to Helena with a smile. "I'm Edra. You are welcome to remain here for as long as you wish."

Helena glanced at him before she bowed her head to Edra. "Thank you. My name is Helena."

Edra's eyes widened as she went to Helena and took her hands. "I have long wished for you to find us. We are very pleased to have you here." Edra's gaze swung to Jarin briefly before she moved closer to Helena to wrap an arm around her. "How does a hot bath sound?"

"Like Heaven," Helena replied with a grateful smile.

Jarin watched the women walk away. Without having to be told, Edra realized what Helena needed. The bath would do wonders, as would a meal and more rest. He wanted Helena with him when he fought the Coven. Her strength hinted at her magic, which he couldn't wait to see.

He suspected it would be glorious.

"I'd hoped to meet a warlock," Synne said.

Valdr moved between Jarin and the Hunter. She cocked a brow at the wolf. Jarin moved his staff to his other hand. "Now you have. Synne is an unusual name."

She shrugged, her amber eyes glancing away. "There is not much about my life that is normal."

He jerked his chin to the bow. "You any good with that?"

Her gaze narrowed as she raised a brow and looked at his staff. "You any good with that?"

"The best," he replied.

A small smile pulled at her lips. "Me, too."

Jarin liked her immediately. He didn't know if it was her boldness or her soul, or both, but within her, he saw a kindred spirit. Someone fighting not just for survival but also for their place in the world.

"Do you think we will get to see Blackglade?" Synne asked.

He shrugged, unaware of any such talk between Malene and Edra. "Why do you ask?"

"Malene told Edra that since she was able to come here, a visit to Blackglade was in order if we were to be allies."

Jarin could well imagine Armir's reaction. "If Malene said it would happen, then it will. She does not go back on her word."

"That makes me like her even more." Synne then turned on her heel and strode away without another word.

Jarin watched her before he let his gaze wander amid the buildings and over a vegetable garden. He heard the distant sound of water trickling, no doubt from a river.

"I think I stood in exactly that spot the first time I saw this place."

He turned his head and spotted a man walking toward him with dark brown hair tied in a queue, and clever brown eyes. Jarin turned toward him as Andi landed on the tip of his staff.

"You must be Jarin," the man said with a smile. Then he held out his arm. "I'm Radnar."

Jarin clasped his arm and returned the smile. "You and Edra have made a good home here. Thank you for welcoming us."

"Us?" Radnar asked with raised brows.

Jarin dropped his arm to his side. "I came across a witch. Helena."

"Ah," Radnar said with a nod of his head. "Leoma will be pleased with the news."

"Are she and Braith here?"

Radnar sighed and shook his head. "After they were married, Braith took Leoma to his land. He knew the Coven would eventually come for the Blood Skull, and he wanted to protect this place so that it would remain a haven for those who need it."

"I would have left, as well."

"It is Braith who bade Carac join us. Braith said more

would be coming to his keep. He's building an army that will stand with us to fight the Coven."

Jarin thought over Radnar's words. "I assume you told Malene and Armir this?"

"Aye. Malene said the Varroki would join with us."

"Good." Jarin smiled. "Very good."

Radnar looked around. "Did Edra take Helena?"

"The witch has been on the run from the Coven for some weeks," Jarin explained. "I found her in a cave, exhausted and nearly to the point of starvation."

"She will be looked after here. I assure you. And so will you."

Jarin looked away. "I am used to being on my own."

"I was too at one point. Things change. From what Armir and Malene told us, much is altering for your people."

Jarin's mind immediately went to Helena. He made a point of not touching her, but that was because he *wanted* it so badly. Just letting her hair run through his fingers had been enough to make his balls tighten with longing. "Aye. Change seems to be everywhere."

"Helena will be occupied for some time, I'm sure. Come with me, and I'll give you a tour of our home. You can also meet the others, and then we can eat."

Jarin looked at his pets.

Radnar smiled. "They are welcome to come with you wherever you go."

Jarin stroked a hand down Andi's feathers. Her head swung to him, their eyes meeting. With a loud call, she flew over the abbey.

Radnar was true to his word. He took Jarin all over their compound. Jarin got to meet Berlaq, the barrel-chested, muscular blacksmith with a long, black beard and bald head.

Berlaq was quiet, preferring the solitude of his workshop to anything else.

Jarin was greatly impressed with the detail the blacksmith put into each weapon. Whether it was a sword, knives, a crossbow, or a bow, every piece was meticulously made to perfection.

Jarin could have remained there for hours, looking over each weapon, but Radnar moved on. Jarin got to meet the other knights. Some trained any who wished to learn to fight, while the others were preparing for the inevitable showdown with the Coven.

Next, Jarin was introduced to Asa. He instantly noticed the Nordic heritage of the petite witch from her long, wavy, pale blond hair to her deep blue eyes.

He was curious as to how she'd come to be with the Hunters, but the question died on his lips when he saw all the sketches on parchment lying around her chamber.

There was pride in Radnar's voice when he said, "Asa is more than just a witch. She sees images that she then tattoos on those who want them."

Jarin held her gaze. "Impressive."

She smiled at Radnar before sliding her gaze to Jarin. "I have love for imprinting meanings from someone's life onto their skin. Armir and I had a nice discussion about his markings. Do you have any?"

Jarin didn't answer her. Instead, he asked, "Do you give someone what they want? Or do you see what a person needs?"

"Both," she replied. "Sometimes, they come to me wanting something but not knowing what it might be. I listen to them while my magic enfolds us. I then get an idea of what that person needs. I draw it and let them choose whether it is right or not."

"She also speaks to animals," Radnar added.

That piqued Jarin's interest. "Is that so?"

"I have an owl," Asa said proudly. "Frida goes out to keep an eye on the Hunters, reporting back if something is wrong. She cannot get to all of them, but she does try."

Jarin was taken aback by that news. "One owl does all of that?"

"She is no regular bird," Asa stated testily.

Radnar then said, "As Asa explains it, Frida feels a connection to the Hunters, and she feels it is her duty to check up on them. She is the one who let us know that Carac and Ravyn were in trouble."

"Have you thought about using more owls?" Jarin asked her.

Asa walked to a table and sat. "Perhaps one day."

When she began drawing, Radnar motioned them out. They walked along the long corridor of the abbey as the knight explained how everything worked with their sanctuary. Everyone had a job. They gave refuge to any who asked for it, but the occupants had to pull their weight.

The two walked through a doorway to a hall set with rows of tables. No words were spoken until they were seated and Radnar poured ale from a pitcher into two goblets.

He handed one to Jarin and asked, "What is your plan?"

"I began tracking Sybbyl after my last encounter with her. She is not traveling in a straight line. She is moving in various directions, sometimes backtracking or going in circles."

"Do you think she knows you follow her?"

Jarin shrugged. "If she did, I think she would attack me. Nay, I believe she is looking for something or someone."

"You are not contemplating facing her on your own, are you?" Radnar asked with a frown.

He was quiet for a long moment. Jarin took a drink of the

ale. "The fact that she has the staff makes her powerful, but she is also easily provoked. That means it is simple to push her to that point where she makes careless decisions."

"Malene spoke very highly of you," Radnar said as he placed his ankle over his knee. "She said you were the best warrior the Varroki have. I also heard from Leoma, Braith, and Carac just how good you are."

"But am I good enough to face Sybbyl on my own and win?" Jarin finished for him.

Radnar issued a half-shrug with one brow quirked. "Something like that."

"My goal was to find Sybbyl. I do not know what I will do when that happens. There will be little time to send word to Malene for reinforcements."

"Or us."

Jarin gave a single nod. "Precisely."

"It would be a shame for the Varroki to lose their finest warrior for something like that."

"The Coven must be stopped."

Radnar took a long swig of ale before lowering the cup and shifting in his chair to face Jarin. "Is that why you have Helena with you?"

"The witch is with me because I could not leave her to die. The Coven can trace her magic, but not mine."

"So you brought her here for us to care for."

Jarin held Radnar's dark gaze for a silent minute. "She and I will track Sybbyl together. I brought her here so that she could see how prepared the Hunters are and maybe get her to trust you and Edra. Helena has her own issues with the Coven. From what I gather, it is a battle that will happen regardless. I plan to make sure she does not face them alone. Two is better than one."

"And an army is even better," Radnar countered.

8

It was amazing what a hot bath and a good scrub from head to toe could do for someone. Helena didn't want to leave the luxurious bath, but the water had grown tepid, and she had no desire to be cold again.

She stood, and the droplets cascaded down her body. Quickly drying off, she wrapped a blanket around her and went to stand before the hearth, her feet kept warm by a thick fur rug.

No longer could she look at a fire and not think of Jarin. So much that had happened with him in the last few days had been around a fire.

He was inscrutable, but it was that mysteriousness that intrigued her. The times she had caught him looking at her made her very aware of herself—and her decidedly horrible appearance.

While not overly vain, she was well aware of how terrible she had looked and smelled before her bath. Now, there was excitement running through her at seeing him after she'd been washed, like shedding her old skin.

A knock on the door jerked her from her thoughts. The entry cracked open, and Synne poked her head in. A smile filled her face when she found Helena.

"You look a sight better," she said.

Helena laughed softly. "I feel much better, as well."

Synne swallowed. "Mind if I come in?"

"Please do."

Synne slipped inside and pushed the door closed behind her. Her pale locks were pulled away from her face in a variety of braids that must have taken hours to do and seemed to complement the woman's beauty.

Synne smiled and walked to her with a confidence that Helena envied. "I may be out of line, but I overheard Jarin and Radnar talking. The warlock says both of you are going to track down Sybbyl."

"Aye, we are."

"It will be easier if you are not hampered by a gown."

Helena perked up. "If you are suggesting breeches like you wear, then, aye. I was going to ask if there were extra around."

"There is always extra," Synne said with a laugh. "I'll get everything you need."

She rushed off. Helena wondered if this was what it was like to have a sister. She had no siblings, but she had always dreamed of having one. Someone she could share secrets and dreams with.

It felt like only moments had passed when Synne returned with an armful of clothes and several pairs of boots. And just as quickly, the Hunter handed her each piece, telling her how to put them on. With each item of clothing that went onto her body, Helena grew more confident.

Clothes shouldn't change someone's outlook, but that's precisely what the pants, shirt, and vest did.

"I was not sure of your foot size, so I brought a few pairs for you to try on," Synne stated once Helena was dressed.

Helena walked a few paces and laughed at the feel of the trousers on her legs. "It feels odd."

"You'll get used to it quickly enough. It makes it difficult to put a dress back on," Synne confessed with a grin. "Move around, you'll see what I mean."

"I am moving."

Synne shot her a look. "You're walking. I mean, run, jump, twist. Lunge. Imagine chasing after someone and having to leap over a fallen tree."

"Oh," Helena said, eyes wide. "I have never done that. But, it would have been easier these past weeks to be in this rather than my gown."

Synne suddenly frowned. "I hope you were not expecting the gown, cloak, shoes, or your undergarments back. I burned them."

"There was no amount of washing that would have saved any of it. They are better off in the fire."

"Good. Now, let us fit you for boots."

Helena followed Synne and sat when the Hunter pointed to the stool. One by one, Synne helped her put on each pair until they finally found some that fit.

Synne straightened with her hands on her hips and smiled at Helena. "You look like a Hunter now."

"I rather feel like one."

They shared a smile, but Synne's dropped quickly. Helena touched her damp hair when she realized that's what the Hunter stared at.

"We should see to that promptly," Synne stated.

Helena blinked, not quite sure what Synne wanted of her. She was used to taking care of herself. She had done it for so long, she couldn't remember any other way.

Synne stopped by the fire and looked over her shoulder at Helena. She then pointed to the fur rug. Helena hesitated a moment before she rose and made her way to the hearth.

With a little push on her shoulder by Synne, Helena found herself sitting. The Hunter began brushing her hair one section at a time with gentle, sure strokes. They didn't talk, and soon, Helena found her eyes drifting close from the movements. Her mother must have once brushed her hair, but she couldn't dredge up even one memory of it.

The feeling of the brush running through her hair was amazing. There were no words to describe how relaxing it was. A simple action could take away all her cares and thoughts.

Well, that wasn't entirely true. She couldn't stop thinking about Jarin.

As if reading her thoughts, Synne asked, "What do you think of the warlock?"

"I think he is extremely powerful."

"Obviously," the Hunter replied sarcastically. "I meant, what do you think of him...as a man?"

"Um..."

Synne chuckled. "That's what I thought."

"What do you mean by that?"

"It was the way he looked at you when Edra led you away."

Helena's heart missed a beat. "And how did he look at me?"

"Hungrily."

Helena's eyes snapped open when her stomach quivered in excitement. *Hungrily.* No, that couldn't be right. "You must be mistaken. I've spent days with Jarin. He has not done or said anything that—"

"You would not be saying that had you seen his look. He is also very protective of you."

"Really?" Helena asked softly, the idea making her smile.

"Aye. He is handsome. And those eyes of his."

"He has a quiet confidence I like."

"Mm-hmm," Synne murmured as she set down the brush.

Helena closed her eyes when the Hunter started braiding her hair, but her thoughts were on the warlock. How she wished she could have seen the look Synne described. No one had ever gazed at her *hungrily* before.

No matter how she thought about it, what Synne said didn't mesh with what Helena had experienced in the days she had been with Jarin. He was detached and rarely spoke, but he always made sure she had plenty of food and found a comfortable place for them to bed down for the night.

She wasn't used to anyone taking care of her, and if she hadn't been so weak, she never would have stood for it. But as the days went on and she grew progressively stronger, she still allowed Jarin to hunt for their food.

Not that she could've been much help. She had always used magic before to help her catch her meal. Since she couldn't chance it with the Coven, she'd had no choice but to leave it to him.

Yet...even she had to admit that it had been nice. They had fit well together. Hopefully, when they left the abbey, she would be strong enough to keep up with the pace he normally used. She was all too aware that he had slowed considerably for her.

"There," Synne said after a long time. "All done. It looks quite fetching if I do say so myself. You have the most amazing hair. I wish mine was red."

Helena felt her cheeks warm as she opened her eyes. She hadn't blushed in years. "Thank you," she said and reached back to touch the braids.

Synne grabbed her hands and fisted all but Helena's index

fingers. Then she ran them along each of the three small plaits on either side of her head above her ears that met at her crown.

"Feel those?" Synne asked.

Helena nodded.

"I braided the plaits on each side into two thicker ones before binding them together here," she said, using Helena's fingers as she explained everything.

"I wish I could see it. I can never repay you for this kindness."

Synne moved to stand before her. "It was my pleasure. You look beautiful, by the way. Ready to eat?"

"Is it time already?"

"Aye," the Hunter said with a grin.

Helena got to her feet and glanced down at herself. She was much skinnier than she had been a few months ago. What strength she'd lost would replenish quickly. It had to. She had no idea when they would encounter the Coven, but it would happen, and she needed to be ready.

She wouldn't be a liability for anyone. Especially Jarin.

"Come on," Synne said at the door.

Helena drew in a deep breath and followed the Hunter out of the chamber. When Edra had first led her to the room, Helena had been tired with the remnants of weakness hanging on. It was like the bath had washed away all of that along with the dirt. For three days now, she'd regularly had food in her belly, and her strength was returning.

Synne talked as they walked through the corridors and past chambers, pointing out this and that. Helena listened, but her mind was on Jarin. She wished she didn't think about him so much, but her thoughts went to him before she had a chance to stop them.

The closer they got to the hall, the more nervous Helena

became. She wanted Jarin to notice her. Nay. That wasn't true. The truth was much more straightforward.

She needed to see the hunger in his gaze that Synne had mentioned.

They turned a corner, and before Helena knew it, they stood in the hall. They must have been the last to enter because the food was already out and seats taken.

Several tables were empty, denoting Hunters who were out searching for Coven members, but she barely noticed them. Her gaze had found Jarin immediately upon entering.

Her stomach plummeted to her feet when he glanced her way without a smile. Then he did a double-take, his pale eyes fastening on her with such intensity that it made her stomach flutter and her heart race.

"Hungrily," Synne leaned over to whisper. "I told you."

Jarin slowly rose to his feet. Valdr padded to Helena. She looked down long enough to smile at the wolf before returning her attention to the warlock. Dimly, she realized that Synne had left her.

Unsure where to sit, Helena looked around and saw Edra waving her over to their table. The table where Jarin was. Helena started toward them with Valdr by her side. Moments later, Jarin started toward her. She came to a halt when he reached her in the middle of the room.

"You look as if you feel better," he said.

If she thought he would mention her attire, she'd been dead wrong. "A bath seems to be a miracle worker."

"I also like the clothes."

She smiled. "I'm enjoying them immensely."

A slow grin pulled at his lips. "They suit you."

She stilled when he reached around and lifted the half of her hair that Synne had left free of the braids. Helena couldn't take her eyes from his face.

Just as with the first time he'd touched her hair, he let it drop without a word. Then he shifted to the side and waited for her to move past him.

On her way to the table, Helena glanced at Synne, who shot her an I-told-you-so look. Helena hastily looked away as she and Jarin reached the main table. She found herself sitting between a tall knight she learned was Radnar and Jarin.

"You were right to bring her, Jarin," Edra said with a knowing look at Helena. "She looks refreshed and ready to face anything."

"Thank you for all the kindness I've received," Helena said. "As well as for the clothes."

"Both of you are always welcome here," Radnar said.

"Eat," Jarin said as he nudged her to grab food.

Soon, her anxiety disappeared amidst the excellent food, ale, and conversation. She laughed at the stories being told and listened raptly to tales of the encounters the Hunters had with the Coven.

Helena filed it all away. It wasn't until the meal was nearly finished that she looked over at Jarin, who was staring into his trencher.

"Everything all right?" she asked.

He glanced at her, giving her a quick smile. "Aye."

That's when she realized he was usually on his own. He wasn't around this many people too often. "Is it too much for you? Shall we go?"

His head jerked to her. "I'm fine."

She cocked a brow, telling him without words that she didn't believe him.

"I do not converse well with others," he admitted with a sigh.

"I beg to differ." Without thinking, she put her hand on his arm to offer him comfort.

There was a beat of silence as they both became aware of her touch. They looked down at her hand as one before she hastily jerked her palm away.

She couldn't catch her breath after, thinking of the strong muscles she'd felt beneath her palm—all while wondering what the rest of him felt like.

9

Uncertainty wasn't an emotion Jarin was familiar with. At least, not until recently. Twice, he'd joined with the Hunters and knights to fight the Coven, and he alone knew the growth of their magic.

He walked from the abbey, wanting and needing the sting of the icy air in his lungs after sitting next to Helena, who looked radiant and so damn pretty he couldn't stop staring.

She rattled him like no one before. And when she'd touched him...it had sent a hot, lust-filled jolt straight through him.

Jarin couldn't allow his thoughts to deter him from his goals, which was putting the Coven back in their place. The fear he had kept to himself was that the witches might be too powerful now. It helped that the Hunters were agreeable to joining with the Varroki.

But would it be enough?

His gaze lifted to the clear night sky. A multitude of stars looked down upon him. Most of his life had been spent staring up at the evening sky before he fell asleep. There was something comforting and soothing about the moon and stars.

Or maybe he was just so used to living on his own outdoors that he didn't know how to act in an enclosed space.

"You do not want to be here, do you?"

His head turned to the side at the sound of Helena's soft, sensual voice behind him. He didn't turn around to look at her. The image of her face had imprinted itself in his mind from the first day he met her.

Seeing her looking healthier and stronger than before and wearing clothing that showed every amazing curve had only fanned the flames of desire that he had been battling. While he wasn't inexperienced when it came to bedding a woman, he had few skills.

And he wasn't sure he wanted to act on anything. It was easier to ignore his feelings and everything else involving Helena.

"If you want to leave, we can," she said. "Or...perhaps you would rather go alone."

He faced forward, unsure how to answer.

There was a stretch of silence. Then Helena said, "You saved my life. I can never thank you properly for that."

"There is no need," he replied.

"I disagree."

He knew the moment she moved closer. He could feel her, as if invisible strings connected them. Jarin fisted his hands at the sensation of the raw, visceral urges running rampant through him the closer he was to her.

Even now, he could feel the touch of her hand on his arm. It wasn't the first time he had been freely touched, but it was the first time he had wanted it. *Yearned* for it.

And missed the feel of it when it was gone.

"We spoke about going after Sybbyl together," Helena continued. "I will not hold you to that pact."

He realized that she was giving him a way out. Why then did it anger him so? "You do not wish to be associated with a warlock?"

"Nay, that's not it," she stated quickly. Then she was before him, glaring daggers at him with her vibrant green eyes. "I see how uncomfortable you are among others, and I wanted to give you an opportunity to go out on your own if that is your wish."

Her red locks glowed in the moonlight as if on fire. Jarin had never seen anything so mesmerizing. She had no idea of her appeal—or how much he wanted her.

"Say something," she demanded.

"You should always be bathed in moonlight."

Her lips parted as her face went slack. "I berate you, and you compliment me?"

"I say what needs to be said."

He watched the subtle play of emotions on her face. Surprise, confusion, and, finally, delight. The nervous lift of the corners of her mouth gave him more insight into her than words ever could.

Few had ever given her such praise. She, like Jarin, had let few people close. Fear of the Coven and those without magic kept her isolated, while he had chosen his solitary path.

Odd that they would find each other.

Helena shivered, wrapping her arms around herself. "I do not always know what to say to you."

"The truth. Always the truth."

"Even if I do not want to say it?" she asked.

He gave a nod. "Especially then. And I will do the same."

"I like that."

Jarin swallowed and tried, unsuccessfully, to look away

from her. "When I leave here, you will be by my side. Unless you have changed your mind about accompanying me."

"Nay," she said hastily, shaking her head.

That pleased him much more than it should. "Then ease your mind. I'll be here in the morn."

"But you do not like it."

"That is not entirely correct." He'd promised her truth, so it would be honesty that he gave—even if it was hard for him. "I think this place is almost as amazing as Blackglade. The problem is that I do not feel as if I belong here."

Valdr walked toward them, coming to sit between them. The wolf leaned against Jarin. Without thinking, Jarin began to slowly pet the animal's head.

Helena studied Jarin for a long, quiet moment before she looked at the abbey. "I disagree. I think you most certainly belong, and I know that everyone is quite taken with you." Her gaze swung back to him. "You do not see the respect and awe others give you."

Jarin glanced away, uncomfortable with her statement. He knew the path of a warrior was one seen favorably by his people. He'd grasped his destiny with both hands and never looked back. The toughest part hadn't been the seclusion or even tracking down the Coven.

It had been leaving Blackglade and his family.

What was it about Helena that brought everything he believed he had buried years ago back?

He jerked his gaze to her when she gently took one of his fists in her hand. He stared at the top of her head as she slowly, tenderly unfurled one finger at a time. Then she placed her hand atop his before lightly running her fingertips over his palm.

She was closer now. So close, Jarin could smell the

lavender on her skin. The scent filled his nostrils and sank into him. When had she closed the distance?

Enthralled, Jarin stood still as stone when she lowered his hand to his side and reached for the other, repeating the movements again. Then she lifted his palm and pressed her lips to his skin.

His blood ran hot, pounding in his ears as his breathing became ragged and harsh. Without a doubt, he wanted Helena. Craved her.

Hungered for her.

Her head lifted, her gaze spearing him. Her smile was soft with just a hint of seduction, as if she knew her action had rattled him—and she liked it.

To his surprise, she released him and turned to walk away. Jarin grasped her hand before she could leave. She turned back to him, but he didn't take her in his arms as he yearned to, didn't lower his head to her mouth.

He simply stared at her, trying to find the words to convey what he felt.

Her lips curved into a grin before she took a step back, their fingers sliding from each other. She pivoted and walked away, but right before entering the abbey, she looked at him over her shoulder.

How in the world was he going to spend days, weeks, and possibly months alone with her and not give in to the desire that pounded through him?

His chance to leave Helena behind was gone, but he didn't regret it. The witch was full of surprises. And he was quite keen on learning more about her.

For the first time, he was immensely grateful that Malene had changed the Varroki laws because he knew he didn't have enough willpower to ignore his need for Helena.

Jarin looked down at Valdr, who blinked at him with

yellow eyes. Jarin frowned as he thought about the Coven once more. The elders were gone. The witches would convene soon where Sybbyl could claim the position to rule them.

She would be the one to take over the role of leader, and there was no telling in what direction she would take the Coven. The more Jarin thought about it, the more concerned he became.

Sybbyl had changed after she got the Staff of the Eternal. As far as he knew, the same lust for power had not happened to Braith when he claimed the Blood Skull.

Then again, Braith was the Warden, destined to be the skull's keeper and make sure it never fell into the hands of the Coven. They had been content to let the skull go and search for other pieces of the First Witch.

But would Sybbyl feel the same? Or would she go after Braith, intent on killing him to claim the skull as her own?

Radnar had assured Jarin that Leoma and Braith were prepared for such an outcome, but Jarin wasn't so sure. And he wouldn't be until he found Sybbyl again. The glimpse he'd gotten of the witch before she disappeared left him thinking that they were all in for more than they could possibly imagine.

The elders had fought amongst themselves for power, with all four rarely agreeing on anything. The Varroki and the Hunters had actually benefited from that. But Jarin couldn't help but think that things were about to get much, much worse if Sybbyl took the Coven in hand as he suspected she would.

He and Helena needed to leave at first light the next day to begin their hunt for Sybbyl. His instincts were demanding urgency, and he always listened.

If he were going alone, he would leave right then. But he wasn't. He'd made a vow to Helena, and he aimed to keep it. A few more hours wouldn't hurt. He would allow her a night in a soft bed before they began their journey.

Jarin pivoted and headed back into the abbey with Valdr by his side. He had been shown his chamber earlier, and he headed there now. As he walked, he went over the details of his last encounter with Sybbyl and everything she'd done to Ravyn. The Hunter had nearly died, and would have, had Carac and his men not arrived when they had. And that was all thanks to Helena.

While Jarin had expected to fight Sybbyl on his own, he wouldn't turn away any reinforcements that offered aid. In his dealings with Braith and Leoma, he'd learned just how much someone would fight for another when love was involved.

He entered his chamber and smiled when he saw Andi sitting on a perch, already asleep. Valdr curled up next to the fire, and Jarin lowered himself to the bed. He lay back with an arm beneath his head, staring at the palm that Helena had kissed.

10

S he felt the witches enter the Witch's Grove. One by one, they made their way to the center where they stood in a circle around Sybbyl. Her call had forced those nearest to heed her demand. The number was not even a quarter of their members, but the sight of the witches made her smile.

Their looks of alarm and disbelief at finding her and not an elder made her incredibly happy. So many who had told her she would never have the magic to become an elder were about to discover just how wrong they were.

"Behold!" she stated loudly and held up the staff. "The elders' mishandling caused us to lose the Blood Skull, but I was the one who found the Staff of the Eternal. And, as you can all see, I am now its owner."

"How do we know it is the real thing?"

The voice came from behind her. Sybbyl drew in a steadying breath. She had expected such an outburst, and now it would give her the opportunity to prove just how powerful she was with the staff.

She let the words and the voice of the witch roll through

her head as she pulled magic from the staff. Sybbyl only had to think the spell for the staff to react.

There was no gust of wind, no smoke or colored magic shot from her or the staff. But the sound of the offending witch gasping for air filled the silence. Within seconds, the woman's life was taken from her.

Sybbyl lifted the staff, daring anyone else to question her authority as the witch's body fell to the ground before disintegrating into ash.

Looking straight at the witches ahead of her, Sybbyl waited for them to kneel before she turned. Every witch she looked at fell to her knees, their heads bowed in acknowledgment that Sybbyl was the new leader.

"Rise, my sisters," she told them. "This Grove is mine. It is the oldest of them, and I am claiming it as my domain. Each of you will disperse and make sure to spread the word of what has transpired this day to our other Coven sisters who were too far away to come."

A young witch with brown hair and close-set eyes stepped from the others. "Will we continue the mission to find the bones of the First Witch?"

"Aye, my child, we most certainly will. I will retrieve the next one," Sybbyl said.

"May I join you?" the young one implored.

Three more witches quickly raised their voices, letting Sybbyl know they also wanted to go with her. Sybbyl had thought to do it on her own, but perhaps it would solidify her new station by proving she could obtain more than one of the First Witch's bones. The fact that she wasn't going after a bone but a person was something she would keep to herself for the moment.

"Aye," she replied with a nod of her head. "The four of you may remain and join me on my quest."

Just as she was about to dismiss the others, there was a shout and a struggle near the back of the circle. Sybbyl waited as the group parted, and two women hauled a third before her, throwing her down at Sybbyl's feet.

"And who is this?" Sybbyl demanded.

One of the women, a portly older witch with thick, white hair and faded blue eyes, pointed a gnarled finger at the one on the ground. "She tried to sneak away."

Sybbyl bit back her grin. How many times had she escaped early when the elders had called them together? Too many times to count. But the longer she stared at the witch, the more she realized that wasn't what this was about.

She squatted down and waited for the woman to lift her head. When she did, Sybbyl looked into her brown eyes and moved a lock of the woman's dark blond hair from her face. The witch was shaking, she was so terrified. Tears coursed down her cheeks, but Sybbyl wasn't moved by them.

"Were you leaving?" Sybbyl asked.

The witch cried harder and attempted to turn her head away. Sybbyl stopped her with a finger to her chin and forced her face back to her.

"Tell me," she demanded softly.

"A-a-aye."

Sybbyl was pleased with the truthful reply. "Now, tell me why."

The witch's crying ceased for a heartbeat before she raised her bloodshot eyes to Sybbyl. "Why?"

"I want to know the reason."

The witch swallowed loudly and pushed up with her hands to lift her torso. She looked at Sybbyl for just a second before glancing away. "I am terrified of you."

"As much as I like that sentiment, I do not think that is

the entire truth." Sybbyl looked at the two women who had stopped the witch. "What do you two think?"

The portly one was quick to reply. "That she does not want to acknowledge you as our new leader."

"Do you?" Sybbyl asked the portly one.

The woman jerked her chin up and stated, "Of course, I do. All in the Coven do."

"They hate me," the witch on the ground said as more tears came. "I would not agree to stand with them against you. I decided to leave and return later to tell you."

Sybbyl touched the witch's head for a moment then rose to her feet with the help of the staff. Sybbyl looked from one witch to the other. Not a word left her lips, but a moment later, both of the women were blaming the other.

She touched first one, then the other with the staff. Both died instantly. As ash piled on either side of the third witch on the ground, Sybbyl offered her hand to help the woman to her feet.

"All of you are aware that the only way to leave the Coven is through death. Once you are a member, you are one for life. I detested the elders and their rules, but I followed them," Sybbyl said. "And while I am not the elders, I am now leader of the Coven. I set the rules now."

She looked at each of them, waiting to see if anyone else wanted to question her. When no one moved, she said, "Leave me."

When the witches started to leave, Sybbyl kept her hand on the witch to keep her by her side. It wasn't long before all that remained in the Grove was Sybbyl, the four witches who'd asked to join her, and the blonde.

"What is your name?" Sybbyl asked.

"Avis."

Sybbyl touched the witch's face. "You are a fair one, to be

sure. I doubt there is a man out there who does not lust after you."

Avis's smile was confident. "If there is a man I want, I get him either with my face or my magic."

"I imagine you do. There is a man I am sending you after. A warlock."

Avis jerked back, her brow furrowed deeply. "They do not exist."

"Oh, but they do." Sybbyl shifted so that the other four could hear her. "The Varroki are real. This warlock is a Varroki, and I want him."

Avis seemed to think about it for a moment, then nodded. "Then I shall get him for you."

"You will know him by the staff he carries and his pale blue eyes that look almost white. He is to be mine. Find him and return him here," she commanded.

"I will begin immediately." Avis turned on her heel and hurried from the Grove.

Sybbyl then faced the remaining four. "The next part of the First Witch I seek is not a bone, but a person. A direct descendant."

The witches looked positively thrilled at the news.

"You will accompany me when I set out for her. But understand that she is mine. We have a history, and I want her to know that she can no longer escape her destiny," Sybbyl told them.

She drew a circle in the ground with the end of the staff and laid it down before her. Then she got on her knees and bent over to put her hands on the petrified bone within the staff.

Sybbyl focused her mind on Helena. The spell to find a person was normally fairly easy, but not so when it was another witch she needed to locate. Whether on purpose or not, Helena had put up wards to stop from being found.

But that wasn't possible. Sybbyl had located her days earlier. Why couldn't she do the same now?

Then she knew—the staff.

Somehow, the ancient bone was now attempting to stop her from finding Helena. But Sybbyl wasn't going to give up that easily.

She summoned all her magic, including what the staff gave her. The force of the power straightened her back. She dropped her head back, her eyes closed as it welled within her. Sybbyl felt as if she were choking, but she didn't stop saying the spell, over and over.

Suddenly, black smoke poured out of her mouth and cascaded down her front. In her mind's eye, it felt as if she were speeding over the countryside, faster than a bird. Everything was a blur. Then it stopped, showing her a dense forest.

Sybbyl searched for trees or sights that she could later use to identify the location before the spell ended and she returned to herself.

She reached for the staff as the last of the smoke fell from her lips. Once on her feet again, she walked from the Witch's Grove with the four witches at her heels.

Helena stoked the fire in her chamber. She couldn't believe she had been so forward with Jarin, but she was glad she'd done it. Her breathing hitched when she recalled the hungry look in his eyes.

She rose to her feet and spun in a circle, happier than she had been in a while. She quite enjoyed being at the abbey. It was too bad they couldn't remain for another day or two. Everyone had been so nice. She really hadn't expected that.

Yet she was excited to be alone with Jarin. He claimed that his vow of celibacy had been broken when he went after a Coven witch, but how much did he know about what happened between a man and a woman?

She was wondering if she could be bold enough to kiss him when her heart clutched painfully. Agony rushed through her body like fire licking at her veins. Her legs gave out, so she fell to the floor, landing hard on her knees. She fought to breathe and get the pain under control.

As soon as the pain lessened enough that she could breathe easier, she jumped to her feet and raced from the chamber and down the corridor. She had no idea where Jarin was, but she needed to find him quickly.

She turned a corner and nearly tripped over Valdr. Helena righted herself only to crash into something hard. Strong arms came around her, steadying her.

"Easy, Helena," Jarin said.

She looked up at him while trying to catch her breath. The pain was nearly gone from her now, but it still wasn't easy to find the words to explain.

His frown deepened as he gazed intently at her. "It's all right. You're safe."

She shook her head rapidly. "I'm not. We have to leave. Now. Right now!"

"What happened? Did someone hurt you?"

She shook her head again and tried to pull him after her. "Come on."

"Not until you tell me what is going on."

He was an unmovable force, rooted to the spot until she gave him what he wanted. Helena briefly closed her eyes, battling the scream of fear that threatened to erupt and spill from her lips.

She opened her eyes and met Jarin's. "I felt magic. It came straight for me."

"I felt nothing," he stated and glanced around.

Valdr stared off into the night and growled softly. There was a rustle of feathers before Andi came flying out of the chamber.

Jarin looked at the animals then at her. "All right. Let me get my staff and bag and we'll be off. After we inform Edra and Radnar."

"Fine," Helena relented thankfully. "But we need to hurry."

He released her to rush back into his chamber and collect his things. His cloak billowed out behind him as he strode from the room.

She fell into step beside him as they made their way to the opposite end of the abbey and knocked on a door. It opened almost instantly with Radnar filling the space.

He looked at them, then said, "Edra. You should come."

The witch joined her husband and took in what Radnar saw. "You're leaving."

"We must," Jarin said.

Helena swallowed. "I cannot explain other than to say magic found me." She touched the place over her chest where her heart was. "The pain was...unbearable. It brought me to my knees, and I knew I had to leave. If I do not, the Coven will find this place."

"Come with me," Edra said as she brushed past them.

Radnar joined them as they walked to another chamber. Edra then handed her a new cloak, a waterskin, and a bag of food.

"Good luck," the witch said.

Radnar gave a nod. "Remember, you are both welcome here."

Helena waved at them, then hurried from the abbey to put some distance between herself, the Hunters, and whoever was after her.

But she knew who that was. Sybbyl.

11

Helena ran from the abbey and didn't look back. She kept thinking of the children housed within those walls and how Sybbyl wouldn't hesitate to annihilate each and every one of them, no matter the age.

She had no idea where she was going. For all she knew, she was headed straight for the witch. Maybe that was for the best. The sooner Helena could face her nemesis, the better.

"Helena."

She heard Jarin's call, but she still didn't stop. She couldn't. There was too much at stake. Valdr ran slightly ahead of her, letting her know the safe routes and where she needed to jump.

It could have been moments or hours that passed before Jarin's arm looped around her waist and hauled her back against him, halting her.

"We cannot stop," she said, fighting to free herself.

But Jarin was too strong, his hold unmoving no matter how much she wiggled and fought.

"We need a plan," was all he said.

All the fight went out of her. She leaned her head back against his shoulder, her breath billowing out into the night. "It was wrong for me to go there. The children should be kept safe. They will never be as long as I am around."

"If Edra thought for a moment it was not safe for the bairns, she wouldn't have allowed us entry," he replied softly. "Everything Edra and Radnar have done and still do pits them against the Coven. Every day, they remain alive and stay in the fight, they win."

Helena closed her eyes as the fear that had gripped her began to lessen. Mostly because of Jarin. He was calm, as if it didn't matter how bad the storm raged around him, he would never let it beat him down.

If only she had that ability.

She took a steadying breath as his warmth surrounded her. His arm was firmly in place, but not restricting her. Without even trying, she felt the hard sinew of his body. In less than a heartbeat, her fear was replaced by something stronger, something more primal.

He leaned his cheek against her head. "Now that we've put some distance between us and the abbey, tell me what happened."

"It was Sybbyl."

"How do you know?"

"I..." She shrugged, grateful that he had yet to release her. Whether she liked it or not, she needed the strength he offered. "I cannot be sure. Just a feeling I have."

His head lowered, putting his lips near her ear. "We will find a place to rest for the night and come up with a plan. At first light, we head out."

Helena shivered at the warm breath that fanned her ear and neck. She gave a nod, unable to form any words.

For a heartbeat longer, his arm remained in place. Then,

he released her and quickly took a step away. She stumbled back and righted herself.

"Follow me," he stated.

Helena hurried after him when he began walking. She had been so intent on putting one foot in front of the other when they left the abbey that she hadn't realized she'd taken them to the fringes of the forest.

Thankfully, there was a steep incline that must offer some kind of shelter by the way Jarin made straight for it. By the time she reached the peak and saw the half-hidden entrance, she was out of breath.

Valdr trotted past her into the dark. A moment later, there was a spark, and a fire flared to life. She caught sight of Jarin, who was staring at her, his face illuminated by the flames.

As she entered the cave, she spotted Andi cleaning her feathers. That must be how Jarin had known about the place. Not that it mattered. Helena realized she would likely follow him anywhere.

She sat near the fire and unclasped her cloak to lay it beside her. Her gaze went to Jarin when she saw movement. She couldn't look away, watching the way his body moved as he set aside his staff, bag, and cloak. Only then did she realize the ends of his hair were damp.

He glanced at her before he raked a hand through his locks, shoving the long, dark blond strands from his face. "I had just finished with my bath when Valdr started pawing at the door. He knew you were distressed."

"How?" she asked, trying to stop picturing Jarin's naked body and the water moving over him. "I did not call out."

The warlock shrugged. "Valdr is a special animal. So is Andi."

Needing something to talk about before they went into

what happened, she asked, "How did you come to have them as pets?"

"I do not own them. They are free to come and go as they please. I rescued Andi from a baron who had captured her. She was still very young, just learning to fly. When I saw him about to sew her eyes shut to begin her training, I knew I had to save her."

Helena looked at the bird. She had her eyes closed, but Andi's face was aimed toward Jarin. There wasn't a doubt in Helena's mind that the bird loved him.

"When the baron refused to agree to my terms, I broke the tresses holding Andi, which allowed her to fly away. I, too, was content to leave, but the baron threw a knife at me. I easily dodged it, but before I could retaliate, Andi swooped down and clawed out his eyes, ensuring he would never imprison another bird."

Helena had new respect for the falcon. "I gather she has been with you ever since?"

"Aye. I thought she would return to her nest, but day after day I saw her flying above me. At night, she remained near me. She is the one who led me to Valdr."

With a smile, Helena reached over and ran her hand through the wolf's thick fur after he'd settled between her and Jarin.

"His mother had been killed," Jarin continued. "Valdr was still a young pup and standing his ground against a boar intent on killing him. I got there in time, but unfortunately, he was the last of his litter left alive. I could not leave him on his own. I took him with me, feeding him until he was strong enough to leave."

"But he remained," Helena finished.

Jarin's lips softened when the wolf looked in his direction. "Both animals recognize magic. I believe they feel it on a different level than either you or I. That could be how Valdr knew you were in trouble."

"Thank you," she said to the wolf. Helena swallowed, the smile gone. "I joined you to fight the Coven, especially Sybbyl."

"Aye," he murmured.

She wrapped her arms around herself. "Yet, every time I think about facing her, I want to run the other way. Not because I'm afraid that I might die, but because I know she wants me."

"Because you escaped them twice?"

Helena searched her mind for the answer but couldn't come up with one. Finally, she shook her head. "I know not. It could be. I do not know any other who has escaped them twice. It is rare to get free the first time."

"How did you do it initially?"

Images of that day flashed in Helena's mind. She wanted to shut them out, but if she and Jarin were going to work together, then he needed to know. All of it.

"I was very good at hiding my magic," she began. "I learned early on that no one could know. My mother had magic, but she refused to use it, even when my father beat her. She feared for her safety as well as mine, so I made sure I was far from anyone whenever I tried magic."

Out of the corner of her eye, Helena spotted Jarin's gaze locked on her. The story was difficult enough, so she kept her eyes trained on the fire.

"My father was a drunk and a brute of a man who used his fists instead of words. I lost track of the times I watched him beat my mother. If I made any noise that called his attention to me, Mum would make sure to turn it back to her. I begged her to stand against him, to defend herself, but she said we needed him. Without him, we had no one to provide for us, no one to protect us. I urged her to use magic, but she scoffed at me."

Helena swallowed, pausing a moment. "I was in a foul mood when Da stumbled home one evening. It took nothing for me to anger him, as usual. Perhaps I wanted that, but I was unprepared when he backhanded me. I will never forget the taste of blood that filled my mouth or the numbness along my cheek. Or the rage.

"Mum stepped in before he could hit me again. I scrambled out of the way, watching as I normally did. But this time was different. This time, he did not relent. This time, he kept hitting her even after she was unconscious. I could stand it no longer, so I used magic to break his neck."

She could still hear the sickening sound, even all these years later. Helena scratched her cheek and drew in a quick breath. "I rushed to Mum and checked her injuries. When she came to and saw what I had done, she cried for *him*. The man who had nearly killed her. Even now, I cannot understand that. She knew without asking that I'd used magic. She told me I had to leave, to run far away so no one could find me. So, I did."

"How old were you?" Jarin asked.

"Not yet five and ten. I ran for weeks, stealing food when I could and relying heavily on my magic to survive. But I knew if I wanted a life, then I had to forget magic. It took a while, but I did it. I learned to survive on my own. I met a kind, older couple who gave me shelter, and I suppose, a home. They never asked any questions. They simply accepted me for who I was.

"I learned that they'd lost their daughter years before to a fever, so I suppose they thought of me as theirs. It was nice having such a kind, loving couple looking after me. I helped them around their home until I was the one taking care of them."

Jarin stretched out his legs as he leaned against the wall. "It sounds perfect."

"I suppose it was. Except that I had to lie about who I really was. So many times, I could have used magic to help them, but I refused. Then, I met a man. He was charming and handsome, and I fell for it all. A month later, I discovered I was pregnant the same day he left the village, never to be seen again. But the couple did not throw me out. They were actually excited about the prospect of a baby in the house."

Helena turned her head to Jarin, briefly meeting his gaze. "Their love knew no bounds. Not once did they ridicule me or cast me out. I carried the babe without trouble and birthed her quickly. She was beautiful and healthy." Helena paused, overcome with the memories of holding her daughter. "Three months later, when she grew sick, and no medicines worked, I turned to magic to heal her. What I had no way of knowing was that there were Coven members nearby. They came for me. Sybbyl was one of them. I refused to join them, and they killed the couple. Then—" She stopped as her throat clogged with emotion.

Valdr crawled closer to her and laid his head on her lap. She blinked through the tears she hadn't shed in years and ran her hand along his head.

"They killed your child," Jarin finished.

Helena nodded slowly. "When it happened, it was as if time stopped. I was detached from myself. The only thing I felt was anger. The rage swept through me so fiercely that I had no desire to stop it. I unleashed it on the witches, striking them down with barely a thought. Sybbyl was the only one quick enough to block my assault. I wanted to finish the fight, but I was so bereft, I couldn't manage to gather my magic again. Sybbyl might not have been hit with my magic directly, but it disoriented her. That gave me time to flee. I did not have the opportunity to bury my child or the couple, though. I ran. Again."

In fact, she had been running ever since.

When Jarin said nothing, Helena looked at him, wondering why he was so silent. The simple act of petting Valdr did wonders to calm her after reliving that horrible time in her life.

"I know why the Coven wants you," the warlock finally said.

"Because I killed some of their witches?"

His chest expanded as he pulled in a deep breath. "How many did you kill that day?"

She frowned as she tried to remember. "There were six—no, seven of them. Six died, with Sybbyl remaining."

"You say you only had to think about their deaths and they were gone?"

Helena gave a nod.

Jarin's brows shot up in his forehead. "You have no idea how powerful you are, do you? An untrained witch using magic without a spell or an object to help you. You used your mind."

"Is that rare?"

"Very," he replied softly.

As soon as Jarin heard about Helena's ability, he began to rethink their action of finding the Coven. In fact, the more he considered it, the more he thought it might be better to take her to Blackglade.

The power of the Varroki might be enough to protect her. Then again, if the Coven was tracking Helena, then returning would mean leading the witches straight to Blackglade. No longer would his home be secret. Did he really want to be the one responsible for having the Coven follow him to the gates?

"You're rethinking having me with you."

His gaze snapped to Helena. Her face was turned toward the fire, and her voice was even, just a hint of resignation in her tone. She had been running for so long. There were very few times she had felt safe or cared for. He wanted her to feel that way with him.

And he wanted to be the one to keep her that way.

"I'm not," he stated.

She forced a smile as she glanced at him. "It's all right. I understand. You have a mission, and I would only be in the way."

Jarin rose and walked to squat before her. He waited until her gaze met his, then he said, "I am not abandoning you. I will not let you leave on your own. The fact is, you're a powerful witch, and the Coven knows it. They want you. You can run forever, but they will find you."

"If Leoma had not been there last time, I'd be dead. I do not believe I can escape a third time."

"You forget, you have a Varroki with you."

Her lips curved into a brief smile. "I am tired of running, but I cannot be the reason any more innocents are killed."

"I understand."

She jumped up and began to pace. "You cannot. They murdered my child. And there was nothing I could do to stop it."

He moved before her and grabbed her shoulders to halt her. "The Coven cannot force you to join them. You have to agree on your own. I think they want you because they fear you standing against them."

As he gazed into her green eyes, he saw comprehension fill them. Her shoulders relaxed as the tension slowly faded from her body.

"You have not seen me do any magic," she said with a frown. "I could be making this up."

He should release her. He knew it. But just like earlier when he held her against him, he couldn't. The simple truth was that he liked touching her.

Liked... Hell. He treasured every moment, eager for every heartbeat he could have her against him.

He wanted her near him. Needed her like he needed air to breathe.

"Aye, you could. The fact that the Coven is tracking you

when you have done no magic makes me more inclined to believe you."

Helena sighed loudly as she gave an exhausted shake of her head. "Maybe I was wrong about what I felt at the abbey."

"I saw your face. You felt something, and whatever it was, it scared you enough to have you on the run again."

Her hand reached up and touched his arm, reminding him that he still had a hold of her. The atmosphere shifted within the cave. He couldn't look away from her any more than he could make his fingers release her.

The way Helena gazed up at him so trustingly, made Jarin want to lean down and sample her lips. He could never remember craving something as badly as he did her mouth.

Valdr let out a low, rumbling growl. Jarin's head snapped to the wolf to find the animal staring out of the cave. A glance at Andi showed that she, too, was looking at something outside.

Jarin moved his hand, about to wave it over the fire to put it out with magic, when Helena stopped him.

"Wait," she whispered.

They remained together, listening for any sound. The night had gone eerily quiet, the silence deafening as they heard each other breathing.

"I need to put out the fire," he told her.

She hurried to the fire and began moving aside the limbs that he had conjured. "Not with magic."

"The Coven cannot track my magic."

"Maybe not before," she said, glancing at him. "Sybbyl has the staff, remember? We do not know what she can do now."

Jarin flattened his lips. Helena had a point. It was better to be safe. Instantly, he was beside her, helping put out the fire with what little dirt they could scrape from the rocks. Finally, he used his cloak to stamp out the last lingering flames.

The animals hadn't moved. Whatever was outside still held their attention, though. When Helena made to walk to the entrance, Jarin pulled her back.

"You said I would have to stop running."

He turned her toward the back of the cave. "This is not the place for a battle."

"We have the higher ground," she argued.

"And nowhere to move. The witches would back us in here, trapping us."

She gave a reluctant nod of agreement. "I suppose we should get some sleep."

"I will take first watch," he told her. "Rest. Valdr will keep you warm."

Jarin waited until Helena laid on her side, using her arm as a pillow before he moved toward the entrance to peer out. If he were alone, he would happily confront whoever was out there, but his instincts told him to protect Helena. She was vital to the Coven, and because of that, he would do whatever it took to keep her out of their hands.

Because, while he'd said they couldn't force her, it had been a lie. If Sybbyl had magic powerful enough, along with the Staff of the Eternal, she might very well be able to make Helena do whatever she wanted.

The simple truth was that no one really knew what the bones of the First Witch could do. The fact that the First Witch feared what would happen to her after she died so much that she'd instructed her followers to distribute her bones far and wide spoke volumes.

She had also ensured that her skull had a Warden that would keep it out of the hands of evil. Whether the First Witch was good or not didn't matter. She'd made a decision at the end of her life that set everything in motion.

Jarin wondered if she had seen what was to come. Is that

why she'd put such things in place to make it difficult for the Coven to gather all her bones? And what would happen if all of them were found and brought back together?

Even more worrying was the question of whether the Coven needed all of the bones. Or were only certain ones required?

Jarin squeezed the bridge of his nose with his thumb and forefinger. This was a time he wished he could communicate with the Lady of the Varroki. Malene saw glimpses into the future. She, like Helena, had only scraped the surface of her magic. Who knew what she could do.

He looked over his shoulder at Helena to find her breathing evenly, and Valdr lying against her back, his big head resting on her bent legs.

Jarin crossed to Andi. He held out his arm, and the falcon jumped on it without hesitation. For several moments, he petted the bird as she closed her eyes.

"I need your help," he whispered.

Andi's eyes opened, and she looked at him. She cocked her head as if waiting to hear what he had to say.

"Fly to Blackglade. I need you to go to Malene. I have nothing to write on, nor will I take the chance of using magic to deliver a message. She will know you are mine. I need..."

He paused and closed his eyes for a heartbeat. He needed so many answers, but he needed to choose one question to ask. Andi couldn't talk or convey what was needed to Malene, but it was a chance he had to take.

"I need to know more about the First Witch."

The falcon blinked at him and then, as silent as the dawn, flew away.

Jarin watched her until he could no longer make her out in the darkness. He continued his vigil for several more hours, looking for anything lurking in the shadows. There was no sign of anyone, and gradually, the sounds of the night returned. He wasn't convinced that whatever was there had moved on, however.

It felt as if someone had been peering down at the area, like one did to an insect. And no good could come of that.

A few hours before dawn, Valdr came to sit beside him. Jarin rubbed the wolf's head before he rose and stretched his back. The wolf would keep watch with keener eyes and better hearing than Jarin did.

He looked at Helena and saw that she was curled into a tight ball. The night had gotten significantly colder, and with the fire out, the only thing she had to warm her had been Valdr.

Jarin only hesitated a moment before he stepped over her and silently lay down beside her. As soon as he did, she scooted back against him, seeking his warmth. He closed his eyes, doing his best not to think about the desire she caused within him or the trousers she wore showcasing her legs—or the fact that her perfectly shaped bottom was pressed against him.

The sleep he needed wouldn't come. Not as long as lust ruled him. And certainly not as long as Helena was so near. Yet he couldn't leave her shivering.

"Do you never get cold?" Helena murmured.

He frowned and turned his head toward her, surprised that she was awake. "Aye."

"You would not know it." She then turned and faced him. "You felt it this time, didn't you? The magic."

"Aye. Though I cannot explain what it is."

"It leaves a shadow over everything. It makes me feel as if I will never see the sun again."

"If it searched for you, then it missed you."

She raised a brow. "Did it?"

"You think it's toying with you?"

Helena shrugged and flipped her red hair over her shoulder. "I know it's Sybbyl, but I cannot prove it."

"We have a few more hours until dawn. We will find out more then."

Her hand touched his jaw, and she slowly caressed her fingers over his beard. "Thank you for staying with me."

"There is no need to—"

He didn't get to finish because she leaned in and placed her lips on his. For several seconds, he couldn't think much less breathe, he was so surprised by her actions. When she began to draw back, he shifted towards her and wrapped an arm around her back, holding her tight.

Jarin moved his mouth over hers, learning her. As soon as her lips parted, he swept his tongue inside. He moaned and deepened the kiss when she wrapped her arms around him. This was the last thing they should be doing, but he no longer wanted to deny the attraction.

He accepted it, and the captivating, persuasive desire that had him tightly in its grip.

Her fingers slid into his hair as he gripped the back of her head, winding her red locks around his hand. The kiss was fiery, the passion building with every stroke of their tongues. It felt as if every action, every moment had driven both of them to this moment—to the yearning that consumed them.

His cock was hard and aching, longing to be buried within her. And when she rocked her hips against him, he thought he might expire from the pleasure.

They were about to reach a precipice. If Jarin didn't pull back now, then he wouldn't. He would give in to the carnal pleasures that awaited and gladly take every second with Helena—consequences be damned.

Then he thought of the Coven, Sybbyl, and the staff. He

recalled the terror on Helena's face and in her voice at the abbey before they'd left. Whatever desire he had withered like a plant in winter.

He ended the kiss and bit back a groan when he saw her swollen lips. She didn't question him, simply lay her head on his chest when he rolled onto his back. Jarin kept his arm around her, locking her against his body. If he couldn't claim her now, he could at least hold her.

If it were Sybbyl out there, then he and Helena would have one hell of a fight ahead of them. Warriors always died fighting the Coven. It was a reality Jarin had accepted the moment he took up the mantle.

Given all his years of fighting the Coven, he had few serious wounds to show for it. He had a suspicion that whatever luck had kept him safe might well have run out. He knew he was one of the best warriors, but would it be enough to best Sybbyl?

He was fortunate enough to have encountered her recently, but now that she had claimed the staff and made it her own, she might well have become something...more. The Coven was already dangerous and unpredictable. He wanted to be as prepared as he could, but he worried that there would be nothing for him to learn since this was all new to everyone —including the Varroki.

His people had spent generations and endured countless deaths ensuring that the Coven never rose to any great power. Things couldn't go wrong now.

"Rest," Helena murmured. "There is time for thinking later."

Jarin closed his eyes and held her tighter.

13

Northern Scottish Isles
Blackglade

The quiet before the storm. With gray skies overhead blocking out the morning sun, Armir took the final step winding up the tower and stood outside the door of Malene's chamber. He stared at the wood, wondering what she was doing within—or if she was even inside.

Malene liked to stand atop the tower and stare out over the sea. So many times, he'd found her there. He glanced up the steps and decided to go ahead and check.

Ever since their trip to visit the witch hunters, he'd been...adrift. He hadn't wanted Malene to leave Blackglade, but even he had to admit that she'd made the right decision. The alliance with the witches and Hunters at the abbey might very well come in handy.

As soon as he ascended the final step, he caught sight of Malene's skirts that rippled lazily around her legs. She stood with her back to him and her gaze straight ahead. How he wished he knew what she was thinking.

It was his duty to bring her to Blackglade and have her take up the mantle as Lady of the Varroki. She wasn't the first mission he'd been tasked with. But he prayed she was the last.

None of the Ladies had been of the Varroki. No one, least of all him, understood why an outsider was chosen, or how the radiance that picked the Ladies worked. It was a part of Varroki culture going back to the time of the First Witch. Who was he to question it?

Malene's flaxen hair was gathered in multiple braids before being bound into two thick plaits that fell over her shoulders. Her fur-lined cloak of soft gray matched her eyes. Ever since she'd changed their laws, she had become different. No longer did she chafe at the bonds that bound her to the Varroki or her position. Instead, she seemed to have accepted her role, perhaps even embraced it.

When she asked him to teach her to read, he'd never expected such an outcome. She had been bored and needed something to fill the time. By giving in to her wish, he might very well have given the Varroki the Lady they not only needed but also the one that had been prophesied.

The foretelling that stated that a Lady with double radiance would usher in a new era to the Varroki. Yet, Armir couldn't bring himself to tell her of the prophecy. Malene already had too much on her mind. She didn't need anything else.

He was her commander. It was his job to make sure she had all she needed, to keep her on the path of leadership, and to help guide her in the ways of the Varroki.

The one thing he'd never expected—and fought hard against—was his attraction to her. Malene was...everything to his people. She was hope and strength and power. Without her, Blackglade would be unshielded, allowing the Coven to find them.

But to him, she was so much more. Her wisdom surprised him. Her willpower inspired him. And her beauty took his breath away.

Until she changed the laws, he hadn't been permitted to even touch her. His position had also been one of celibacy. With the rapid decline of the Varroki over the last several generations, Malene realized the problem and changed it.

He walked toward her until he came to stand alongside her. The view from atop the tower was magnificent. She had the same view through her windows, but that never seemed enough for Malene.

"Have you come to tell me that our people have revolted against my changes?" she asked without looking at him.

He turned his head, gazing at the profile of her heart-shaped face. Her cheeks were red from the frigid, blustery wind. "Nay."

Her shoulders drooped as she closed her eyes. "They do realize I am trying to help, then?"

"They do. As I warned, not everyone is keen on the change, but that tends to be the older ones. The younger Varroki are excited."

Her lashes lifted, and gray eyes met his. "What would I do without you?"

Armir realized it wasn't really a question, but he knew the answer. She would do quite well with or without him. Malene needed no one. She was that strong.

He was privileged to be the one to stand with her and watch the amazing changes that she was bringing forth.

"What is it?" she asked as she faced him, a frown creasing her forehead.

"Nothing."

"I do not like when you lie," she stated.

He bit back a grin. "This is a lot of change for everyone."

"Including you."

"Including me," he added. "I'm merely thinking of the future."

Her plump lips pressed together before she gave a small nod and moved her gaze back to the horizon. "You should find a wife, Armir, and have many babies. You're a handsome man. I doubt you would have trouble finding a woman."

The pleasure at her saying that he was handsome was like warmth filling him. The trouble was, the woman he wanted to claim as his own and fill her belly with his bairns was Malene.

He'd touched her, held her. Granted, it had been when she was unconscious, but he knew how right she felt against him. Yet she was the one woman he would always yearn for.

The one woman he could never have.

She smiled up at him. "Is there someone who has caught your eye?"

"Aye," he answered.

"Then woo her. Do not wait. The Varroki need to grow if we are to continue fighting the Coven."

He bowed his head and turned on his heel. Armir had taken only two steps when he heard the cry of the falcon. His gaze scanned the skies until he spotted the bird that flew directly toward them.

Armir paused and looked over his shoulder at Malene, who was also staring at the falcon. It reached them, circling the area before landing on one of the tall stones that were now bent inward from Malene's magic.

He strode to the bird and gazed at it. "It looks like Jarin's falcon."

"Andi?" Malene said.

In response, the bird issued a call and flapped its wings.

"It has something tied to its leg," Malene said.

Armir held out his arm. The falcon dove from its perch, spreading its wings at the last moment and landed on his leather arm bracer. "Easy, girl," he murmured.

The bird swiveled its head to Malene as she walked closer. She slid her fingers softly down the bird, speaking quietly to it. Then she removed the tightly rolled strip of parchment from the falcon's leg.

Malene unfurled the note and read it, her brow furrowing deeper with every word. Her head snapped up to him. "It's from Jarin. Bring Andi."

Armir followed Malene down the flight of stairs into her rooms. A fire roared, keeping the chamber warm. He watched as she gathered some meat left over from her noon meal and gave it to the falcon.

"She has had a long flight," Malene said.

He wanted to know what the note said, but he didn't press Malene. She would tell him in her own time. After he'd found a place to perch the bird, he turned to Malene and waited.

She licked her lips. "Andi went to the abbey and spoke with Asa. She's the one who wrote the note."

"Ah," Armir said with a nod, recalling the witch who was able to talk to animals. Then his heart missed a beat. "Jarin is not hurt, is he?"

Malene quickly shook her head. "Nay. Let me start at the beginning."

He listened as she told him how Jarin had encountered Helena and their journey to the abbey and then from it. When Malene finished the tale twenty minutes later, Armir raised a brow and glanced at the rolled-up message.

"All of that was written?" he asked.

Malene's gaze lowered to the floor briefly. "Asa used magic in some of the words to show me what occurred at the abbey."

"And the rest?" But he really didn't need to ask. More and more, Malene had been getting visions. Most times, it was of things occurring in the present, but a few had been of the future.

"I saw it as I read the missive," she replied.

"Your magic is growing every day. I can hardly keep up with it."

She raised her palms, showing him the blue light that radiated from both, signaling her the Lady of the Varroki. "I, too, am trying to keep up. But this is about Jarin."

"He wanted to inform us of Helena?"

Malene lowered her hands to her lap. "He wants to know more about the First Witch."

"Why do I think you are more focused on the significant power that Helena has?"

"Because it could be connected."

Armir blew out a breath as he tried to recall all the stories he'd learned of the First Witch. "How?"

"Why else would the Coven want Helena so badly?"

"Because she killed some of their members?"

Malene gave him a hard look. "So have the Varroki and the Hunters."

"And the Coven wants all of us."

"That is true. However, they aren't using magic to find us. They are expending considerable power to locate Helena."

Armir had to admit that was odd. "I thought the Coven was after the bones of the First Witch. Helena is very much alive."

"What if she is part of the First Witch?"

Dread filled him at the thought. "A descendant?"

"It would explain Helena's strong magic."

"Jarin is going to need our help." Armir started to rise, but Malene put her hand on his arm and halted him. He slowly lowered himself back into the chair and raised his gaze to her.

His heart thumped slowly, heat spreading through his clothes from her touch. It took every ounce of his control not to pull her against him, to show her how much he ached for her.

"He sent his falcon with only a verbal message," Malene said and pulled her hand away. "He did not use magic, which means he is trying to mask himself and Helena. My guess is that he has figured out that she is important to the Coven."

Armir focused his mind on the task at hand to keep his thoughts from Malene. He might not be a warrior like Jarin, but he had trained as one. It was his duty to find and kill any witch who happened to take the life of any of his warriors.

It was a responsibility he took seriously. Thankfully, the warriors were so good that he'd had to carry out such actions very few times. If it weren't for the Quarter, who were the seers of the Varroki and knew when one died outside of Blackglade, they might never know anything.

"We have no way to contact Jarin," he said. "He could be trapped, but if I know him at all, he will prepare for battle. That means, he'll find a place that puts him at an advantage."

"Can Jarin and Helena fight off the Coven themselves?"

Armir met her eyes and shrugged. "It depends on how many there are. We have not even spoken about Sybbyl. We have no idea how the staff is altering or adding to her magic."

"No one does, because no witch has been in possession of any of the First Witch's bones. We have no idea what we might encounter."

He quirked a brow. "We?"

"You plan on going to find Jarin. I'll be with you."

"Nay."

"I am La—"

"Nay," he said louder. "You are needed here. You keep Blackglade shielded from not just the Coven but the world. We took a huge chance with you leaving to visit Edra at the abbey. This is a battle, Malene."

She rose, her back straight and shoulders back. "A battle you're going to need me for."

"That battle is coming."

"How do you know this is not it?" she demanded.

He didn't, and if he had any say in it, she would never come face-to-face with the Coven. "You trust me to give you my counsel on all matters. I'm asking you to remain behind. I have no idea what awaits me, and I'll not be responsible for your death."

"I can take care of myself."

He took a step toward her. "It is my duty to protect you."

"And you cannot do that and help Jarin," she said. Her expression resigned, she gave a firm nod. "Know this, Commander, if I have a vision of you in trouble, then I *will* be there. You protect me, but it is *my* duty to protect all the Varroki. And that includes you. Now, go help Jarin."

Armir hesitated. There were so many things he wanted to tell her, but they stuck in his throat. Instead, he bowed his head and strode from the chamber.

14

Dawn came far too fast. Helena would've preferred to lay on Jarin's chest and think about their kiss. The breath-stealing, heart-thumping kiss that even now made her stomach flutter.

It had been everything she'd imagined and more. She could kiss him for eternity and never get enough.

His hand splayed on her back, pulling her closer. She didn't need to look up at his face to know that he was awake. He'd likely never gone to sleep, just as she hadn't been able to after their kiss.

Her thoughts went from Jarin to what might be out there to the confrontation she knew was coming with the Coven. Helena wondered if she were strong enough to survive a battle with Sybbyl.

"I think I am developing a love of caves," she murmured.

He chuckled, the sound rumbling in her ear and causing her to smile.

"Is that so?" he asked.

She nodded. "They are very...homey."

"Aye," he whispered and grew silent.

Helena's eyes closed. The dark cloud that had hung around them since their quick departure from the abbey was back in full force. Her jest had only cracked it a little.

"We can remain for another day," Jarin offered.

It was a tempting offer. Very alluring, in fact. She rose up on her elbow and gazed into his pale blue eyes. "That is not who you are, and while it might be the easier thing to do, it is not what I believe we should do."

He ran his fingers gently along her jaw. "There is much about me that is changing."

"Not this," she replied with a grin.

He glanced away. "Perhaps not."

"You're a warrior in every sense of the word, and I'm so thankful you are with me."

"You need no one. Your magic is strong enough to carry you through anything."

She sat up and looked out the entrance of the cave. "How can you say that when I have not done any magic around you?"

"Trust me." He rose in one movement, pulling her cloak with him. Then he held out his hand.

Helena glanced at it before she accepted it, and he hauled her to her feet. She waited as he tied her cloak into place. He then grabbed his bag that he looped over his head and under an arm before fastening his cloak and wrapping his fingers around his staff.

"I'll go first," he stated.

She opened her mouth the same time Valdr got to his feet.

"Nay," Jarin said to the wolf. "Stay with Helena."

Valdr didn't look at all thrilled as he trotted to her side and sat. She turned with Jarin as he started toward the opening.

"Wait," she said. "You're just going to walk out?"

"I would prefer to kiss you, but if I do, I won't be able to stop."

She swallowed, recalling the delicious taste of him. "Oh."

"Valdr will let you know when I call for you. Remain here until then."

He turned to leave, but she rushed to him, grabbing his face and pulling it down for a kiss. With a half-moan, half-growl, he spun them and pressed her against the wall.

The passionate kiss left her clutching him in an effort to remain on her feet. It sizzled, it blazed.

It burned—just as her body did.

She cried out when he tore his mouth from hers and took a step back. Their chests rose and fell rapidly, but it was his eyes that had gone nearly solid white that she couldn't look away from. She grasped the rocks behind her to keep on her feet instead of reaching for him.

"We will survive this," he stated. "And I *will* kiss you again."

His vow made her breath catch. Before she could reply, he was gone. Helena wanted to rush to the entrance, but Valdr moved in her path, preventing her.

With every heartbeat, she waited to hear sounds of battle, but there was only silence. The world was waking. Birds chirped, flying from limb to limb. More light poured through the entrance, but still, there was nothing to let her know that Jarin was fine or if he'd been injured.

It was the not knowing that was the worst. All sorts of images ran through her head, each one worse than the last.

Something hit her hand. She looked down to find that Valdr was bumping his head against her fingers. He walked to the entrance and looked back at her.

"Is Jarin calling for us?" she asked.

In response, the wolf left the cave. She was quick to grab

her bag and follow him. The first step outside, she paused and looked around. The vantage point allowed her to see far, though the thick trees hid much.

After a moment, she made her way down the rocky slope to find Valdr waiting for her. The two of them moved swiftly to find Jarin. The warlock smiled when he spotted them.

"I've found no evidence of anyone being here," he told her.

She frowned. "None? Someone was here."

"Some*thing* was here."

"I was hoping I'd jumped to conclusions last night in believing it was Sybbyl, but I was right, wasn't I?"

A muscle worked in his jaw. "I cannot say either way. Magic was used, I know that much. You were right to warn me not to use mine. If they were searching for magic, then perhaps they've moved on."

"Now what?" she asked. "Your words made sense last night. I need to stop running."

"That means fighting."

She shrugged one shoulder. "I have watched knights, Hunters, and other witches fight against the Coven. The only times I fought was to get away from them. I should have been standing against them the whole time."

"You have been," he told her. "You refused to join them. That took bravery."

"Regardless, it is my turn to fight." Even though it might mean her death. She didn't want to die, but it was time she did something more than run.

Whether Jarin knew it or not, he had given her the courage to do what was right.

"Then we need to find someplace that suits us before we let Sybbyl and the Coven know where we are," he said with a cocky grin.

"Do you have someplace in mind?"

"I might. And it isn't far."

That made her frown. "I want to be as far away from the abbey as possible."

"For all we know, the Coven members have walked right past the entrance to the abbey. Edra has done a good job of concealing it. Trust that."

He was right. Helena knew it, but she couldn't stop the worry. It would always be there no matter what she said or did. She looked at the sky, so used to seeing the falcon that Andi was missed.

"Did she make it to Blackglade?" she asked as she returned her gaze to Jarin.

He gave a nod. "I have no doubt."

"How will you get the information you need?"

"I do not know. I'll sort through that when Andi returns. Until then, we have a long walk ahead of us."

That made her grin. "Lead the way. I have no skirts to hamper me."

Hungry eyes traveled down her legs. "I'm aware."

Helena laughed as Jarin turned and began walking. Just hours before, she had been fearful of leaving the cave. Now, she was laughing. Things had changed so swiftly. But she wasn't alone anymore. She had thought she was fine on her own, but she'd been wrong.

Valdr brushed past her as he hurried after Jarin. Not to be left behind, Helena ran, her smile widening at the freedom the pants gave her.

"I love wearing trousers," she said when she caught up with Jarin.

He glanced at her. "Have you given up gowns for good?"

"I do not think so."

Talking ceased as they moved swiftly. Every once in a while, Jarin slowed to a walk. Twice they halted to rest, drinking heavily from the waterskin. Helena was amazed at how much ground they'd covered.

By noon, they found a cluster of trees to rest beneath. Helena delved into her bag and pulled out a loaf of bread, some cheese, and dried meat. They set aside the cheese and ate the meat first. She tore off some bread for each of them.

There were clouds in the sky, but the temperature was warmer than it had been in days. After such exertion, sitting still too long made her cold. Oddly enough, she was eager to get back to moving to stave off the chill.

She looked up to find Jarin watching her. "What is it?"

"I was wondering if the Coven is searching for all witches who have escaped them or only you."

"Oh." She'd hoped he wanted to talk of other things, but how could they when they had such worries? "Part of me hopes it is all witches because then they haven't singled me out. Then again, I would hate for anyone to be hunted by the Coven."

"Edra knows what it feels like."

"She spoke a little about the seven years she ran from them while we waited for my bath. She finally took a stand, as well. I can only hope my outcome is as good as hers."

Jarin gave her a confused look. "It will be better."

They remained for another twenty minutes before they were up and alternating running with walking as before. Valdr was never far from them, his tongue lolling out the side of his mouth, his ears perked.

The hours passed, and the sun sank. Perhaps it was because Helena now had a mission, something to plan for and focus on instead of just running. Maybe it was because she was with Jarin, but it was the best day.

It had begun on a tenuous note, but with every step, she

felt more confident, more self-assured. There was a smile on her face when Jarin slowed them to a walk again.

The steep peaks turned into rolling hills. Jarin had taken them south, but she couldn't figure out to where. She trusted him, though. He had been seeking witches for years and had no doubt been all over England and Scotland.

They reached the edge of the forest, and she gasped, her feet halting when she saw it.

Jarin nodded toward the large structure. "That is where we will await the Coven."

"Stonehenge? Why?"

He continued walking. "The Celts favored it."

"And?" she asked, jogging to catch up with him.

"The Varroki are Norse and Celtic. I know how powerful that ground is for me."

That's when it dawned on her. "As a Witch's Grove is for the Coven."

He shot her a grin. "With the right spells within the stones, I might be able to temper the power of the staff if Sybbyl comes."

"Doesn't the fact that she has the Staff of the Eternal mean that the entire Coven is stronger?"

Jarin gave a snort and shot her a flat look. "I do not imagine that any Coven member would share power."

Helena hadn't thought about that. "You think she'll come?"

"If she's the one looking for you, then aye. If not, I'm sure destroying whatever witches she sends will be enough to get her here."

The closer Helena got to the megalith, the more at peace she felt. When they finally reached it, she paused beside one of the giant rocks and placed her hand on it.

"It...feels as if it's humming," she said.

Jarin passed between two stones and made his way to the center. "They vibrate with magic. Usually, only the Celts and the Varroki can feel it."

His words surprised her. She followed him to the center where there was another large slab placed horizontally on another piece of rock. "I am neither a Celt nor a Varroki."

"Are you sure of that?" he asked.

She wasn't sure of much anymore.

15

J arin couldn't take his eyes off Helena as she walked among the stones. Based on the way she stared in awe and touched with such reverence, she was mesmerized by them.

He knew witches. He'd encountered all kinds, and the one thing he was certain of was that Helena was different than all of them. He longed to see her use magic to confirm it.

"We are safe here," he said.

Her red head swung to him. "You say that as if I questioned it."

"I say it, so you will comprehend that this place is magical."

She cocked her head to the side. "Then it will shield our magic?"

"Aye," he said before pointing his staff at the ground. Fire erupted from the earth, sparks flying upward from the burst.

She walked to him, her lips parted and her gaze on his face. "Do magic again."

He frowned, confused, yet he did as she requested. The

words in his head went through his hands and into his staff where magic lit the end. The flames soared higher.

Helena halted before him and slowly reached up to touch his cheek. "Your eyes go white when you do magic."

Being on his own so often had made him forget things such as that. But Helena didn't seem repulsed by it. In fact, it seemed to captivate her.

"Does that happen to all Varroki?" she questioned.

He gave a shake of his head. "It is passed down through my father's family. It is considered a gift among my people, but it makes it difficult to hide my magic when I am away from Blackglade."

"I think it's beautiful."

Desire rose quickly, blood rushing to his cock so he was hard in an instant. Their first kiss had been beautiful, the second scorching. And he craved more.

It was all he thought about, all he wanted.

Helena. A witch with as much fire in her blood as in her vivid red locks. A woman with immense beauty and a soul so solid, so vibrant that it couldn't be extinguished.

Her hand caressed down his jaw to come to rest upon his chest over his heart. "The Coven will not find us?"

His body burned like liquid fire. He physically ached from not touching her, not pulling her into his arms and tasting her kiss once more.

He vaguely realized that she had spoken, but it took him another few moments to put a response into actual words. "Not until we wish them to."

"Then tonight is ours?"

"Aye," he whispered, his blood pounding in his ears.

She moved back and untied her cloak before laying it near the fire. After flashing him a grin, she bent and removed her boots.

Jarin leaned his staff against one of the ancient pillars and took off his own boots with hands that shook—not from nervousness, but from need. He almost used magic to take away their clothes, but he liked the idea of getting a glimpse of her a little at a time.

If he could restrain himself.

Helena unfastened the vest over her shirt and tossed it aside. He then removed his vest. Next, she reached for her pants. His mouth went dry when he saw her lean legs. When it was his turn, he opted for his shirt, which he tugged over his head and discarded to the side.

"Oh," she said, her eyes locked on his chest.

She moved toward him and raised her hands. She hesitated before placing them on his chest. "Such intricate work."

His eyes closed as she looked over his tattoo that covered his chest and upper back to his neck, and ran over his shoulders and down both arms to his wrists. He had chosen the design himself. It was both Norse and Celtic knotwork with a Viking wolf head on either pectoral.

"What does it mean?" she asked as her fingers trailed along his back as she walked around him.

Her touch made it difficult for him to focus. He waited until she stood before him once more. His eyes opened, and he looked down at her. "It is my armor. Norse," he said, pointing to the wolf heads and the Norse designs. Then he pointed at the other knotwork. "And Celtic. Every Varroki warrior has such armor."

For long moments, she continued to caress the skin covered with the tattoo. Finally, she stepped away and met his gaze. With slow movements, she gathered her shirt that fell to her hips in her hands. Then she lifted her arms over her head, pulling it off.

Jarin's mouth went dry at the sight of her. Her skin was the color of cream, a direct contrast to the vivid red of her hair and green eyes.

Her breasts were full, her pink nipples already turgid. Jarin couldn't wait to run his hands down her body to the indent of her waist and over the swell of her hips before cupping her ass.

"I have never seen anything more beautiful," he murmured.

Jarin stole her breath again and again. With his hungry looks, as well as his words. Then there was his body. She couldn't get her fill of it. The thick muscles covered by the tattoo that was as much a part of him as Valdr and Andi.

The cool wind didn't touch her, she was so heated from her desire. She licked her lips, waiting for Jarin to remove his breeches. She could make out the impressive outline of his arousal, and she wanted to see all of him.

Finally, he unfastened his trousers and slowly pushed them down his legs before stepping out of them. Her lips parted as she took in the size of his rod. Belatedly, she glanced down at his legs dusted with blond hair and corded with muscles.

While she wasn't well versed in sex, she also wasn't inexperienced. And she knew she wanted Jarin. She never understood why others fought their attraction. If two people were unattached to anyone else and attracted to one another, why shouldn't they find pleasure in each other's arms?

She held out her hand to him, noting that hers shook a little. His fingers touched hers, softly, gently. Then, he jerked her to him, wrapping his thick arms around her and slanting his mouth over hers to kiss her as if there were no tomorrow.

He was tall, well built, and knew what he wanted. If she

thought he would be hesitant or clumsy, she was so very wrong. He was the opposite.

Jarin lifted her, and she wrapped her legs around his waist while their frantic kissing continued. When he knelt down then leaned over to lay her on her back, she shoved at his shoulder until he relented and allowed her control.

She ended the kiss when she had him on his back, straddling his hips. His pale blue eyes stared up at her with such raw longing that her heart skipped a beat.

Helena bent over and kissed his neck and then his chest. She slid her body down as her mouth moved lower over his abdomen and then to his hips. Her lips touched everywhere but his straining cock.

Her head lifted until she locked gazes with him. Then she wrapped her fingers around his rigid staff and moved her hands up and down the length.

His deep moan caused desire to tighten within her. She flipped her hair to one side as she lowered her head to him. His chest was rising and falling rapidly as he watched her. She didn't break eye contact, not even when she parted her lips and wrapped them around the head of his arousal.

Jarin's eyes closed, and his hands fisted in her cloak as she took him deeper into her mouth. Her head bobbed up and down with the movement of her hands as she pleasured him. His hips moved in time with her while his breathing grew harsher with every heartbeat.

She had always loved the decadence of pleasuring a man's arousal. To have him begging for release or panting for more, she was the one making the decisions, the one deciding how much enjoyment to give.

"Helena," Jarin groaned.

She paused and raised her head to look at him. His body was straining, fighting the desire she wished to give him. He grasped her shoulders and jerked her up his body to take her lips.

No one had ever kissed her as he did. Jarin made her forget everything when his mouth was on hers. Perhaps that's why she didn't realize she was on her back, his body between her legs until his hand was fondling her breast.

She gasped when he thumbed a nipple. Desire shot straight down to her sex, making it clench. Her hips rocked against him when his mouth latched on to her breast, and he began to suckle her nipple.

His lips moved from one breast to the other, teasing her until her breasts were swollen and her nipples aching for more. Then he kissed down her body, locking his gaze with hers as she had done him.

Helena bit her lip when he grabbed hold of her hips and hovered his mouth over the red triangle of curls at the juncture of her thighs. His gaze grew fierce, heated with a promise of pleasure right before he spread her woman's lips and put his tongue on her.

Her breath left her in a rush. Only once before had a man touched her in such a way. Warmth spread through her, flushing her body and causing desire to tighten low in her belly. She arched her back when he found her clit, his tongue circling around the swollen nub.

The way his tongue, so soft and slippery, held her at his mercy made her ache to have him inside her. He knew the most sensitive parts to tease, how to push her ever closer to peaking. If only he would suck harder, she might find release.

He could feel her body quivering beneath him. She had

brought him to the brink of oblivion with her mouth, and he wanted to do the same for her.

To have her held in such thrall simply by licking and teasing her made him want to keep her in this state forever. Her soft moans drove him mad. And the way the firelight danced over her body as she undulated caused his balls to tighten even more.

As good as she tasted, he wanted to bury himself inside her, to feel her slick folds envelop him. Jarin continued teasing her with his tongue as he slowly pushed a finger inside her.

Her moans turned to soft cries as he worked his digit in and out of her. The more her hips rose, seeking deeper contact, the more he craved to be inside her.

He finally gave in and rose up on his hands over her. Her eyes opened. The desire, the blatant need he saw there made his breath catch.

Shifting his hips, he aligned the head of his cock against her. He moved forward, letting it slide over her sensitive clit. She cried out, her body jerking from the contact.

"Please, Jarin. I need you," she urged.

He moved over her sex twice more before he slowly pushed inside her. The sight of her lips parted, and her eyes rolling back in her head nearly made him climax right then.

But Jarin clenched his teeth and moved his hips forward and back, sliding deeper and deeper until she had taken all of him. She wrapped her legs around him, locking her feet. He was so far gone that there was no holding back for him now.

He began to thrust, his tempo building until he was moving hard and fast. The moment Helena's body stiffened, and he felt the first clench of her walls around his cock, he could no longer hold back his orgasm.

With her body clamping tightly around him, they

climaxed together. He watched the pleasure wash over her face, felt her nails dig into his back.

He remained inside her until the last of her orgasm waned. Then he kissed her, stroking her face. She looked up at him and smiled softly.

Jarin pulled out of her and rolled onto his back. Helena moved with him, curling up against his side with her head on his chest. For the first time in years, he felt content, as if peace had finally found him.

He knew that even if Malene hadn't revised the laws, he still would have taken Helena as his lover. The attraction that pulled them together was unrelenting as well as unavoidable. He could no more deny her than he could make his heart stop beating.

What Jarin did know was that he would do whatever it took to keep Helena away from the Coven. She was his, and he was hers. The bond was there, already tightly knit.

No one could break that.

16

Everything seemed to be brighter, more intense. Or perhaps it was just her. Helena watched the clouds drift lazily across the darkening sky. Jarin's fingers lightly caressed her back, causing goosebumps to rise on her flesh, it felt so good.

Her gaze landed on Valdr, who lounged on the opposite side of the flames. With Jarin's heartbeat in her ear, the popping of the fire, and the sounds of nature, Helena had never been more content.

At one point in her life, she had dreamt of a home with a husband to love and children to raise. That had been her goal. Even after all the years of wandering from one village to the next, staying only a few weeks before moving on again. The entire time, she had looked longingly at the homes people disappeared into at night to be with their families.

She'd had that once, and she was determined to have it again. Or she used to be. Being with Jarin had shown her that having a building to call home wasn't everything, because she had all she wanted right then in the open air, staring at the beauty around her.

"It is so peaceful here," she said.

Jarin put his free arm behind his head. "Most do not understand the standing stones. They fear what they do not know, so they stay away from them. Those are the ones missing out on what is within them."

"I have seen some megaliths, but nothing like this."

"They have stood for thousands of years and, hopefully, they will stand for thousands more."

She loved listening to Jarin's voice. The deep resonance was soothing. "I'm thinking about how much I'm enjoying being here, but you're thinking of the Coven."

"Actually, my thoughts are on you."

Helena shifted her head to look into his eyes. She couldn't help but smile. "Me?"

"Aye," he murmured in a husky voice.

There was an intensity in his pale orbs that made her stomach flutter. "What about?"

There was a long pause before he said, "Everything."

Her heart missed a beat as he flipped her onto her back and leaned over her. She ran her hand down his beard-covered jaw. Her body heated the moment she felt his cock harden.

"I want you," he said.

Valdr's head snapped up, and his ears perked. The next second, Jarin was on his feet, facing the direction the wolf stared. Helena watched the warrior, her gaze shifting to the rippling sinew and the power that rolled off him in waves.

She slowly got to her feet once Valdr lowered his head again. Aside from rising, Jarin hadn't moved. She came up behind him and put her hand on his back.

"You deserve better than me," he said.

Helena pressed her lips to the indent of his spine then laid her cheek against him. "I wholeheartedly disagree."

"I have no life to give you. I roam, tracking down the Coven."

She flattened her palm on his arm and caressed downward until she reached his fisted hand. It took some effort, but she pried his fingers open and then linked her hand with his.

"You have given me more than I've ever had. I like how I feel with you. I thought you felt the same."

The sound that fell from his lips was half moan, half snort. "More than you will ever know."

"Then stop talking nonsense and kiss me."

In the next breath, he had her flattened against one of the stones, pressing his body against hers. She sank her fingers into his silky hair while he ravaged her lips.

His large hands slid around the backs of her thighs and spread her legs as he lifted her. Once her legs were around him, he thrust into her.

Helena tore her lips from him, gasping at the feel of him. She tightened her arms around his neck and met his gaze.

"I would never have been able to refuse the call of your body regardless if I was supposed to be celibate or not," he admitted.

"Take me. I am yours."

He growled and began driving into her hard and deep. His eyes briefly flashed white when his pace quickened. She forgot about everything as desire took her, flinging her toward the precipice of her climax.

She clung to him, her legs tightening the faster he moved. While she didn't understand how or why he had such control over her body, she accepted it—welcomed it, in fact. She had told him the truth when she said that she was his. Because she was.

From the first time she'd seen him, though she didn't realize it then. It became apparent when they kissed. Despite —or perhaps because of—the danger surrounding them, she recognized the enticement, the pull that Jarin had over her.

Her thoughts vanished like smoke when his lips latched on to her neck, kissing and licking the sensitive skin. She cried out when she peaked, her body bucking against his from the orgasm.

He never stopped moving, prolonging her pleasure until she shook with it. When the climax finally faded, her breaths came in great gasps. She held Jarin tightly, and it wasn't long before he gave a final thrust and filled her body once more with his seed.

She had been so wrapped up in the desire that she hadn't thought of the consequences of their coupling. And if she were going to face the Coven, she couldn't think about them now either.

Her eyes closed as she buried her head in the crook of his neck. Without asking what was wrong, Jarin carried her to the fire and laid her gently on the ground.

"All will be well," he whispered before giving her a long, tender kiss.

She curled up on her side facing the fire with Jarin pressed against her back. Helena couldn't stop thinking about what it would be like to hold a child she had made with Jarin.

She didn't even know she had put her hand on her stomach until his palm covered hers, silently acknowledging what could happen. It was wrong for her to allow her mind to travel down such a road.

Losing her first babe had nearly destroyed her. She had reconciled herself to never having another child again, but then Jarin gave her hope.

"Sleep," he bade.

With her body lethargic from their lovemaking, her eyes closed of their own accord.

Jarin kept his hand over Helena's on her stomach. The thought of her belly swelling with his child made him giddy. When he decided to become a warrior for the Varroki, he'd known he would never have a family or children of his own. It hadn't bothered him.

Until he saw Helena holding her stomach. Jarin had known immediately what was going through her mind, and his own thoughts followed down that same path. A kernel of hope was planted in his heart then. A wish he dared not share with anyone.

He had no idea what was coming with the Coven, and that worried him. As he and Helena traveled, his mind had gone in many directions regarding why the Coven wanted her so desperately—and none of the conclusions were good.

Would he be enough to keep her out of the Coven's reach? Jarin had never questioned his magic before, but he did now. Because he cared for Helena.

He waited until her breathing evened with sleep before he rose and dressed. He covered her with his cloak and gently stroked a hand down her red tresses. With a nod to Valdr to guard her, Jarin left the confines of Stonehenge to search for food.

Hunting was something he'd always done without magic. The Earth gave up her bounty to feed him, so the least he could do was respect the animals enough to give them a fair chance.

He ignored a deer that would supply too much meat—he hated being wasteful. Instead, he focused on other small game.

Jarin's patience was well worth it when a hare hopped across his path.

Withdrawing a strip of leather and a smooth pebble, he placed the rock in the band and began to wind it up. He released the rock, watching it sail through the air and make contact with the rabbit. The animal was dead upon impact.

Jarin made his way to the hare and placed his hand upon it. "Thank you for your sacrifice," he whispered.

He lifted the animal up and turned to retrace his steps back to the stones when a bird flew over him, landing on a branch a few feet away. As soon as his gaze fell on the falcon, he recognized Andi.

"You made it back," he said to the bird and held out his arm.

She didn't hesitate to come to him, landing on his arm and staring at him with her intelligent eyes.

"Thank you for making the trip," he told her.

He was about to continue walking when the hairs on the back of his neck stood on end. Jarin hadn't brought his staff with him, but he didn't need it in order to do magic.

"She did much more than make the trip," said a deep voice behind him.

Jarin turned and locked eyes with Armir, who strode from between two trees. "What are you doing here?"

"Giving you what you need," the commander said. "Information."

Jarin smiled at Andi. The falcon never failed to impress him. "How did you figure it out?" he asked Armir.

Light green eyes met his. "Your bird went to the abbey and found Asa."

Jarin couldn't believe he hadn't thought to send Andi there. He rubbed the bird's chest. "Smart girl. Well done."

"Aye, she is a special one."

Jarin returned his attention to Armir. He held the commander's stare for a long moment. "It has to be very important for you to make the journey."

"I shall tell you everything, but first, bring me to Helena. I would like to meet her."

Jarin hesitated. The laws might have been changed, but he wasn't sure how Armir felt about them. More than that, he didn't want the commander finding Helena naked.

He whistled to Andi, who flew off in the direction of Stonehenge. Hopefully, the bird would be able to wake Helena so she could dress.

"I see," Armir replied.

Jarin raised a brow. "What is it you think you see?"

"Quite a lot, actually. In case you were interested, I agree with Malene's reversal of our laws. Even if I did not, you need not hide your affair with the witch."

"It's private."

Armir bowed his head. "As it should be. Shall I let you go ahead and prepare her before I arrive?"

"As concerned as I am with you seeing her without clothes, I am more troubled by the news you bring. It is as bad as I fear, isn't it?"

Armir glanced away, his lips flattening briefly. "How strong, mentally, is Helena?"

"She will be able to handle whatever you tell her."

"I hope you're right."

Jarin did, as well. He motioned for Armir to follow as they made their way to the stones. The commander filled him in on life at Blackglade, but Jarin barely heard him. His thoughts kept going to the worst things that would bring Armir to them.

When they reached Stonehenge, Helena stood beneath

one of the great lintels, awaiting them. She gave him a welcoming smile before turning her gaze to Armir.

Jarin walked to her and took her hand. "Helena, this is Armir. The commander has come from Blackglade to give us answers."

Her gaze slid back to Armir before she offered him a smile and stepped aside. "Please, join us."

17

There were many things Helena had imagined when Jarin spoke about the Varroki. She might have even envisioned someone in her mind when he mentioned Armir. But the tall, muscular man standing before her who looked like a Viking with his piercing light green eyes and long, blond hair gathered at the back of his head, the thick length wrapped in strips of leather every four inches until the end that reached down to his mid-shoulders, was nothing like she expected.

She couldn't look away from Armir's head that was shaved on either side and adorned with tattoos. No beard dusted his hard jaw or covered the sharp cheekbones and hollowed cheeks. With just one look, she realized Armir was a man you wanted as a friend, not an enemy.

She had been surprised when she woke to find Andi perched on one of the massive rocks and looking down at her. Helena had immediately sat up to look for Jarin. When she didn't see him, she dressed, all the while, her gaze scanning the area for signs of movement. The fact that Valdr was calm helped to keep her that way, as well.

Finally, Jarin had appeared, but he wasn't alone. She instinctively knew that things were about to change—and not just because she and Jarin were no longer alone.

Jarin grabbed her hand and gave it a little squeeze before releasing it and trailing Armir to enter the circle of stones.

Helena looked out into the dark night. Somewhere out there, the Coven wreaked havoc on innocents or unsuspecting witches. How much longer until she was next? As daunting as that prospect was, Helena would almost rather face the Coven than whatever knowledge Armir intended to pass on.

As soon as Jarin had introduced Armir, she deduced that the commander had come to them with information. Most likely information that could help her and Jarin fight the Coven.

But it might also be something else.

If she intended to come out alive when she fought the Coven—which she did—then she needed to know everything. No matter how difficult it was to hear.

Or acknowledge.

She turned on her heel and made her way to the fire. Valdr rose and trotted to her while licking his lips as Jarin stood off to the side, preparing their meal to roast over the flames.

Helena gave the wolf a good rub before she lowered herself to the ground and found her gaze going to Armir, who sat on her left. They were near enough to the fire to feel the heat and for the red-orange glow to fall over them.

The movement of the flames caused the light that fell upon Armir's head to give the illusion that the tats on his head moved.

"You are wary of me," he stated.

Helena's gaze moved to Jarin when he paused and looked up at her. She was happy when Valdr lay beside her, for petting him gave her hands something to do.

She met the commander's gaze. "You are the second Varroki I have encountered, and you are a stranger. I am leery of all strangers. However," she said after a long pause, "I trust Jarin, and he trusts you. So, I will trust you."

He issued a nod in acceptance of her words. "I understand that few witches are allowed to learn of their magic as we are in Blackglade. You hide from those who fear what you can do."

"I've lost count of the number of women I've seen viciously killed for being a witch when they had no magic. Fear and superstition run deep through the land."

Jarin paused and said, "Everywhere."

"So, aye," she told Armir. "I have always hidden my magic. First from others, then from the Coven. It is all I have known, and it is all most witches know unless they are part of the Coven."

Armir snapped a blade of grass from the ground and rolled it between his fingers. He stared at it a long time before he said, "There are other, smaller covens to help protect witches."

"You and I both know that the Coven went after them first. If any are still around, they are barely hanging on," she replied.

His green eyes might be light, but the paleness only made them more intense. Helena wondered if all Varroki had eyes like Jarin's and Armir's.

"I suppose you think the Varroki should have done more."

Out of the corner of her eye, she saw Jarin still, and his head snap up to watch them. Helena sensed that she was being tested, and she wasn't sure how she felt about that. Obviously, the trust issue went both ways.

"Since I knew nothing of the Varroki, how could I possibly think that?"

"What about after you learned about us?" Armir pressed.

She shrugged. "What is the point of lamenting all the wrongs I believe have happened to me and all those who might be responsible?"

Armir turned his head to look at Jarin. "Malene would like her."

"Aye," Jarin said, a smile pulling at his lips as he met Helena's gaze.

She found her own lips lifting in a grin. Then she remembered why Armir was here. She waited until Jarin put the rabbit over the fire to cook, then she said, "Whatever it is you've come to tell us, please, just say it."

Armir held her gaze a long minute before he nodded. "As I told Jarin, the falcon did not come directly to Blackglade. It stopped at the abbey first."

"Asa," Helena replied. "Of course."

Jarin's lips twisted. "I should have thought of that."

"You were worried," Armir said. "You knew sending the bird to us would bring someone to you. Andi sharing what had transpired with Asa allowed Malene to do some research before I came."

Jarin drew in a breath and released it. "What did she find?"

Helena's heart slammed against her ribs, and her hands grew clammy, all because she was nervous and frightened to hear whatever Armir was about to say. She tried to swallow, but all the moisture had left her mouth.

Armir's light green eyes swung to her. "What do you know of your family?"

She was taken aback by the question. Helena gave a small shake of her head as she shrugged. "They farmed the same piece of land for two generations. My family was poor but respected."

"What about your ancestors?" Armir pushed.

Helena glanced at Jarin. "I know nothing."

"Armir," Jarin said, his voice pitched dangerously low.

The commander cut his eyes to Jarin as the two silently faced off across the fire. Finally, Armir returned his gaze to her. "I ask because I wanted to know how much you knew of your heritage."

That's when she realized what he wanted. "You wish to know if there were other witches in my family. My mother was one, as was my grandmother and great-grandmother. The one thing I can tell you is that it seems only females are born to my mother's line. The fact that my father didn't have a son is the one thing he hated above all. My mum had seven babies, all girls. I was the only one to survive."

"Interesting," Armir murmured to himself. He took a quick inhale then said, "Jarin was right in his suspicions that the Coven was after you in particular."

She clasped her hands together to keep them from shaking. "Because I escaped from them twice?"

"That might have something to do with it, but Malene has another theory."

Helena hated how quiet Jarin had become. The more Armir spoke, the deeper the frown on Jarin's brow furrowed, which only made her worry grow. "What is that theory?"

Armir rubbed his hand over his jaw. "The Coven is after the bones of the First Witch."

"That is not news to me."

Jarin mumbled something under his breath. Helena glanced at him then turned her attention back to Armir, who watched her carefully. A chill ran down her back, a warning that she needed to prepare herself.

"The Coven wants all parts of the First Witch," Armir continued. "The bones are all that is left. At least that is what we thought, but it seems as if Sybbyl has learned something from having the Staff of the Eternal."

Helena's mind raced to try and put all the pieces together. Everything kept coming back to her. She shook her head, not wanting to believe it.

"While the bones of the First Witch hold great power, there is something that has massive amounts more," Armir said. "A descendant."

Helena was suddenly cold to her very soul. She wrapped her arms around herself. "Nay."

Armir didn't let her look away. "Malene has read every book in her library three times, and it is a considerable collection. There is an old text that speaks of the First Witch. In it is one line that mentions her three daughters. One remained in Norway, one traveled to Scotland, and the other traveled southeast. The one thing that connects them to the First Witch is that only females are born to the line."

Helena was going to be sick. It was bad enough when she believed the Coven wanted her for retribution, but to discover that they were after her because she was a descendant of the First Witch was another matter entirely.

Helena looked down to find Jarin's hand on hers. She hadn't even realized he'd moved to sit beside her, but she was glad he was there. She tightened her hold, freely taking the comfort and strength he offered.

"Finish it," Jarin demanded of Armir.

The commander said, "In the pages of the book, it mentions that the bones of the First Witch were scattered across countries, and there is even speculation that some are in the sea, but Malene recalls one section that said 'the Living Heart can find all the bones.'"

"I see," Helena murmured.

Jarin eyes flashed with anger. "The Coven is not getting near her."

"I agree," Armir said. "I believe we should take Helena back to Blackglade to hide her."

Helena shook her head before he finished. "I won't run anymore. It does not matter where I go or how far I travel. Sybbyl and the Coven will find me. I left the abbey for that reason, and it's why I refuse to go to Blackglade."

"She's right," Jarin added grudgingly. "Sybbyl will find her. We have worked too hard to keep Blackglade hidden from the Coven and anyone else. It needs to remain that way."

Armir's brow puckered in a frown. "You intend to fight them?"

Helena nodded, her chin lifting as her courage returned. "I won't submit to Sybbyl or any of them. It doesn't matter what they do to me, I will give them nothing."

The commander lowered his eyes to the fire, the expression on his face sad. "While I approve of your bravery, they would only need to take one look at the two of you to know that by getting their hands on Jarin, you would do whatever they wanted just so they would not harm him."

Helena turned her head to Jarin, the truth slamming into her. "I would."

Jarin made a sound in the back of his throat. "As if the Coven could capture me."

"You're used to fighting them before the Staff of the Eternal came into play. Things are different now, my friend," Armir cautioned.

"Then what do we do?" Helena asked as she looked at the commander. "I do not want to run."

Armir shrugged before leaning to the side on his hand. "There is only one thing you can do. Face them. Alone."

"Absolutely not," Jarin stated in a cold tone.

She contemplated the commander's words while feeling Jarin's heated gaze on her, silently begging her to agree with him. Finally, she looked at Armir. "What if you're wrong? What if I'm not a descendant?"

"What did you plan to do before you had this information?" he asked.

Helena swallowed and said, "I was going to face them with Jarin. Live or die, I want it to end. I won't run anymore."

"How does you being the Living Heart change anything?"

Jarin pulled his hand from hers and rose to his feet, his face mottled with anger. "It changes everything."

She reached up and retook his hand. When his light blue eyes met hers, she said, "It changes nothing. I have to do this."

"With me by your side," he said as he lowered himself to one knee to face her.

Helena smiled, her heart aching. "There is no one I'd rather have by my side, but I have to do it alone."

Though he didn't argue more, she saw all the words he wanted to say, but didn't, in his eyes. She was terrified of facing the Coven alone, but she also knew she would do anything they wanted, give them anything just to make sure Jarin was safe. That's how much she cared.

That's how much she loved him.

It gave her another incentive to best the Coven. Even if she couldn't beat them, she would make damn sure they knew not to mess with her again.

18

"Nay." Rage simmered just beneath the surface, and Jarin was tired of holding it back.

Armir paused as the two of them glared at each other over the flames. Helena had risen and gone to stretch her legs with Valdr by her side.

"I know what you are about to ask," Jarin continued, letting the anger drip from every syllable. "And I will not do it."

"To remain with her is to hinder her," Armir argued.

Jarin fought to reclaim the usual calm that surrounded him. "I am the one who convinced her to fight. I promised her that I would stand beside her when she did."

Armir leaned forward and turned the spit over the fire. "Things have changed since then. Helena is too important for her to fall into the Coven's hands."

"You say that as if I'm not aware," he bit out, not bothering to hide his growing ire.

"You care for her."

That drew Jarin up short. "What does that matter?"

"It means everything. It means that you will fight to the death for her. It means that you will move Heaven and Earth for her. It means, old friend, that you would die for her."

Jarin held Armir's gaze for a long moment, letting it all sink in—and accepting it all for the truth that it was. Jarin hadn't intended to develop feelings for Helena. They'd progressed before he even realized what was happening, but he wouldn't change any of it.

What he had with her was...beautiful and perfect. It was something he never believed to be within his reach, and yet he now stood in the glow of it—and he never wanted it to fade.

"I can see by the look on your face that you will never part from her," Armir said.

Jarin shook his head. "It wouldn't matter who she was. The Living Heart or not, I would stand beside her, protecting her and fighting with her."

Armir was silent for a moment. "What if Malene had not changed the laws. Would you still be with her?"

Jarin looked away, his mind drifting to the past and his desire to be a warrior. "From the time I was very little, I knew I wanted to be a warrior for the Varroki. It mattered little what was asked of me because I cared about nothing more than protecting Blackglade and my people. It was no sacrifice to give up ever having a family, not when I was doing such work. You know the extremes I have gone to in order to track down the Coven."

"Aye," Armir murmured.

Jarin slid his gaze back to the commander. "Being with a woman then meant nothing because abstaining was just part of my mission. I say all of that so you will understand when I tell you that the undeniable pull I feel toward Helena is inescapable. Even if I were a thousand miles away, I would still be drawn to her. I believe everything I have done, every step I have taken has led me straight to her. So, aye, I would have broken my vows for her."

"I suspected as much. I think no less of you for such an admission. You're very lucky."

Jarin was so wrapped up in his own thoughts that he nearly missed the flash of regret and pain in Armir's eyes. He studied the commander for a long time.

"What of you?" Jarin asked. "Your position also allows you to take a wife now. Is there someone you want?"

Armir's green gaze locked on the flames. "Would it surprise you to know that I, too, would have broken my vows?"

"Before Helena, I would've said aye. Now that I know what it feels like to be in her arms and know her body, nay. Now you can have this woman you want."

"Can I?" Armir asked. He snorted softly and shook his head. "I don't believe I can."

"There is not a woman in Blackglade who would not want to be yours. Your position alone commands the utmost respect. You are only second in line after Malene."

Armir shrugged one shoulder. "Position in our world means nothing if the other person does not feel the same."

"Have you spoken to this woman?"

The commander's eyes lifted to Jarin. "Nay. And it is better this way. I am used to looking at her from afar."

Armir had chosen his words carefully, but the fact that he had been so cautious allowed Jarin to figure out who Armir longed for—the Lady of Varroki herself, Malene.

Jarin kept the information to himself. If Armir didn't wish to say her name, then he wouldn't either. Jarin had spent little time with Malene, but he had liked her immediately when they met. Everyone did. She had an elegance about her that commanded respect. Added to her intelligence, she was the perfect leader for their people.

Armir cleared his throat. "What is it you feel for Helena?"

"I have not put a name to it."

"Is it love?"

Jarin shrugged. "Does it matter what it is? My feelings run deep, and that is enough for me."

"I believe Helena is the Living Heart. That means she has as much—if not more—magic than the Staff of the Eternal. She can face the Coven on her own."

They were back to that. Jarin wasn't in the mood for this conversation. "Do you really believe it will just be a few Coven members facing off against Helena? It will be Sybbyl, and she won't be alone."

"One way or another, no matter what, it will come down to Sybbyl and Helena," Armir stated. "From what we learned from Ravyn and Carac, Sybbyl is very confident. Now that she has the staff, she will believe she can get whatever she wants."

"If Sybbyl is coming for Helena, it's because she knows Helena is the Living Heart, which also means Sybbyl understands how powerful Helena is."

Armir's lips flattened. "Helena can handle it."

"Have you seen her in battle? Do you know something about her magic I do not?" Jarin demanded angrily.

"Do you believe she isn't capable of facing the Coven on her own?"

Jarin shook his head. "That is not what I said."

"You implied it," Armir replied. "You do not think she can survive without you beside her."

He started to answer, then closed his mouth. Did he think that? Nay. The truth was that he was so terrified of losing her that he couldn't bear to think of her fighting the witches on her own.

"Ah," Armir murmured. "Now I see what you mean. I would suggest being very careful with how you speak because Helena might not think you believe in her."

Jarin lifted his eyes to the black sky above them. "My options are to stand with her and take the chance that the Coven will use me against her. Or, I can let her go on her own and hope that she wins, but also come to terms with the fact that she might die. And I would never be there to hold her or say my final farewell."

"Aye," Armir answered. "Neither is a good choice, but this is about more than just you and Helena. This is about the Varroki and even all those living without magic. We have fought the Coven for thousands of years to ensure this moment never happened."

"Yet, here we are."

"Aye, yet, here we are. It is the choices we make at this time that will either put us in the position to win or allow the Coven the foothold they are trying to grasp."

Jarin drew in a deep breath and looked at Armir. "No matter what, I've lost Helena."

"She knows what is at stake. She will not allow herself to fall into the Coven's hands. For you, for our people, and for the rest of the world, she will do what is right."

Because he couldn't. Jarin's heart hurt at the thought. He had found something so amazing, so wonderful...and he was about to lose it all. If he didn't already hate the Coven, he would now. The little time he'd had with Helena wasn't enough. It was just a taste of what could be his, and he ached for more.

"Am I being punished because I did not care about what laws were in place? Is it because I desired her so much that I only thought of myself and what it felt like to be in her arms?"

Armir blew out a long breath. "If you are being punished,

then so am I. We cannot help where our hearts lead us, or the feelings that develop. I wish there were another way for you and Helena."

No one wanted that more than Jarin. He ran a hand down his face, suddenly weary to his core. He looked around, only just realizing that Helena had been gone for some time.

Jarin jumped up and anxiously looked around the stones for some sign of her, hoping that she had returned and paused to listen to their conversation. Because the alternative was too much to contemplate.

Armir joined him in the search, and soon, they were outside the boundaries of Stonehenge with no sign of Helena.

Jarin strode inside the circle again to where Andi was perched nearby. Valdr had gone with Helena, which meant that he couldn't ask the wolf to track her. But Andi could find them.

"Find Helena and Valdr," Jarin requested.

The bird stared at him silently, her intelligent eyes unblinking as she remained.

"Please," he begged.

Armir came up behind him and put a hand on his shoulder. "Even the falcon knows what needs to be done. Take comfort in knowing that Valdr is with her. The wolf will protect Helena."

That was his job. Jarin turned away, feeling helpless and furious. He spied his staff and grabbed it as he once more went outside the stones.

"Jarin," Armir called as he followed. "What are you doing?"

"Whatever I need to do."

Just as he was lowering the tip of his staff to the ground to use a spell to determine which direction Helena had gone, Armir shoved it aside.

"She left because she knew you would not leave her," Armir stated. "And if you think for a moment that it was easy for her, then you know nothing."

Jarin frowned as the realization hit. "You knew," he said through clenched teeth. "You knew what she planned while we talked."

"I suspected," Armir corrected.

"And you didn't tell me."

"Had you watched her face, you would have seen it yourself. There is nothing more she wanted than to remain with you."

Jarin took a step away from Armir. "I'll find her."

"Then you will destroy any chance she has of succeeding. Have faith that she will return to you."

"When was the last time you fought the Coven?" Jarin demanded. "Three years ago? Or was it longer?"

Armir's face tightened. "You know I left to avenge one of the warriors killed by a Coven member."

"You face one witch every few years. I battle them daily. I faced off against the elders and other witches like Sybbyl who got hold of powerful artifacts. Do not presume to tell me Helena's chances against them. I know much better than you."

"Then think of Helena. If the situations were reversed, would you not want her to accept your decision? Would you not do anything to keep her safe? Even if it meant confronting the Coven on your own?"

Jarin turned away, hating that Armir was right. "I should be with her."

"We both should. Every witch and warlock should. But we cannot. This is Helena's battle. She wants and needs to decide her own fate. She might not have chosen to be descended from the First Witch, but destiny has forced her to shoulder the responsibility of choosing a side."

"What am I supposed to do in the meantime?"

"Continue doing what you always do."

Jarin faced Armir once again. "If you were in my place, would you be able to let Helena go?"

"I'm honestly not sure."

"I hope you never have to find out."

Armir's shoulders sagged. "I envy that you got to experience what it is like to hold the woman you long for. I dream of it every night but, honestly, I do not know if I would be strong enough to let her go."

"I will never stop fighting for Helena," Jarin declared. "I will never stop hoping she'll return to me. And I will never stop hunting the Coven."

19

Sybbyl stared ahead into the inky blackness of night. Somewhere out there, Helena hid. The witch somehow knew she was after her, but Helena would only get so far. Sybbyl was quickly gaining ground. It was just a matter of time.

It took a great deal of magic for her to move herself, not to mention the three witches with her, across miles in a blink of an eye. But it was worth the pain it caused to catch up to Helena so quickly.

She wanted the witch on her side, but Sybbyl was well aware that after everything that had occurred between Helena and the Coven, the witch might refuse.

Sybbyl anticipated that along with the thought that Helena would go down fighting. That would simply never do. Sybbyl would have to come up with some way to hold Helena captive and get her with child. Once the babe was born, there would be another descendant of the First Witch, and Sybbyl would have no need of Helena.

She could kill the witch and raise the baby as her own,

which meant that the Living Heart would then belong to her and the Coven just as the Staff of the Eternal did.

Sybbyl knew it wouldn't be easy to hold Helena and get her with child. But with magic, all things were possible. She just had to find the right spells. Once she had something to focus on, Sybbyl was as tenacious as they came.

She was so focused on her chase that she was surprised by Avis's sudden arrival. The other witches were just as shocked to see the witch.

"What are you doing here?" Sybbyl demanded. "I sent you out to find the warlock."

Avis gave a shake of her head. "He is not an easy one to locate, but I was able to track him."

"Here?" she asked.

The witch nodded.

Sybbyl narrowed her gaze as she resumed looking into the distance. What were the odds that the warlock and Helena were together? Things couldn't be that easy for her.

Could they?

Sybbyl smiled and glanced at the staff in her hand. It was all thanks to one object that everything she wanted was falling into place so easily.

Then she paused, her head jerking to Avis. "How did you find the warlock?"

"It was a spell my mother showed me long ago. I cast it, searching for magic different than my own. It is similar to a locator spell, but since I do not know the person, I look for magic instead."

Sybbyl walked to the witch and smiled at her. "What did you find?"

"Strong magic, unlike anything I have ever seen or felt before. We can feel when a witch does magic, but I sensed nothing in the locations I visited."

"How do you know you are heading in the right direction?"

"The magic is fresher with each location," Avis replied. "Then it stopped. Nothing. Until just a little while ago."

"In this direction?" Sybbyl asked.

Avis nodded, smiling.

She looked at the three witches behind her. "It looks like I am going to get both Helena and my warlock this night. Come," she ordered them.

With the four witches trailing behind her, Sybbyl made her way through the trees. She frowned as she walked. She had been here before, but she couldn't remember when or why. As she searched her mind, she came to the edge of the woods and saw the great stones dimly illuminated by the moon.

"Stonehenge," one of the witches murmured behind her.

It had been many years since Sybbyl had been to the place. She hadn't liked it the first time, and she liked it even less now. But she instinctively knew that Helena and the warlock were there.

"I do not like this place," Avis whispered.

Sybbyl had once believed the standing stones repulsed all witches, but obviously, she was wrong if her two targets were there. Perhaps the circle repelled only those of the Coven.

A Witch's Grove was for all witches and warlocks, but it was known that some with magic never felt welcome within them. Perhaps the same was true for the stones.

"It matters not," she told the women. "We are going to surround them. They will try to run, but they will not get far."

She walked from the trees, confident the witches would follow her. The closer they came to Stonehenge, the more something kept telling her that Helena was no longer there.

Sybbyl paused and turned to the right. She closed her eyes and whispered to the staff to show her the closest items of the

First Witch. This time, the staff refused to answer, but she was undaunted.

A faint flicker of light from deep within the stones let Sybbyl know that someone was there. It could be a trick designed by Helena to give her more time to put distance between herself and Sybbyl.

"Where are you going?" Avis asked when Sybbyl pivoted away from the circle of stones.

"Helena is not there," she replied.

"What of the warlock?"

Sybbyl shrugged. "He will be mine soon enough."

The witches said nothing else as they followed Sybbyl. With every step, she knew she was heading in the right direction.

Armir met Jarin's gaze. They had both felt the approach of the Coven and quietly got into place for battle, but before they could get close enough, something stopped them.

The night was dark, with the moon shedding little light for them to see who was leading the witches, but Armir knew. It was Sybbyl. She had come for Helena, and somehow, she'd figured out that the witch wasn't within the stones.

"They're going after her," Jarin said.

Armir nodded reluctantly. "It would seem so."

"And you want me to stand by and do nothing?"

"I never said that."

Jarin's pale blue eyes narrowed dangerously before his lips curved into a grin. "I think you should hunt more often."

"I have my hands full with quite enough at Blackglade, thank you."

"I can see how guarding and helping a beautiful woman like Malene would be taxing."

Armir cut Jarin a dark look. "Do you want to follow the Coven or not?"

"You know I do."

"I want a glimpse of what the Staff of the Eternal can do. Not to mention, I want to see how Sybbyl wields it."

Jarin moved his hand from left to right, extinguishing the fire. "Then what are we waiting for?"

"They cannot know we're here."

"I do this every day, Armir." Jarin then gave a soft whistle that had Andi soaring into the sky. "Shall we?"

Armir walked to the scorched earth where the fire had been and grabbed the still hot stick with the roasted hare on it. He was starving and not willing to let food go to waste.

When he reached Jarin, the warrior tore off a large chunk of meat and sank his teeth into it. Then they were off. Armir wasn't sure what awaited them. He still believed it would be better if Jarin were far from Helena, but at the same time, if they could help the witch, there was no reason they shouldn't.

He could only hope that the decision didn't come back to haunt him.

Leaving Jarin had been the hardest thing Helena had ever done. She felt as if she had left part of herself at Stonehenge— a piece she would never get back until she was in his arms again.

No matter how many times she tried, she couldn't get Valdr to return to Jarin. The wolf stayed within steps of her at all times. He helped lead her through dense sections of the forest, over rocky terrain, and across the shallowest part of a stream.

She knew that if Valdr were still with her when the Coven found her, they would kill the wolf first. She wouldn't be able to handle that. Whether the animal could understand her or not, she began talking to him about it.

The action might have been lost on Valdr, but it helped her. She listed out all the reasons why the wolf needed to return to Jarin once she had found a suitable place for battle. Because she would win—or die trying.

Helena walked all night. She didn't pause until she saw the sky turn a soft gray. A look over her shoulder showed her a magnificent sunrise. One that she had thought to share with Jarin in the comfort of his arms.

How drastically things had changed within such a short amount of time. She should be used to it, but it was something Helena would never grow accustomed to.

She watched the sun rising higher while her mind replayed the hours she'd had in Jarin's arms. She hadn't wanted to fall in love. It just happened, without her even realizing it. Now that the emotion was there, she couldn't ignore it.

While talking to Armir earlier in the night, she'd come to the conclusion that in order to protect Jarin, she had to leave. While she didn't know Sybbyl, she knew the witch's kind.

Sybbyl had to have everything. She'd already had a run-in with Jarin, and there was little doubt in Helena's mind that Sybbyl now knew that Jarin was a warlock. The witch would want to add him to the Coven and maybe even keep him for herself.

Helena didn't know the witch's thoughts—and she didn't want to. The Varroki had hunted the Coven, and with Jarin in their midst, there was no telling what information they could get from him—willing or not. If Sybbyl got her hands on

Jarin, Blackglade and all the Varroki were in danger. Same with those at the abbey.

But that was only one of the many excuses Helena used to convince herself to walk away from Jarin. The truth was that she knew he would never divulge anything to the Coven. He was strong enough mentally, physically, and magically to withstand whatever Sybbyl tried to do to him—with or without the Staff of the Eternal.

Helena didn't know how things would play out between her and Sybbyl, but she knew it wouldn't be pretty. She prayed she had strong enough magic to stand up to the Coven. Both Armir and Jarin thought she did.

If she really were the Living Heart and a descendant of the First Witch, then she would do her ancestor proud. She knew next to nothing about her Viking heritage, but she was determined to find it within herself somehow.

Too much depended on it.

Helena turned back around and began walking once more. Valdr brushed against her leg, a reminder that she wasn't alone. She took comfort in the wolf. He looked up at her, tongue lolling as if asking her if they could go faster.

She smiled and started jogging. It felt good to move in such a way. Plus, it was a reminder of how she and Jarin had covered large amounts of ground.

The better part of the day was spent alternating between walking and running. She stopped and filled her waterskin often. There was little food left in her bag from the abbey, so she was careful about how much she ate.

Her mind wandered, her thoughts going to her ancestors, Jarin, and the Coven when she saw it. Helena came to a halt and looked at the hill before her. There was nothing particularly spectacular about it, but she knew instantly that it was the place where she would face the Coven.

She hurried to the knoll and stood atop it, looking out at the land around her. Then a voice filled her mind.

"*Never fight unless you know the odds are in your favor.*"

Helena lifted her chin and felt magic crackle along her fingers. "The odds are in my favor."

20

J arin took his duty of eliminating the Coven seriously. But this was different. This was to help save the woman he... He what?

He was afraid to go down that path and say the word.

Instead, he focused on Sybbyl and the Coven members. He and Armir moved silently and quickly. The witches never got too far ahead of them. It helped that the women never looked over their shoulders, but Jarin wasn't going to take that for granted.

He used a shielding spell that would make it difficult for anyone to see him, and Armir followed suit. Jarin wanted Sybbyl for himself. After his first run-in with the witch that had ended with her getting away, he wanted retribution—and he wanted to ensure that she never got her hands on Helena.

Jarin motioned to Armir that they should split up, each moving to flank the witches. Armir never slowed in his steps, but he looked ahead, his mind seemingly working out each scenario. He finally gave a nod of agreement.

That's all Jarin needed to diverge to the right as Armir

moved left. Jarin wanted to rush to the witches, to bellow the loud war cry of his ancestors and head straight for Sybbyl. But he didn't. He held himself in check, slowing so he didn't get ahead of the Coven.

The sky lightened, but he paid little attention to it. The trees were sparse, and the ground rocky. He was focused solely on the witches. It took Andi flying so close that her wings touched his cheek to get his attention. Jarin inwardly grimaced.

That kind of lack of concentration could get him killed. The fact that Sybbyl and the others seemed unconcerned about anyone following them should be caution enough.

He slowed to a walk and held out his arm for the bird. Andi landed on his wrist. He stroked her chest. "What have you seen?" he whispered.

She turned her head forward and let out a call.

Jarin frowned. "Have you found Helena?"

The bird flapped her great wings in answer.

"Keep an eye on her," he told the falcon.

Andi flew up so high, he could barely make her out. Jarin then turned his head to the Coven members. He didn't know where Armir was, but the commander was a superb fighter. He wasn't at all worried about Armir. If anything, Jarin was concerned about Armir getting to Sybbyl first.

"She's mine," Jarin stated.

He continued following them. His body was tense with anger and frustration, and he couldn't even run any of it off. With the witches walking as if they weren't in a hurry, he had to do the same.

Jarin contemplated running ahead and finding Helena, but he didn't—as hard as it was not to. He respected her decision, even if he didn't agree with it.

As he thought about all the things he wanted to say to

Helena, he noticed that the witches had begun to spread out from one another. It was so subtle and done over a half hour that he almost missed it.

That's when he realized that they knew they were being followed. Sybbyl was preparing to attack, but would they go for him or Armir? Jarin decided to give them a wide berth as he ran ahead of the group. When he found an outcropping of rocks, he jumped atop it and waited, watching as the witches came towards him.

Before the Coven reached him, Sybbyl drew to a stop. The four women behind her did the same, their eyes scanning the area. They knew he was there, but they couldn't see him.

He noted the black crown atop Sybbyl's blond hair, but it was the band of black paint that went over her eyes and temples to disappear into her hairline that made him narrow his gaze.

It was very similar to something the Norse did when they went into battle. Was it just coincidence? Or was the staff influencing her?

"I know you're out there," Sybbyl stated. "Show yourself."

Jarin tightened his fingers on his staff. Her gaze had moved over him twice already, which meant his shielding spell was holding. But for how much longer? It might be a good way to test just what the Staff of the Eternal could do.

Then again, they knew Jarin was there, but not Armir. If the shielding spell worked, then that could give the commander time to plan an attack while Jarin kept the witches' attention on him.

Jarin removed the spell, showing himself. Sybbyl's blue eyes locked on him and she smiled as if she had just gotten a prize she coveted.

"I had a witch looking for you. Who knew all I had to do was wait for you to find me," she said with a seductive grin.

He remained silent. There was nothing he could say that would benefit him, so he decided to be patient and find out what Sybbyl wanted.

"The strong and silent type," she said as she walked closer, her hips swaying suggestively.

He glanced at the staff she held. It had once been in his hand, and if he had anything to say about it, it would be once more. But first, he had to kill Sybbyl and make sure the Coven never went after Helena again.

Sybbyl lifted her chin to look up at him. "I cannot begin to tell you how excited I was to learn the Varroki were real. I honestly believed only women could have magic, but you showed me differently. There are more of you, I take it? I want you to show me."

He merely raised a brow in response.

She shrugged, her lips compressing for a heartbeat. "It might take years, but I'm willing to wait for you to tell me what I want to know. In the meantime, I have other plans for you."

Unease slithered through him. What the hell could she want with him?

Her smile widened as if she were reading his mind. "I can tell you every detail you want to know. Perhaps, I will start from the beginning. Witches are tired of hiding. Those too weak to use their magic on others to protect themselves are being killed. The rest of us are very willing to do whatever is necessary to stay alive."

"Like killing innocents."

"So, you do speak," she said with a smile. "I honestly hoped you would not be one to get hung up on things like that. After all, the Varroki keep to themselves. You do not meddle in the affairs of the rest of us, at least not that I knew about until recently. Just what do the Varroki do?"

"We kill anyone in the Coven," he stated.

Her smile disappeared as she frowned. "That will simply not do. Whatever you thought to do to my sisters and me will not happen. You should accept that now."

"Says who?"

Her eyes glittered with power. "Me. I make the rules now. I am transforming this narrow-minded world run by men into one of acceptance. One where women rule."

Jarin wasn't fooled. "Women? You mean you."

"Well, aye," she said with a laugh. "Of course, I mean me. I will be queen, but even a queen needs those she can trust. And those will be women. No longer will we be subservient to men. No longer will we have to fear being forced to lie with a man or marry him. We will make our own decisions."

"And how does that involve me?" But Jarin had a pretty good idea.

Sybbyl moved a few steps closer. "You, my handsome, virile warrior, will help me spawn a new breed of witches and warlocks."

"I would sever my cock from my body before I allowed that to happen."

The fierce anger that contorted Sybbyl's face wiped away any shred of beauty she had. "Did you not hear me? I make the rules."

"Not for me."

Jarin saw the attack coming before the first witch moved. He held up his left hand and sent a blast of white magic into the woman's chest. She died before she hit the ground, her body already turning to ash.

Sybbyl didn't move as the other three witches rushed him. Jarin remained on the high ground, using the leverage to take out another witch. He turned, his staff pointed at another when something slammed into him.

He looked down to find inky strands of smoke wrapping around him so he couldn't move. A look in Sybbyl's direction proved that she was the one responsible, the smile on her face said as much.

No matter how hard he tried to hold onto his staff, it fell from his numb fingers, tumbling from the rocks to the ground below.

Then Sybbyl pulled back on her staff, and his feet were jerked out from under him. Jarin hit the rocks so hard it knocked the breath from him. The black strands continued to wrap around him up to his shoulders. He was rolled roughly from his perch onto the ground and blinked up at the sky.

He spotted Andi and hoped the bird wouldn't attack. Jarin had lost the advantage. At least now, he had an idea of what the Staff of the Eternal could do—as did Armir. The commander could take the knowledge back to Malene so they could prepare.

Sybbyl walked to him and squatted beside him. She went to touch his face, but Jarin moved his head away from her. Her smile was tight as she glared at him. No matter how much power she had, he would never bend to her.

Never.

"You will regret jerking away from my touch," she vowed.

His gaze raked over her. "I doubt it."

She quirked a brow and placed the tip of the Staff of the Eternal on his chest. The entire thing glowed white before it turned purple and ended up lavender.

Anger filled Sybbyl's gaze. "Just as I suspected. You have no problem with witches, just the Coven. Tell me, how is Helena? Did you enjoy your time with her?"

Jarin kept all emotion from his face and eyes. He'd thought to keep his feelings about Helena to himself, but he should have expected Sybbyl to use such tactics.

The Coven leader slowly straightened and shook out the black skirts of her gown. "I took you easily, Varroki. I will do the same to Helena. She will be mine to control."

Jarin hoped that Armir heard all of this to prepare Helena, because no matter how hard he tried, Jarin couldn't manage even a spark of magic. It had to be the black elements that held him immobile.

Sybbyl stamped the staff into the ground. The next moment, he was on his feet. His body was no longer his. Sybbyl controlled it, and that worried him greatly. Because if he couldn't get free, then he couldn't fight. And if he couldn't fight...

He was a Varroki warrior. His life was battle. He had dedicated himself to the eradication of the Coven, to keeping evil from taking hold.

The entirety of his life, he'd been undefeated. But this was no ordinary witch he was up against. This one had the added power of the First Witch. Jarin thought he'd been prepared for that. He'd been wrong.

The next time he fought Sybbyl—because there would be a next time—he wouldn't forget this lesson.

"Come," Sybbyl commanded.

Jarin tried to remain still, but his body moved on its own. The smirks from the remaining two witches set his teeth on edge.

"Keep smiling," he retorted. "Had she not stepped in, both of you would be dead."

That silenced them for the moment. Jarin clenched his fists. He felt lost without his staff. At least Sybbyl hadn't picked it up. If she had, she would have discovered that it was no ordinary stick.

It came from a hazel tree in Norway where the First Witch once lived. He was the only warrior to use a staff, but it wasn't for its magical capabilities. He hadn't even realized it had any until he did magic while holding it.

The staff was a reminder of what he fought for—and against. But the longer he had it with him and the more magic he used while holding it, the stronger they both became. Now, it was a part of him.

A shadow passed over him. He glanced up and saw Andi, who dipped her wing and swung around to the left. It was her way of letting him know that Armir was still there and hiding on that side.

21

The wind had a bite to it, brushing against Helena's cheek like icy fingers. She sat on the cold ground, thankful that what little snow had fallen was already melted.

She didn't know how long she would have to wait for the Coven to arrive, so she took the time to prepare herself. After she'd sent Valdr off to hide, telling him he had to live for Jarin, she faced north. Then she let her soul search for the connections to her ancestors.

This continent was the Celts'. She had no idea if she had any of their blood within her, but she knew she had Norse. Sybbyl sought to find the voice that had spoken to her when she arrived.

"I have run for so long," she said. "If I am the Living Heart, help me find the strength to fight in the coming battle."

"*You already have all you need.*"

Hearing the feminine voice again sent shivers of excitement through her. "Who are you?"

"*You know who I am. I have guided you since you were a*

little girl. I tried to guide your mother, but she refused to accept me."

Helena gasped, struggling for breath.

"You have always known the way. You did what you had to do to protect yourself and your mother."

"I failed with my daughter."

"Nay, my child. You must let go of the past. Look to the future."

All she saw was Jarin's face. "Can I defeat the Coven?"

"You can do anything you wish. Difficult choices await you. Be ready. You are the Living Heart. In you beats the blood and magic of the First Witch. Never forget that."

"Wait," Helena called, but she knew the voice was gone.

She understood why some feared magic. It could do terrible, horrendous things. But it could also do amazing things—like connecting her to the First Witch.

"I will never forget," she vowed.

Helena had been scared before, but she wasn't any longer. No matter what happened, it would occur by her choice. She wanted to end the Coven and return to Jarin, but if all else failed, she would ensure that she wasn't a pawn in Sybbyl's game.

The First Witch had been powerful. She'd determined her own fate. Helena would follow her ancestor's example and do the same. Her destiny was her own, and she accepted whatever happened.

It was the call of a falcon that caught Helena's attention. She lifted her gaze and spotted the bird. When it swooped low, she recognized Andi.

"Nay," Helena murmured as she climbed to her feet and turned around.

She had hoped Armir would keep Jarin away, but the commander must not have been successful. As much as she knew it was better to be separated from him when she faced Sybbyl, Helena's heart beat faster at the thought of having Jarin with her.

When the man came into view, she knew immediately that it wasn't her warrior. Apprehension filled her when she saw that it was Armir who approached instead.

"What happened?" she demanded when he was close enough.

The commander's face was stoic, but anger sizzled just beneath the surface of his light green eyes. "Sybbyl and four Coven members came to the stones. They somehow knew you were not there, so they turned and headed this way."

"You followed them," she said, guessing their next move.

Armir bowed his head. "Aye. We flanked them, and then Jarin got ahead of Sybbyl. We used a shielding spell, but she knew he was there. In order to give me time to get to you, he revealed himself and killed three of the witches before Sybbyl captured him."

Helena took a step back as if she had been struck. "Nay."

"She is on her way to you now. Helena, you need to prepare. Whatever she has done to Jarin, he has no control over his body. And...she plans to use him to create a new breed of witches."

Helena moved her gaze over Armir's shoulder where Sybbyl would likely approach. "Let her try."

"She's powerful," Armir cautioned. "More formidable than either Jarin or I anticipated. Do not underestimate her as we did."

She frowned as Armir held out a hand to her. In the next instant, Jarin's staff appeared. Armir handed it to her. Jarin was never without it. She knew he wouldn't have let it go unless he had no choice.

Armir pushed the staff toward her. "Take it. When Jarin

first became a warrior, he traveled to Norway where the First Witch died, and her body was cut up and distributed. The Varroki have long believed there was magic in those woods. A storm came, and lightning struck a tree. This was a piece that fell off. He made it into a staff that he's carried ever since. There is magic inside it. Magic, I believe, from the First Witch."

Helena slowly wrapped her fingers around it. When it was securely in her palm, she felt warmth spread from her hand, up her arm, and through her body.

"*Remember who you are.*"

She smiled at the voice she recognized and met Armir's gaze. "All this time, Jarin had some of the First Witch's magic."

"I do not believe he knew it. Whether he did or not, he did not take advantage of it."

"She knows."

Armir's brow puckered. "She?"

"The First Witch. She has protected Jarin with this gift. Her body might be gone, but she is not."

"You have spoken with her."

Helena nodded. "I have. But it is also a feeling I get from the staff. From her."

Armir blew out a breath, nodding. "I will fight with you."

"Nay," she said, standing in his way when he would move beside her. "The Varroki need you. Malene needs you. Take what you have learned here and tell others."

"You wish me to leave you to face Sybbyl alone?"

"I do."

He hesitated. "And Jarin?"

"He's a warrior. What do you think he will do?"

"Fight," Armir answered.

Helena grinned. "We both will."

"Will it be enough?"

She gave a nod toward Andi and then to where Valdr waited. "Take the animals. Sybbyl will go after them, and I refuse to allow them to be hurt. Besides, their deaths would destroy Jarin."

"What will destroy him is losing you."

"He will not lose me," she promised.

Armir bowed, his long, blond ponytail falling over his shoulder. When he straightened, his penetrating gaze met hers. "You have the pride and strength of a Varroki. You will always be welcome within our gates, for you are one of us."

Her eyes misted at his words. She smiled before he turned on his heel and walked to where Valdr had emerged from the tree line. It took Armir three tries before Valdr finally followed him. The wolf stopped and looked at her once more before disappearing into the forest.

Andi flew over her seven times before she too finally followed Armir.

Helena was thankful that the animals realized they must leave. She drew in a deep breath and slowly released it. Anyone looking at her would think she was alone, but she was far from that. She had the First Witch with her—and Jarin in her heart.

It wasn't long after that she saw the approach on the horizon. Sybbyl was in the lead, with Jarin behind her and witches on either side of him.

Everything was about to come to a head. Helena had hated the Coven for so long, but to allow such emotions to rule her now would be her downfall. So much more was riding on her. She had to think of the bigger picture.

Helena adjusted her grip on the staff and squared her shoulders when the group reached her. She glanced at Jarin, who lifted one side of his lips in his way of telling her that he was on her side. The brief exchange bolstered her spirits.

While Sybbyl raked a gaze over Helena, showing her disdain, Helena merely looked at her.

"Are you really going to stand against me?" Sybbyl asked.

Helena lifted her chin. "Aye."

"Do not be a fool. I'll win. Nothing can stand against the Staff of the Eternal. Just look what I caught," she said and motioned to Jarin.

"Are you so desperate for men that you have to capture one?" Helena asked.

Sybbyl's nostrils flared. "Do not pretend that you don't know him. You and Jarin know each other...intimately. You recently shared your body with him. I want you to know that he is mine now."

"Did you not tell Ravyn how women would no longer be under the rule of men? But you have no issue with subjecting men to the same?"

"You catch on quick."

Helena gave a shake of her head. "I like the idea of women making their own decisions, but you are doing this the wrong way."

"Magic is the only way," Sybbyl stated angrily. "Why would we be given such a gift if not to use it?"

"You mean to kill innocents? Like my baby?"

Sybbyl rolled her eyes. "You refused the Coven. What did you expect us to do?"

"And that is all that is wrong with the Coven. Have you thought about how large your organization is, but witches still fight against you, still hide? You, who want to give women the right to make their own decisions, are giving us none."

"This is different," Sybbyl replied.

Helena grinned sadly. "That is something any fanatic in power would say."

"Enough of this," Sybbyl said, annoyance in her tone and

in the expression on her face. "You have one more chance. Join us, or die."

"My answer hasn't changed from the first two times I was given that ultimatum."

Helena shrugged, a slow smile forming as a look of pure glee filled her. "Then you die. Only, not today. I will hold you until the life growing inside you is born. Then, I'll kill you and raise it as my own. I will then control the Living Heart."

For a moment, Helena could hear nothing past the rush of blood in her ears. She stopped herself from touching her stomach at the thought of life growing inside her. A life she and Jarin had created.

Sybbyl couldn't know how desperately she wanted more children, and for all Helena knew, it was a trick.

She didn't dare look at Jarin either. This news made it so that she was barely holding it together. One look at him, and she would shatter the cool façade she had erected for this battle.

Armir had cautioned her not to underestimate Sybbyl, and yet that's exactly what she had done. Luckily, she'd realized her mistake in time and could perhaps correct it.

"You are very confident," Helena said.

Sybbyl grinned. "I'm holding the staff."

"And *I* am the Living Heart. You hold a piece of the First Witch. I have her blood. Do you really think you're stronger than I am?"

Helena stepped back and let her magic fly. Purple coils sprang from her hand, directed at Sybbyl and the two witches. Sybbyl used the staff to block hers, but the others weren't so fortunate.

Helena didn't waste any time throwing more of her magic. This time, it was directed not just at Sybbyl, but at the smoke bindings that held Jarin.

Sybbyl's lips peeled back to show her gritted teeth as she pointed the Staff of the Eternal at Helena. The force of Sybbyl's magic caused Helena to stumble back several steps and drop to one knee.

But she was far from finished. Helena lifted her head and locked gazes with Sybbyl. She got to her feet while letting her magic gather within her, pulsing faster and faster. She readied for Sybbyl's next attack, but it wasn't directed at her—it was aimed at Jarin.

Sybbyl placed the tip of the staff against Jarin's temple. His face contorted in agony, his entire body spasming. He then released a bellow of pain before he dropped to his knees.

Helena yelled as she threw her magic at Sybbyl, using Jarin's staff to amplify it. The purple coils wrapped around Sybbyl, sinking into her skin. She screamed in rage and agony as smoke rose from where the magic burned her, but she still kept the staff against Jarin.

There was a loud blast that threw Helena backward. She landed on her back but quickly rolled over and jumped to her feet. When she readied to release more magic, there was nothing but smoke that billowed from where Sybbyl had been. Helena rushed to it, hoping to find her dead, but the witch was gone.

And so was Jarin.

22

"Nay." Helena looked around wildly. "Jarin. Jarin!"

She turned in a circle, looking for any sign of him, but there was nothing. It was as if he'd disappeared without a trace.

"He's gone."

She ignored the deep voice of Armir because to accept his words was to admit that Jarin was indeed gone.

"Helena."

Tears clouded her vision. She didn't stop them as they crested over her lids and fell down her cheeks. She had expected to be the one to die. But Jarin was in Sybbyl's clutches, which was so much worse.

Something soft brushed against her hand. She sank her fingers into Valdr's fur as the wolf leaned against her. Overhead, Andi released a loud call as if she too were searching for Jarin.

"I have to find him," she said.

Armir came up on her other side and released a loud breath. "You heard what Sybbyl said."

Helena turned her head to meet his gaze. "I told you to leave."

"She never saw me or the animals, but I was not going to leave you or Jarin."

"You did not help either."

"She was gone before I had a chance."

Helena turned her head away, squeezing her eyes closed. "I'm sorry. That was unfair. It was my battle."

"I was on my way to help when she left, and it isn't just your battle. It is all of ours."

She opened her eyes to see Andi flying away, continuing her search for Jarin. "Where did Sybbyl take him?"

"Could be any number of places."

"That isn't helpful."

"I know."

Helena swallowed and drew in a shaky breath. "I will find him."

"Aye, you will. With our help."

She cut him a look. "Our?"

"I want you to come to Blackglade with me."

"Nay," she said with a shake of her head. "I cannot give you that kind of time. Besides, I can use a locator spell."

Armir clasped his hands behind his back. "Do you really believe Sybbyl would let you find her so easily? Every witch knows how to do one of those spells. It's going to take much more to find Jarin."

"It will take weeks to reach Blackglade," she argued.

"It will take but moments."

She frowned at him. "I have heard of that magic before. It is dangerous."

"And painful, but it takes mere seconds to cross such distances. Once Jarin is located, we can do it again to reach him."

What were her choices? Walking around for months if not years, hoping to stumble across him? Or by taking a chance with the Varroki. If she wanted to get to Jarin, there was only one option open to her.

"I am not leaving Andi or Valdr," she stated.

Armir opened his mouth, then closed it. He looked down at the wolf. "We do not take animals when we do such magic."

"We will this time. At least Valdr. We can send Andi flying to Blackglade."

Armir flattened his lips in disapproval, but he finally relented. "I'll need to make the wolf sleep first. Otherwise, it might be too painful for him."

"Do what you must," she said and whispered Andi's name while sending magic along the wind to call the falcon back. Then she went down on her haunches to look into the wolf's eyes. "I need you with me to find Jarin. Please trust me. Lay down."

The animal lowered himself to the ground and turned his head to Armir as if waiting. Armir squatted beside the wolf and stared into his eyes as he began whispering a spell. Valdr was asleep within moments.

As soon as Andi returned, Helena bade the bird return to Blackglade where she, Valdr, and Armir would be waiting. The bird let out a forlorn cry before she returned to the sky.

"Now what?" Helena asked Armir.

The commander met her gaze and twisted his lips. "Prepare yourself."

Helena tightened her hold on the staff. When Armir squatted down next to the wolf and touched Valdr, she did the same. Armir then covered the hand she had on the staff with his own. He whispered two words. A heartbeat passed with nothing. Then, no sooner had she blinked than it felt as if her world were being ripped apart, as if *she* were being ripped apart.

She tried to hold back the scream, but it was torn from her. The entire world shook around her, and just when she didn't think she could stand it anymore, everything stopped.

Helena took in a breath and looked down at Valdr, who still slept. The next moment, she turned away, clutching her stomach as she retched. It felt as if there were thousands of hammers slamming against her head, but the worst part was that her eyes couldn't focus on anything.

"Easy," Armir said, his voice hoarse. "It will pass."

She shook her head, not believing him as she continued to heave. Tears of pain fell from her eyes and sweat covered her. Her arms gave out, and she collapsed to the side, grateful for the cold stone pressed against her forehead.

Moments passed with her eyes closed. Her stomach finally started to settle and her skin to cool. Helena didn't know how long she lay there before she felt the wind. She rolled onto her back and found herself gazing up at a sky thick with gray clouds. It was then that she noticed the tall columns that were curved inward toward her.

She turned her head to Armir. He was fuzzy around the edges, and no matter how many times she blinked, it didn't clear. He was seated but leaning to the side, one arm propping him up. His eyes were closed, and the fingers on the ground gripped the stone.

It made her feel better that he was as affected as she. Magic came at a price. Always. Some magic had very little repercussions—or in the ways of the Coven, was directed elsewhere so they felt nothing. But other magic, like jumping locations, had effects that made it difficult to continue using such spells.

Armir's eyes snapped open a heartbeat before a woman appeared. Helena didn't have time to react to her vision clearing because she saw him looking at the woman with such longing that it made Helena catch her breath. But as quickly as it appeared, Armir hid it.

Helena returned to her side and pushed herself up by her hands. She grasped Jarin's staff and shifted to face the woman. Without having to be told, Helena knew the stunning female with the long, flaxen hair and gray eyes was Malene. She was slight in stature, but there was steel in her bones and fire in her eyes that only one who led understood. Helena stumbled to her feet, and Malene was there to help her, lending a hand.

She smiled at Helena. "Welcome to Blackglade."

Helena returned the smile as a tear slipped from the corner of her eye. "Thank you."

Malene glanced at the staff before she turned her head to Armir. They exchanged a silent look before he hefted Valdr in his arms and climbed to his feet.

"Come," Malene urged.

Helena walked with her to the edge of the tower. Helena wanted to look out at the wonders around her, but her vision still hadn't cleared completely. They went down a flight of stairs and entered a large chamber.

Malene walked to a table and motioned toward a bench while Armir kicked the door shut behind him and rested the wolf near the roaring fire.

Armir began to talk, but Malene held up her hand, a blue light coming from her palm. "I saw it. All of it," she stated.

Helena frowned and glanced at Armir. "I do not understand."

"Her powers continue to grow," he explained. "Malene is sometimes able to see things as they happen."

Helena jerked her head to the Lady of the Varroki. "You saw what Sybbyl did?"

"Aye," Malene replied with a nod. "I knew Armir would

bring you here, so I began preparing. First, you need to build up your strength from the effects of the spell. Eat."

Helena glanced at the table, just noticing the array of food before her. Armir didn't hesitate to reach for food, but she was more hesitant.

"Trust me," Malene said. "It helps."

Helena took a piece of bread and pulled apart a small section that she put into her mouth. As soon as she ate it, she discovered she was ravenous. She finished off two more pieces of bread and some meat before she touched the goblet of water.

She listened to Malene speak of mundane things that happened around the city, and Helena realized that the Lady of Varroki was attempting to put her at ease.

With her belly full, Helena folded her hands in her lap and met Armir's gaze.

He set down his goblet and sighed. He then glanced at Malene. "What are your thoughts?"

She walked serenely to the table and sat beside Helena. "My vision, if you wish to call them that, began with Sybbyl's arrival. I heard your exchange with her, as well as witnessed the battle. You did well. So well, in fact, that you were besting her. She fled, and took Jarin with her."

"I was winning?" Helena asked.

Armir chuckled. "You sound surprised. You shouldn't be, especially after talking to the First Witch."

Malene's soft gray eyes widened. "She spoke to you?"

"Aye," Helena admitted.

Malene's smile was wide. "I knew she was still with us."

Armir leaned his arms on the table as he looked between the two of them. "We have to find Jarin."

Helena waited for Malene's agreement, but the Lady remained silent. Helena asked, "What are you not saying?"

Malene's gaze lowered to the floor for a long moment then she looked up. "Did Jarin tell you what he does?"

"Aye," she said. "He told me how the Varroki have fought the Coven for generations."

"And, all that time, the warriors spent weeks and months seeking out the Coven."

Helena's heart sank as she comprehended what Malene was saying. "Jarin and the other warriors search out witches because you have not been able to use a spell to find them."

"Aye."

"But we aren't looking for witches. We search for Jarin," Armir added.

Helena looked from the commander to Malene, and the two of them shared a smile. "Do you think it will work?"

"We can try," Malene said.

"Now?"

Armir rose to his feet. "Perhaps you should rest."

Helena glared at him. "You know what Sybbyl has planned for Jarin. Do you want to give her time to carry it out?"

"We can start now," Malene said as she put a hand on Helena's arm.

Helena looked down at the hand and instantly regretted her harsh words. "My apologies to both of you."

"No need," Armir said. "We understand."

Nothing more was said of it as Malene rubbed her hands together, the blue light coming from each palm growing brighter. She held her hands facing each other and closed her eyes. Words Helena didn't recognize tumbled from Malene's lips.

Seconds became minutes, and sweat started to bead on Malene's brow. Finally, the Lady of the Varroki gasped for air and lowered her hands, her chest heaving.

Helena waited expectantly, but the moment Malene's eyes

met hers, she knew the spell hadn't worked. "Sybbyl is too strong."

"I'm not giving up," Malene said.

Helena got to her feet and walked around the chamber while Armir saw to Malene. Helena stopped at the window and looked out over the turbulent seas with waves that crested into white before rolling back into the expanse.

Sybbyl's words kept playing over and over in her head, but there was something she could no longer ignore. Helena put her hand on her stomach. Did a life grow there? Did she dare hope?

Malene came up beside her and put a hand over Helena's. "I can give you the answer you seek."

Helena looked at her. "You know?"

"Aye. Do you wish to, as well?"

The answer wouldn't change her desire to look for Jarin until she found him. No matter how long it took, no matter what she had to do, she wouldn't give up on him.

"I do," Helena said.

Malene lowered her arm and drew in a deep breath. Then she smiled. "A child grows in your womb."

Another baby. Jarin's child.

And hers.

This time, Helena had much more to fight for, and she wasn't going to lose her bairn or the man she loved.

23

Helena.

That was the first thought rushing through Jarin's mind as he came to. He was on his side, and by the damp leaves and dirt beneath him, he was on the ground.

Instead of opening his eyes, he reached out with his senses, tuning his ears to catch the slightest sound, detecting the faintest shift in the air on his skin, and catching every scent upon the wind.

Sybbyl was with him. There was no denying the smell of her power and evil. And the only place a Coven member went to feel safe was a Witch's Grove. He knew the still air from the places all too well.

But this Grove was different. It was calmer, as if the very trees themselves looked to Sybbyl for...everything.

Jarin tried to remember what had happened before. The last thing he recalled was looking at Helena. She had been magnificent standing defiantly atop the hill holding his staff. Watching her battle Sybbyl had left him breathless.

Not once had he worried about her, not after witnessing

the strength of her magic. She had been as ferocious as any Viking shieldmaiden, as fierce as any Celtic warrior.

And she was his.

He knew it in his bones, in his soul. At that moment, he knew the name of his feelings for her—love. He was in love with Helena.

The elation within him dampened when his mind moved through the events of the skirmish between Helena and Sybbyl. Helena's magic had freed him from the black smoke strands that held him, but he hadn't had time to fight Sybbyl.

The witch had turned that damn staff on him, pressing it against his temple. And in his mind, she repeated one question: *Where are the Varroki located?*

Jarin tried to get away from her, away from the pain that had twisted his muscles and locked his limbs so he couldn't move. The next thing he knew, everything went black.

Now, here he was. The only thing that made his situation better was knowing that Helena wasn't there. She had been too strong for Sybbyl. While Sybbyl had tried to hide that fact, he'd seen the fear in her eyes, in the tightening of her mouth.

Jarin lifted his lids and stared at the wall of trees thirty feet from him, their branches interlaced so tightly no light could get to the floor of the forest. A Witch's Grove, just as he'd sensed.

He spotted movement against one of the trunks and recognized the Gira. With every tree he looked at, he saw at least one of the nymphs. There had to be a hundred or more surrounding him. As that discovery settled in his gut like a stone, he realized two things.

That the Staff of the Eternal must have called the Gira.

And that he would never get past the nymphs to escape.

Jarin slowly sat up and gradually scanned the area. The

Grove was massive, possibly the largest of them all. And like all of them, the ground was covered in bones.

He found Sybbyl in the middle of the Grove with her back to him. She knelt on her haunches, her black skirts splayed out perfectly around her. Her golden locks fell free to her waist, while the black crown remained perched atop her head.

Beside her, protruding from the ground, was the Staff of the Eternal.

She flung her arms out to her sides. Jarin rose to his feet, happy that he was once more in command of his body. But what concerned him was that he suspected that Sybbyl was about to cast a spell. He didn't know if it was meant for him or Helena, but he had to stop it.

He walked to stand before Sybbyl. Her eyes were closed, but she smiled, sensing him. The black paint that went from temple to temple and across her eyes also covered her lids. So, when she snapped open her eyes, the white against the black was eerie.

A trick the Norse used many times.

"You finally woke," she said. "I was beginning to wonder if I damaged your mind."

He shook his head.

She lifted a blond brow. "You want to see what real magic is. Stay there, and I shall show you."

"I know what real magic is," he stated.

Her blue eyes narrowed. "Meaning it is not mine."

"The staff has given you what you have now. Without it, you would be nothing. I doubt the Coven members would even listen to you if you attempted to lead them."

She lowered her arms, resting her hands atop her thighs. "You are trying to rile me."

"I speak the truth. Whatever feelings that stirs within you is meaningless to me."

"I expected you to be a better liar than that. You want to hurt me, to anger me because you do not dare show the fury you are holding back."

Jarin hated that she was able to read him so accurately. Perhaps all the time he'd spent on his own had been detrimental. He'd had no reason to learn to hide his feelings. The few times he had to immerse himself with others to get to a witch hadn't lasted long enough for him to worry about being discovered.

Not to mention, he believed his performance had been adequate enough to pass him off for whatever he'd needed at the time.

This situation was entirely different. It was something the Hunters from the abbey were skilled at. They didn't just learn weaponry and battle tactics, they learned how to blend in with any crowd, becoming whatever person they needed to be in order to complete their mission.

Too bad he didn't have such skills.

"Your silence says it all," Sybbyl stated, a confident grin upon her lips.

He crossed his arms over his chest. "You were so certain that you would best Helena. That did not go quite as you planned, did it? In fact, you ran from her."

The slight tightening of Sybbyl's mouth was the only clue that his words had hit their mark.

"I'm far from finished with Helena. However, I found a new target."

"Me?" he asked.

She laughed, her eyes locking on him. "By capturing you, I have given myself a way to the Varroki. I already rule the Coven. I give all witches—and warlocks—the same choice. Join me, or die."

"You really believe you can take on the Varroki?"

Her smile grew. "Aye."

"Then you're a bigger fool than I first believed."

"If the Varroki are so powerful, then why have they remained in the shadows?"

"To eradicate the Coven."

She shrugged, rolling her eyes. "I think it's because there aren't as many of you as you would like me to believe. I think there has always only been a handful. And, like the Hunters, they believe they can impact us."

Jarin's brows shot up briefly as one side of his lips tilted downward. "I suppose I see how you might come to that conclusion. But let me give you another possibility. The Varroki are made up of many more than you think. They live for one thing—ensuring the Coven never gains power and tips the balance toward evil."

Sybbyl's brows drew together in a small frown.

"In all the years that the Coven has been trying to gain power, when has it happened? Has it always been just out of reach with something occurring that kept the Coven from attaining what they wanted?"

Jarin inwardly smiled when Sybbyl's face contorted as if she had just eaten something sour.

"You lie," she bit out.

"Do I? Or do I speak the truth?"

She shook her head, her long locks moving with her. "It was mistakes made by witches within the Coven that kept us from succeeding."

"If that is what you believe."

"I will find the Varroki."

He gave a snort. "Nay, you will not."

"You will take me to them."

"Do you honestly believe that I would go out looking for Coven members, knowing that I might be taken and not have spells in place that would prevent me from willingly giving you such information—or allowing a witch to extract it from me?"

She considered him for a long moment. "Maybe what you say is true, or it could be another lie. I have yet to figure you out. I will, though. That I promise you. Until then, sit back and watch while I locate the abbey and the Hunters so I can lay waste to them all."

Shock went through Jarin, but he didn't move. Edra was smart. She would know something like this was coming. She would prepare.

But would it be enough?

His mind went to Leoma, who was with Braith at his keep. Ravyn was also away from the abbey with Carac at his castle. Yet it was the children running around the abbey that Jarin kept thinking about.

Then he recalled that Sybbyl had said Helena was carrying his child. He had to get away from Sybbyl. Soon. Jarin wanted to be with Helena, to ensure the safety of her and their child.

Sybbyl once more lifted her arms out to her sides. She held his gaze for a moment before her eyes shut. Her lips moved, but he could not hear the words or make them out.

After a few minutes, she rose up on her knees and held her arms bent in front of her with her palms facing the sky. Sybbyl went silent and then leaned her head back. Black smoke billowed from her mouth and mingled with her hands.

Jarin's arms dropped to his sides as he took a step back. He knew what that smoke could do, and he wanted no part of it. His magic filled his palms, waiting to lash out.

Then, he stilled. Magic? He not only had control of his body but his magic, as well. Was Sybbyl foolish enough to do that? Or was it the Witch's Grove? Everyone knew the Groves helped to heighten magic.

Jarin might not like being in them, but there was no denying what they did. Sybbyl was too intent on her spell to think about him attacking her.

He drew in a deep breath, and right as the smoke began to spiral toward the sky, he pulled back his arms with his hands facing outward and shoved his magic at her.

It barreled into Sybbyl, knocking her onto her back and severing the spell before she could finish it. Jarin immediately responded by sending two more blasts of magic that hit Sybbyl so hard she was lifted off the ground and tossed a few feet away.

He strode to her as she rolled onto her back. He planted his feet on either side of her and held his hands over her, continually pushing his magic into her.

Instead of fear, she smiled up at him, causing unease to run through him.

"Impressive," she said. "But you cannot kill me."

He gritted his teeth and sent every bit of his magic into his hands and then outward into Sybbyl. But just as she said, she didn't die.

Her smile widened. "The Gira will not let you kill me."

"But I can hurt you," he said.

The fact that sweat rolled down her temple to disappear into her hair, and that her hands were clenched into fists was all he needed to come to that conclusion.

"And I can give you pleasure."

His head jerked back. "I want nothing from you other than your death."

He was suddenly on his back. Jarin looked up to find a dozen Gira on top of him, their magic making it so he couldn't move. He still fought them with his body and his magic, though it did little good.

Sybbyl took her time getting to her feet. She swung her

hair out of her face and righted her crown before she faced him. "You did hurt me, and I will do the same to you soon. But for now, I'll give you pleasure."

Worry went through Jarin. He would not be forced to have sex with Sybbyl, not after having something so magical with Helena.

The Gira held him tightly. Frustration ran through Jarin. It wasn't until his clothes were removed that he bellowed his fury.

"What is wrong with him?" Sybbyl demanded.

Jarin stilled. He raised his head and looked down at his flaccid cock. He didn't want Sybbyl so, of course, he wouldn't respond to her.

Then he glanced at the Gira, who were pouring their magic into him, trying to force his body to ready for the coupling. Except it wasn't working.

Jarin smiled and lowered his head. Sybbyl would not be getting what she wanted from him. Not now.

Not ever.

24

The night had been the loneliest of Helena's life. Jarin had become a staple in it, so effortlessly. So quickly. She hadn't realized how much she had begun to turn to him. To depend on him.

Helena looked over her shoulder at Malene. The Lady of the Varroki had invited Helena to remain in the tower, allowing her a bath and a feast. It was quite an honor.

Armir had remained with them late into the night, not departing until well after midnight. It had been evident that he didn't want to leave, but he had, taking Valdr with him. Helena feigned exhaustion to be alone with her thoughts.

Malene had offered her bed, but Helena refused, preferring the floor. She curled up before the fire. The hours crawled by as Helena went through every word and action that had transpired between her and Sybbyl, trying to find something that would give her an advantage.

When she finally dozed, Helena dreamt of Jarin, of being in his arms, tasting his kiss, and feeling him within her. She missed him so much that an ache had begun within her chest.

And not knowing what Sybbyl was doing to him only made things worse.

Helena finally gave up trying to rest and returned to the window. The shutters were closed, and she didn't dare open them for fear of waking Malene. Helena peered through the slits as best as she could, but something kept drawing her back to the top of the tower.

She padded barefoot to the door and cracked it open. After a look over her shoulder to make sure Malene still slept, Helena slipped outside and softly closed the door behind her.

Her breath locked in her throat at the frigid temperatures that met her. But she ascended the slippery stone steps nonetheless.

Helena pulled strands of her hair from her face that the wind whipped about her. Now, she wished she hadn't released it from the braids, but she hadn't wanted to pass up another opportunity to wash her body and hair.

She finally reached the pinnacle of the tower just as the sun rose and looked in awe at the six tall pillars. Each one was curved inward like a beast curling its claws into a fist. The stones creating them were not cracked or crumbled. Instead, they seemed altered, proving that magic had created the phenomenon.

Helena walked to the center of the space and slowly turned in a circle, taking in the vast water, the many isles, and the rocky cliffs and valley that made up Blackglade. She smiled when she saw the cottages below and wondered which one Jarin had been raised in.

There were larger structures, as well. Some that looked similar to a small keep, but it was the large, wooden structure that had the unmistakable dragon head carving of the Vikings upon it that interested her.

She stopped when she found herself facing south. Somewhere, far from here, Sybbyl imprisoned Jarin. Helena knew he would fight the Coven leader until the end of his days to be free. Not just to return to her, but because he abhorred anything to do with the Coven.

Jarin would never surrender to Sybbyl. Not for anything.

Everything Helena had learned about her magic, she had discovered herself. Some of it came easily. Even spells would appear in her mind, as if she learned them without knowing it. Now, she knew the reason. All the times she'd believed she was alone, the First Witch had actually been with her—every step of the way.

Helena shuddered from the frigid wind and the nearly frozen stones beneath her feet. She should be colder than she was, she knew that, but it didn't bother her. Magic was all around her, power unlike anything she had felt before.

It was different than the Coven's, even different than at the abbey. This was old magic, rooted in tradition and two intertwining cultures. It was resilient, compelling.

Potent.

She welcomed it, sought it. It ran over and around her as well as through her. In this place, atop this very tower, she was connected to the Celts and the Norse in ways she had never dreamed possible.

"Show me," she begged. "Show me how I can find Jarin."

There was a flash of lightning that zigzagged through the sky, followed almost immediately by a boom so loud that it shook the tower. Helena ignored it as she let herself be absorbed by the magic.

It was like walking through a dense hedge, but the more she pushed through, the easier it was to move. Eventually, everything cleared, and she found herself looking down upon a Witch's Grove.

Her gaze ran over the huge size of it, noting the impenetrable trees and more Gira than she had ever seen. Then she saw him. Helena smiled at the sight of Jarin. Until she noticed that he was naked.

Gira held him down, trying to make his cock stir. The harder they tried, the louder he laughed. Not too far away, Sybbyl paced, glaring at him.

Jarin was so close, Helena thought she might be able to touch him, but it was all an illusion. Yet it showed her the lengths Sybbyl was willing to go to in order to get what she wanted. Somehow, Jarin was holding out against the witch and the Gira.

"Stay strong," Helena whispered.

Jarin's smile dropped, and a frown puckered his forehead. Almost as if he had heard her.

Helena looked back at Sybbyl. The witch was too intent on getting what she wanted to have noticed anything. Helena didn't want to play her hand early, though, so she pulled back. Jarin became smaller as Helena once more looked over the Grove.

She drew back more, to see the forest where the Grove was located. Then she saw the nearest village and the landmarks she would need to find it all again.

Malene jerked upright in bed. She glanced at the hearth, but she knew Helena wasn't there. Malene jumped out of bed at the same time the door was thrown open.

Armir strode in, the wolf beside him, and water dripping from them both. The commander looked around, his lips compressing. There was another loud crack of lightning and a boom of thunder.

She knew where Helena was. Malene rushed to the door, but Armir blocked her way. "Move," she ordered.

"It's too dangerous."

She lifted her chin, staring into his beautiful, pale green eyes. "Stay here or come with me, but I am going up there."

"So damn stubborn," he grumbled as he turned on his heel. "Stay close to me."

Malene grabbed hold of his shirt as they stepped outside. Valdr raced past them. The wind was fierce, but the rain was only coming down lightly. Malene shook with the cold and wished she'd put on her shoes by the time they reached the top where Valdr stood. As soon as Malene saw Helena, she came to a stop.

"Holy hell," Armir murmured.

Malene had to agree with him. Helena stood in the rain with her red hair flying around her like long, slim fingers. Her arms were out to her sides as she faced southward. Her green eyes were open, but her gaze was directed inward.

The lightning they had seen and heard was striking the tower, inches from Helena. But it was the shadowy figure behind her that had Malene reaching for Armir's hand.

Suddenly, the lightning was gone. Helena fell to her knees, her head hanging. Malene kept her gaze on the figure. The shadows moved away, giving just a glimpse of the woman who looked straight at Malene.

"The First Witch," Malene whispered.

The woman put a ghostly hand on Helena's head, and then she was gone.

"Just when I thought I had seen everything," Armir said.

Valdr rushed to Helena, walking around her in a circle. Malene hurried to Helena, kneeling beside her as she wrapped an arm around the witch.

Helena lifted her head and smiled. "I found him," she said breathlessly.

"Armir," Malene called.

Her commander was there immediately. He helped get Helena to her feet, but she pulled back when they tried to walk her to the steps.

"This place," Helena said.

Malene smiled. "It is something wonderful, is it not?"

"Aye."

Armir adjusted his grip. "We need to get you out of this weather. See? Even Valdr doesn't like you up here."

At the mention of the wolf, Helena and Malene found him impatiently waiting on the stairs.

"I feel none of it," Helena admitted.

Malene and Armir exchanged a glance. It was Helena who pulled away from them and made her way down the stairs and back into the chamber behind the wolf.

Malene sighed and started after her, but Armir grabbed her arm. It wasn't something he would have done even a month earlier, but her changes in the laws now allowed him the liberty.

She turned her head, and their gazes met. The first time she had seen him, she'd thought Armir intense and savage. It didn't take her long to realize he was that and so much more.

"You saw her," he said.

Malene knew he wasn't referring to Helena. "I did."

"She looked at you."

"I saw that, as well."

Armir released her hand and turned away to walk a few steps before pivoting back to her. "I think what we just saw from Helena is just a hint of the depth of her magic. Can you imagine if she had fallen into the hands of the Coven?"

"You speak as if it has all been decided. There are still

many variables at work here. Helena has chosen to side against the Coven, but do not forget, they have Jarin."

Armir's lips flattened. "Do you really think Sybbyl would keep Helena until the bairn is born?"

"Absolutely. Sybbyl craves power like most hunger for love. She's had a taste of it now. It does not help that Helena showed her that she was more powerful. Sybbyl will use and do anything to get Helena. Anything."

Armir ran a hand down his face. He shook his head and glanced down. Then his frown deepened. "You aren't wearing shoes."

There was a grin on her lips when Armir herded her down the steps and into her chambers. He stared into the fire beside Helena and Valdr as Malene changed into dry clothes. She then made her way to the trio.

"I want to leave today to find him," Helena said.

Armir's penetrating green eyes turned to Malene. She gently pushed Helena into a chair and found a towel to begin drying her hair.

Helena caught her gaze. "Do you not agree?"

"I agree that you have done something amazing in finding him. Not even Sybbyl's magic aided by the staff stopped you. I am in awe of that," Malene said.

Helena's gaze hardened. "But?"

Malene straightened and lowered her hand holding the towel to her side. "Sybbyl will continue to search for anything of the First Witch's."

"Unless Sybbyl's dead."

"Do not underestimate her," Armir cautioned.

Helena looked between the two of them. "I defeated her. And I found Jarin."

"She got scared and ran," Armir said. "I would not call that a defeat."

"But," Malene hastily added when Helena started to argue, "the fact that Sybbyl ran does mean you defeated her. However, Armir has a point. You do not want to underestimate her or become too confident."

Helena swallowed and looked into the fire. "Jarin saved me. I was about to give up all hope when he found me starving and cold. I cannot leave him with her." Helena's face contorted with rage. "The idea of Sybbyl touching him makes me..."

She trailed off, and Malene squatted before the chair and covered Helena's hands with own. "You love Jarin."

"Aye," Helena murmured.

"He is a Varroki, one of ours," Malene said. "We will not allow him to remain in Sybbyl's clutches. We do this together."

Armir went down on one knee. "Together?"

Helena pulled Armir's hand to theirs. "Together."

25

His loathing knew no bounds. Jarin let his gaze fill with repugnance as he glared at Sybbyl.

"I will succeed," the witch declared. "I have the Staff of the Eternal. You'll lose control over your body eventually, and when that happens, you'll be mine."

The Gira released him. Jarin peeled his lips back to show his anger as he looked at each of the nymphs. His revenge upon them was going to be sweet. Without a word, he summoned his clothes. Instead of using magic to get dressed, he put each item on himself, never taking his eyes from Sybbyl as a show of power. He wanted the witch to know that he not only didn't care about being naked in front of her, but that she did absolutely nothing for him.

Sybbyl rolled her eyes as she turned her head away.

"I have learned that if someone has to tell another what they will do, then they don't have the power to do it," he stated.

Sybbyl laughed and cut her eyes to him. "Can the same not be said for someone who states what they *won't* do?"

"My reference is to anyone in power. Is that not what you claim you are?"

Her blue eyes narrowed as she faced him. "I claim nothing. I lead the Coven."

"If you say so."

"I do." Her voice had dropped an octave, signaling her anger.

Jarin inwardly grinned. It was so easy to rile the witch. If Sybbyl were truly in charge, she wouldn't feel the need to defend herself at every turn. Either she hadn't officially claimed her position, or the Coven hadn't completely bowed down to her.

What did concern him was the way the Gira stared at Sybbyl as if she were a goddess risen from the dead. And in some ways, the simple fact that she held the Staff of the Eternal labeled her as just that.

Jarin glanced up at the sky, recalling Helena's voice. She had found him. Somehow, someway, she had used magic to locate him.

He was used to fighting alone, counting on no one but himself. He wanted to be able to grab the staff from Sybbyl, but she hadn't released the damn thing since their small battle earlier. That had probably been his one and only shot to get the staff—and he'd lost it.

If he couldn't get it, the next best thing would be to get free of her. That in itself would be nearly impossible with the Gira. Each time he looked at the trees, there seemed to be more of the nymphs.

They had held him down as if he were nothing more than a child. His skin still crawled from their touch. He wouldn't get two steps into the trees before they stopped him. And, frankly, he would be happy never to have another one lay hands on him again.

He knew they ate the humans they caught with their whispers, but he suspected they spent days or weeks toying with the helpless prey first.

While he had been immune to whatever spell they'd used, Sybbyl had not. He saw the way her chest heaved, and her eyes grew heavy-lidded. The nymphs' magic caused desire to flow wantonly through Sybbyl and most likely many, many others.

The witch tilted her head to the side as she regarded him. "I will break through whatever spell you're using to thwart me."

"Spell?" he repeated and gave a shake of his head. "Each warrior who wanders the lands in search of Coven witches does so after years of training. Our bodies and minds have endured countless hours of bombardment by all kinds of magic. You will never force me because I won't allow it to happen."

She tapped a finger against her chin. "Ah. So, all I need to do is get into your mind."

"Do your worst."

"Oh, I will," she promised, her eyes sparkling with the challenge.

Jarin wished he could defeat Sybbyl on his own, but that wasn't possible. Not that long ago, he had told Ravyn that she needed to accept help. Now, he was in the same predicament. But he knew that aid was coming.

He just had to ensure that he lasted until Helena arrived.

Sybbyl slowly walked around him. Jarin didn't move, didn't even look at her. He measured the distance from one end of the Grove to the other from each side because every bit of information could be the piece that gained him an advantage.

"I gather the Varroki have witches."

He shrugged, nonchalantly. "Of course."

"How is it that none of us have birthed a warlock? Why only the Varroki?"

His gaze shifted, landing on Sybbyl as she stopped before him. "For someone who covets the bones of the First Witch, you know very little about her."

"I honestly did not believe she was real until the Blood Skull was found. Since then, I've changed my views."

"Simply because, by attaining her bones, you gain power."

Sybbyl grinned slyly. "That is an added benefit. There is little that was ever said of the First Witch. I would know more."

"And you wish for me to tell you?"

The witch glanced at the staff. "You can tell me what I want to know, or I will have the Gira hold you down again and spend a few hours playing with that impressive cock of yours. We might get lucky and get it to stir."

"Do what you must."

His flippant reply got just the reaction he wanted when Sybbyl's nostrils flared, and her lips tightened. She wanted to intimidate and manipulate men, and for the most part, she had been successful.

But he wasn't like most males.

Sybbyl lifted her chin, defiance in her gaze. "We will get back to your submission later. Right now, I want to know about the First Witch."

He crossed his arms over his chest and held her gaze. He might not be able to best the Gira or even wrench the staff from Sybbyl's hands, but he could undermine her in other ways. Right now, the nymphs were seeing that Sybbyl wasn't in complete control.

And if Jarin had anything to say about it, she never would be.

Sybbyl's lips pinched together the longer he was silent. "I gave you a command."

"I do not recognize you as having authority over me."

She took a step forward, pointing the staff at him. "Do you test me?"

"I state a fact."

The end of the staff briefly slammed into his chest. Magic, hot and bright, sliced through him, buckling his legs until he was on his knees. The smug smile was back on Sybbyl's lips as the Gira watched gleefully from the periphery.

But Jarin wasn't one to give in that easily. The torture wasn't anything he hadn't endured to become a warrior, and the witch was in for a surprise when he didn't give in as she expected.

"Begin," Sybbyl demanded, threatening to use the staff again.

He jerked his chin to the weapon. "The Blood Skull spoke to Braith. Has the staff not spoken to you? Has it not told you all you want to know? Nay? I wonder why that is."

Sybbyl rammed the staff into his chest, hard, but without any magic. Then, through clenched teeth she warned, "Do not test me."

"What the bloody hell do you think I'm doing?" he retorted icily.

A frown deepened her brow as she looked at him with new eyes. "You would rather spend hours being tortured than share stories with me?"

"Aye."

"What a pity," she said with a sad shake of her head. "And here I thought you were smarter than most. Seems I was mistaken."

Jarin snorted at her blatant attempt to persuade him to do

as she wished. "Do you know why the staff has not spoken to you? Because it doesn't believe you're worthy."

Sybbyl's expression clouded with anger and a hint of doubt. "Enough."

"You wished to know. I'm merely sharing," he replied coolly. "Does the staff not believe you should wield it because you did not gain power through the ranks of the Coven? Or is it because of something else."

"Shut your mouth," Sybbyl said louder.

Jarin grinned. "A little of both, I think."

"You know nothing."

"I learn fast."

She pushed the staff against his chest once more. The magic was brutal, relentless as it began to constrict his body, preventing Jarin from taking in a breath.

Sybbyl leaned down until her face was even with him. "You know nothing, warlock. You think you can outwit me, but you're wrong. You certainly cannot best me with magic. I see the hope in your eyes, a hope that says you believe Helena is coming for you. It will *never* happen."

Jarin gritted his teeth against the pain and fought to remain upright. He wanted to be awake when Helena came.

Because she would.

Jealousy and rage contorted Sybbyl's beauty, revealing the ugly truth of her soul. "Not only will Helena never find us, but even if by sheer luck she was able to, the Gira will never let her in. They will rip her apart as soon as they see her simply because I wish it."

Jarin wasn't so sure of that, but he would keep that tidbit to himself for the moment. He would be alive to see Helena's entrance because he knew it was going to be spectacular.

"You...do not have...what it...takes," he said.

She blinked, her face filling with fake concern. "What ever

is the matter? Is it difficult to breathe? Are there spots dotting your vision?"

Jarin took every hit of her magic without returning any of his own. He needed to learn how far she would go and how strong the magic was. Because that would be how he got the upper hand. It might take days, weeks even, but he was prepared.

He knew that no matter what, Helena would find him. Hopefully, Armir had taken her to Blackglade. Helena, Malene, and Armir were an army unto themselves.

The magic suddenly relented. Jarin gratefully drew in a deep breath, filling his burning lungs with it again and again. He eventually looked up to discover Sybbyl watching him with narrowed eyes.

"Why did you not fight back?" she demanded. "Even if I wanted to bind your magic here, I couldn't. This place is magic. You let me hurt you to..." Comprehension dawned on her face. "You're learning my power. Perhaps I should speed up your instruction."

Instead of answering her, he asked, "Do you honestly believe you can conquer those at the abbey, the Varroki, and any other witch who refuses to join the Coven with one bone of the First Witch?"

"I told you, I will have the Living Heart. One way or another," she boasted. "If it's Helena or your child, I will control it."

Jarin climbed to his feet to look down at her. "Helena will never succumb, and neither will our child."

"I wish for my plans to happen now, but I am prepared to wait years."

He laughed then, the sound bouncing around the quiet of the Grove. "We both know what a lie that is."

Sybbyl's blue eyes flashed with indignation. "There is

another bone of the First Witch on this isle. The Blood Skull may be out of my grasp for the moment, and the Living Heart might be a little stubborn, but I can get another bone."

"Then what is stopping you?" he goaded.

She spun, her long, blond hair swinging out behind her. "Do you know what an advantage two of the First Witch's bones will give me?" she asked as she walked away.

Jarin knew exactly how much, and it made him very uneasy. There was no way for him to tell anyone of Sybbyl's plans. Hell, he'd be happy just to let one of the Hunters know that there was another bone close so they could begin searching for it.

Suddenly, he frowned. The Blood Skull, Living Heart, and Staff of the Eternal were all in England. Didn't that defeat the First Witch's demand to scatter her bones far and wide? No one would've been fool enough to bring so many pieces to one place.

Isle.

The word rang like a bell in Jarin's head. Three of the pieces had been in England, but that wasn't the only country on the isle. There was also Scotland.

And if Sybbyl could locate the nearest bone, then so could Braith with the Blood Skull, or Helena as the Living Heart. All Jarin had to do was get word to one of them and let them know.

But first, he had to contend with Sybbyl and the Gira.

26

Somewhere near the abbey...

There was something wrong in the forest. Synne pressed her back against the ancient oak, her palms flat against the bark. She wished she knew what the cause of the faint shift she smelled in the air was.

If only she had magic.

It wasn't the first time Synne had wished she were born a witch. Having been raised by Edra, magic was all Synne had ever known. She used to lie awake at night and pray to whatever god was listening that she had powers yet undiscovered.

Despite her multitude of prayers, magic had never been hers. But Synne had another gift. Her knowledge of witches and their connection to the earth gave her a deeper understanding and love of nature.

There were times when she felt particularly weary, or the rare times she was lonesome, that she could swear the sway of the tree branches was their way of trying to hug her, not just the wind.

Her duties as an archer kept her perched in trees, which only cemented her bond with nature. So, when she sensed a disturbance in the air, she knew it was the trees trying to tell her something.

"I'm listening," she whispered to the oak. "What are you trying to say?"

A quick, violent rush of wind rattled the surrounding treetops so fiercely that it almost seemed as if someone had grabbed them by the trunk and shook them. As soon as it began, it was gone, leaving the forest eerily quiet.

Synne opened her eyes. Her breath billowed out from between her lips in a cloud. The winter had been unusually cold, yet she felt the temperature fall several degrees more in seconds.

She turned and faced the tree, looking up at the crooked limbs that spread out far and wide. Without hesitation, she climbed. Synne went as far up the tree as she could, then looked out over the forest.

At first, all she saw was more trees. It normally had a calming effect, but the disquiet in her had her scanning the foliage again and again and again. There was something out there. She was sure of it. She just had to discover what it was.

That's when she noticed it.

The absolute silence.

There wasn't a single song from a bird. Moreover, she didn't see any flying from branch to branch, either. She quietly moved down a few limbs and searched for any sign of other animals. Thirty minutes later, she came to the glum conclusion that they, too, were gone.

It was almost as if all life had deserted the forest. Fear did that. What was it that the animals sensed that she'd missed? It was time someone with magic took a look.

She pressed her cheek against the bark of the tree. "Thank you for letting me know."

The oak might not have told her what was wrong, but it had alerted her that something was amiss—and that was far more than she'd had before.

Synne hastily climbed down the tree. When she landed on the ground, she put her palm against the bark once more. Then she stealthily made her way back to the abbey.

Synne frequently patrolled the farthest from the abbey, which is why it always took her so long to get back. It was also why she was usually the first to let them know that someone approached with a carefully aimed arrow toward the next sentry.

Despite her haste, Synne was careful as she approached the ruins. She waited several minutes to ensure that no one was near before she hurried through the arched gate and into the magical confines of the abbey.

She didn't talk to anyone as she ran through the grounds and then the abbey itself, looking for Edra. She finally found the witch sitting with Radnar in a sun-drenched room warmed by a large fire. At one time, a child would have perched on one of their knees, much as Synne had done herself.

But now, there were many others to look after the abandoned young ones taken in. It allowed Edra and Radnar to focus on other things—like keeping everyone safe.

Edra's head snapped up, but it was Radnar who asked, "What is it?"

Synne swallowed and slowly walked toward them, trying to think of words to explain what she'd experienced as she carefully placed her bow on the table.

"Take a breath," Edra advised and rose to place a cup of water in Synne's hand.

Synne drained the mug and set it on the table. She looked from Edra into Radnar's brown eyes. "Something is amiss."

"Where?" he asked.

Synne parted her lips and shook her head. She briefly closed her eyes and said, "In the forest. The *entire* forest."

Edra had encouraged Synne's link to nature, and not once had she ever dismissed anything Synne said. Edra took Synne's hands in hers. "Tell us everything."

"There isn't much to tell."

"There is always much to say in such matters," the witch said, her blue eyes crinkling at the corners as she smiled.

Radnar frowned. "Does someone approach?"

Synne gave a shake of her head. "I saw no one."

"Then we have time." Radnar pointed to the chair next to him, a silent order for Synne to sit.

Edra gently turned her to it and gave her a little push. Synne found herself seated between them. Radnar and Edra had saved her. They had given her a home, a family, and more love than she could ever have hoped for. They'd given her freedom and something important to fight for. She owed them everything.

And she would do anything to keep them and everyone at the abbey safe.

"Synne," Edra urged.

She swallowed and began. "I walked the forest as I do every day. I touched each tree as I always do."

"Aye," Radnar said with a crooked smile.

Synne shifted in her seat. "Something made me stop beside one of the ancient oaks. I put my back to it and placed both hands on the bark, and that's when I smelled it."

"Smelled what?" Edra asked.

Synne searched for the right word and shook her head in frustration. "The closest I can come to describing it is...panic.

That's why I climbed to the top of the tree and looked around. It took a moment, but I finally realized what was wrong. There were no birds."

Radnar exchanged a glance with Edra. "None? Surely, there had to be some. Perhaps hiding in their nests?"

"I saw no movement. Heard no song. Not in the trees, and...not on the ground. In fact, it seemed as if all the animals were gone."

Edra sat back, her face blank from shock. She tugged nervously on the end of her long, blond braid that fell over her shoulder. After a moment, she rose and began to pace before the table.

"Tell us the rest," the witch implored.

Synne began to shake her head, then she recalled the wind. "I asked the trees to tell me what was wrong. There was a great gust of wind that lasted mere moments. The stillness after is what prompted me to climb the tree."

Edra was silent a long time as she paced. Radnar took Synne's hand in his own. He shot her a reassuring smile. Though it had been two decades since she arrived at the abbey, Radnar still looked as hale and hearty as he had when he found her, except for the graying at his temples.

Aside from a few more wrinkles around Edra's eyes, she also looked the same. The emotional toll the couple bore for everyone who sought shelter at the abbey did the most damage.

Synne knew the many nights Edra and Radnar stayed up far later than anyone else, checking spells, considering which Hunter should go where, and if any of the outsiders were coming too close to the abbey.

Because, hidden or not, no one was ever truly safe as long as the Coven was out there.

Synne was comforted by Radnar's grip. He had been the

one to first train her. It began as a way for her to protect herself. She hadn't questioned him when he put the small bow he'd made just for her in her hand and taught her how to use it.

Day after day, he spent hours with her, guiding her to become better and better. He didn't treat her differently because she was a female. In fact, in some instances, she thought he pushed her harder than others.

Without a doubt, she was as good as she was with the bow because of him. When he felt he had taught her all he could, he found someone who could take her to the next level.

Not once had she stopped training. Not once had she told Radnar that it was enough. Not once did Synne complain. Because she knew just what was at stake.

And when she told him she wanted to become a Hunter, he had merely replied that she'd been training for that from the very beginning.

She looked into his brown eyes, remembering the first time she had gone after a witch with Radnar. He had sat back, letting her make the decisions. He'd given her the courage to stop second-guessing herself and patiently pointed out areas where she needed more training.

Everyone at the abbey knew how badly Edra and Radnar had wanted a child of their own, and Synne wished she was theirs. The couple was the parents she never had.

Finally, Edra halted. She faced Synne, her chest expanding as she took in a deep breath. "Your bond to nature might just have saved us."

"How?" Synne asked.

Edra walked around the table to Radnar and took his free hand in hers. They shared a long look before Edra shifted her attention back to Synne. "There are only two things that I know of that would cause such a reaction in woods usually teeming with animals."

"The Coven," Radnar said with a sigh.

There was a long pause as Edra stared at Synne. "And Gira."

Synne's chest tightened at the mention of the nymphs. She held a great fear of them despite never seeing one before. "The-they're here?"

"I'm not sure." Edra licked her lips, her unease apparent. "I could use a spell to see, but if I do, the Gira and the Coven will know we're here."

Radnar tightened his fingers around her hand. "Will the nymphs sense the spells you and Asa put around the abbey?"

"They could be out there right now?" Synne asked as she jumped up, pulling her hand from Radnar's.

He stood slowly and caught her gaze. He was calm, steady, and his voice even. "With your keen gaze, you would have seen them. Did you?"

"Nay," she said with a shake of her head.

Edra forced a smile. "They are likely only near, then. Or it could be the Coven."

"Neither scenario is good," Synne said.

Radnar wrapped an arm around her, pulling her against him as he ran his hand up and down her back. "Nay, it's not. But we have survived this long. We will figure something else out."

"What do I do?" Synne asked.

Radnar released her, grasping her upper arms while smiling. "Keep to the trees, my girl. They will tell you all we need to know."

"He's right," Edra added.

Synne was no longer crippled with terror thanks to the couple. Once more calm, she grabbed her bow and walked to the door. When she reached it, she paused and looked back to see them holding hands as they stared intensely into each other's eyes. Synne hurried from the chamber to give them privacy and made her way down the corridor.

Radnar and Edra might not be her birth parents, and the others living at the abbey might not be her brothers, sisters, aunts, uncles, or cousins, but they were family nonetheless.

Perhaps it was seeing Radnar defending those unable to help themselves, or maybe it was Edra using magic to protect a stranger that had made Synne want to be a Hunter. But she couldn't imagine a life where a father, brother, or husband ordered her about. And while she didn't hate gowns, she much preferred wearing pants so she had freedom of movement.

She might never know what had happened to her real family or why she was abandoned, and she might never know what kind of life she could've had with them, but she wouldn't change her present for anything in the world—even if it were a life filled with danger.

That was part of the appeal. Each day was a new adventure. Whether it was patrolling the forest, escorting someone seeking solace to the abbey, fighting the Coven, or honing her skills, Synne was always busy.

So what if she never found the kind of love that Edra and Radnar had. She had other things to think about. Besides, the last thing she wanted was someone trying to change her.

She walked out of the abbey to find the knights training. There were a few handsome ones, but not one of them had looked twice at her. If only she could be more like Ravyn, who was sexy and alluring in whatever she did. But that wasn't Synne.

How she hated when her thoughts took her down that road. She had more important matters to think about than that of men and the puzzling, baffling path of love.

She gave a nod to Asa as the witch stood outside with her small owl perched on her forearm.

"Be careful out there," Asa called.

Synne paused and met Asa's deep blue gaze and nodded to the owl. "Has Frida seen something?"

"You know what she has seen because you've seen it yourself. Things are going to get even more dangerous."

Synne nodded at the truth in her words. "That is what our lives are about, isn't it? As long as the Coven is out there, we live with danger just around the corner."

Asa walked to her and touched her shoulder. "You should come see me soon. I saw a vision of you and the tattoo you will need."

Synne bowed her head. "Consider it done."

She left the shield of the abbey and made her way deep into the forest. Her gaze was sharp, but her mind moved between the possibility of Gira within the woods and what it was that Asa had seen in her vision.

27

The wind blowing the fur lining the outside of the hood of the new cloak tickled Helena's cheek. She walked beside Armir through the streets of Blackglade with Valdr next to her.

"We do not have time for this," she said.

Pale green eyes slid to her, but he only smiled in response.

She glanced over her shoulder to look back at the tower. It stood like a lofty sentry, standing guard over the isle. "Where are we going?"

"It's not far now."

Helena was doing her best to remain calm, but she must not have revealed how critical it was to get to Jarin quickly.

"Be calm," Armir said as they paused to let a group of children of various ages run past them. "You know how resilient Jarin is. If anyone can withstand Sybbyl, it's him."

"All that means is that she will make him suffer longer."

Armir stopped and faced her. She had to take a step back since his action had been so sudden. As she looked up into his chiseled face, she saw the ancient line of Vikings in the steely way he held her gaze.

"Every warrior that leaves our gates spends more time out in your world than in ours. The warriors train for years in anticipation of being caught by either the Coven or those without magic. Trust me when I tell you that every one of those men and women who risk their lives to track the Coven are the best the Varroki has to offer. And Jarin is the best of them all."

Somehow, Helena wasn't surprised by the revelation. "You tell me that, but you still fear for him. I see it in your eyes."

"Of course, I do." He looked toward the group of retreating children. "At one time, Jarin and I played together. We trained with each other with sticks, with magic, with our hands...as well as with our minds."

"You wanted to be a warrior," she guessed as she sank her fingers into Valdr's fur as he leaned against her.

Armir drew in a deep breath. "Every Varroki has a part to play in the continuation of our people and the fight against the Coven. Aye, I did want to join the warriors, but my calling took me in another direction."

"A special one, I think."

He looked at the tower. "Malene is not the first Lady I have guarded and aided, but she is by far the finest of them." His head swung back to Helena. "My duties go beyond that of the Lady of the Varroki, though. I am also in charge of the warriors."

Helena nodded slowly. Everything the Varroki did was in direct contrast to the Coven. Whatever Armir wanted to show her, it was important enough for them to take time away from getting ready to find Jarin. "I understand."

They continued walking. The streets became narrower as the land dipped down and then back up again. Her thighs were screaming in protest when she glanced up and saw the large structure sitting atop an outcropping.

Steps had been chiseled into the rocks leading up to the home, and there were at least two hundred of them. Valdr bounded ahead of them, stopping to sniff things here and there. Helena was out of breath by the time they reached the top.

Armir turned her around and had her look out. She forgot about her aching legs or the burning in her lungs as she beheld the stunning sight of the rocky coastline, a wide beach with sparkling sand, and miles of water before her.

"Can you imagine growing up with this kind of view?" Armir asked.

"Is this your home?"

He smiled at her as the door opened behind them. They turned, and Helena came face-to-face with pale blue eyes that she knew well. Her lips parted as she took in the blond hair with gray at the temples, and the lines of age that did nothing to distract from the man's strong jaw and piercing gaze.

He was an exact replica of Jarin, including the broad shoulders and tall form, except, he was older.

The man slid his gaze to Armir. "It must be important for you to bring the *örlendr* here."

"She is no outsider, Bjorn. She is a descendant of the First Witch."

Helena held still as Bjorn's gaze swept over her. There was so much she wanted to tell him about Jarin, but she kept quiet, waiting to see what Armir was about.

Valdr returned to Helena's side, and Bjorn took note of the action before swinging his gaze back to Armir.

Bjorn braced a hand on the doorway, a muscle ticking in his jaw. "Why bring her to my door?"

"Because Helena is a link to our fight with the Coven," Armir said.

"I know well enough what she is." Bjorn glanced at her again before crossing his arms over his chest. "How about you tell me the real reason you're on my doorstep."

"I believe Armir thought I would like to see Jarin's family," she stated.

Bjorn's attitude changed instantly. His eyes jerked to her as he slowly lowered his arms. Hope filled every inch of his face. "I thought that was Valdr with you. You know my son, then?"

"Aye," she said. "Jarin saved my life."

Bjorn stepped aside and held out his arm. "Enter, please."

Helena was the first one inside, with Valdr pushing past her to lay before the hearth. She looked around the long table, wondering which place Jarin favored. It wasn't hard to imagine a young Jarin in the space. It was obvious that he had been well loved if his father's pride were any indication.

She pushed down the hood of her cloak and walked to the hearth where she spied a carving in the rock. Unable to resist, she ran her finger over the Viking rune.

"It means family," Bjorn said from behind her. "Jarin carved it right before he left."

Helena put her palm over the rune and closed her eyes. Jarin rarely spoke of his family, but now she knew why. In order to protect them and do his duty, he'd pushed his love for them as far back as he could.

She stood and turned to Armir. "You think I have doubts about Jarin?"

The commander watched her for a long moment. "You have no idea what you'll encounter. I want you to be prepared. You saw a side of Jarin that he hasn't shown anyone in years, but he is fierce in protecting those he loves."

"Loves?" Bjorn said, looking between her and Armir.

Before she could reply, Armir continued, ignoring Bjorn's outburst. "Sybbyl wants you. As the Living Heart, if she controls you, she'll be able to win this battle. Everything we have all fought for will be lost. If she does not already know of your love, she will take one look at your face when you see Jarin, and she'll know the truth."

Helena briefly looked over her shoulder at the carving. "You're telling me I need to put it all aside. You could have told me that at the tower."

"You needed to see the depths that Jarin has gone to for his family and everyone at Blackglade. And what he will do for you," Armir said.

Bjorn stepped between them, facing Helena. "Where is my son?"

Helena took one of his large hands in hers and looked into his eyes. "He has been captured by the new leader of the Coven, Sybbyl."

"He fought her to protect Helena," Armir added.

Bjorn's eyes closed for a heartbeat. "Jarin does not reveal his emotions on his face or with his words. It has been like that since his mother died birthing our youngest. His emotions are in his actions. Look for that."

"I will get him from Sybbyl," Helena vowed.

Bjorn took her hands in his and squeezed them lightly. "Just make sure she does not then get her hands on you. If what Armir says about Jarin's feelings for you are true, it will devastate him to lose you."

"I won't lose against her." Helena glanced around Bjorn's wide frame to Armir. "I know now what I need to do to ensure my victory."

She shared a smile with Bjorn before she pulled her hands from his and started for the door. She was nearly to it when his words stopped her.

"I rejoiced when Malene changed the laws," Bjorn said. "I knew then that my son had a chance at a family. I wondered if there was a woman out there who could equal him. Now, I can rest easy knowing my worries were for naught."

Helena shifted to look back at Bjorn as Valdr rose and padded to her. "Thank you."

Armir ushered her out of the house and down the steps. She didn't speak as the three of them made their way back to the tower. Halfway up the winding staircase, she paused, looking out over the land.

The commander said nothing as he stood behind her. He merely waited until she gathered her thoughts.

"Was it difficult for Jarin to leave his family?" she asked.

Armir moved a step closer to her. "Aye."

"Do you think I can bring him home?"

"Without a doubt."

She gave a nod and continued onward. When they reached the top and entered Malene's chamber, there were books and tablets scattered on the table.

The Lady of the Varroki looked up and smiled. "I think I found something that could help in our battle with the Coven."

Helena hurried to the table to stand opposite Malene. "What is it?"

Malene straightened as she pointed to a thick book she'd been reading. "I remembered that there were records of the first Varroki who came to these shores. I had to find the book and reread the story to refresh my memory, but it states that the First Witch, Trea, led all witches for years. It was three of her sisters who grew jealous of her magic and the power she wielded not just with witches but also with the Vikings themselves."

"Sisters, as in other witches, or actual sisters?" Armir asked.

"Actual sisters," Malene answered.

Helena lowered herself onto the bench and propped her elbows on the table. "I can guess where that jealousy led."

Malene nodded, brows raised. "Exactly. Trea was powerful enough to keep them in check, but she knew that upon her death, her sisters would wreak havoc."

"Wait," Armir said. "So, the First Witch...Trea...was good?"

"I do not believe she was one or the other. I think she did whatever was needed for her people," Malene said.

Helena shrugged. "That makes sense. She may have done things we would consider evil, but they might have been her only recourse. We have no way of knowing."

"What is she like?" Armir asked Helena. "When has Trea spoken to you?"

Helena folded her arms on the table and thought back to the voice in her head. "She has guided me. Her words reminded me of who I am and what I'm capable of. She never pushed me in one direction or another, simply held me up when I wavered. She gave me strength."

"She was with you atop the tower," Malene said.

Helena yanked her gaze to the Lady. "What?"

"She was," Armir added. "Malene and I both saw a shadowy figure behind you."

"She's the one who showed me the way to find Jarin," Helena murmured.

Malene slowly sat. "She put her hand on your head before looking at me and disappearing. If she were evil like the Coven believes, wouldn't Trea have urged you to join them?"

"Possibly. I get the feeling that she's helping me fight *against* them."

Armir's lips tilted. "Because she probably is. What else does the story say?"

Malene placed her hand on the page. "The author states that Trea went off with a trusted group of six followers when she was dying. She didn't want her sisters near. They were also the reason she had the followers burn her body once she was dead and then distribute what was left of her bones."

"Let me guess," Helena said. "The sisters began the Coven."

Malene nodded.

Armir blew out a breath. "Family against family. And all because of jealousy."

"If it had not been her sisters, it would have been someone else," Malene said.

Armir shrugged. "True."

Helena tapped her fingers on the table as her mind ran through this new information. "Now we know why the Coven has always been obsessed with finding the bones of the First Witch."

"And had three elders governing them," Malene added.

Helena nodded in agreement. "But how does any of this help with Sybbyl?"

"Think about all Sybbyl has been told since joining the Coven," Malene said. "And think about how little she knows of Trea."

Helena frowned. "I'm not sure knowledge of the First Witch will turn Sybbyl to our side."

"Oh, it won't," Armir said with a grin.

Malene's lips curved into a wide smile. "Nay, it won't."

Helena looked between them before she joined in with a smile as comprehension dawned.

28

Sybbyl ran her hands over the smooth surface of the Staff of the Eternal. The bone within the wood had aged so it was barely identifiable. It looked more like the wood than anything human. How many witches had looked right past it without seeing the relic for what it was?

She was quite happy that no one else had found it before her. It gave her everything she had always dreamt would be hers.

Her gaze slid to Jarin. The warlock sat far from her but also kept his distance from the Gira who stood at the edge of the trees. The nymphs didn't venture into the Grove unless Sybbyl invited them.

Never had Sybbyl imagined she would be able to control them. She'd never even contemplated such an act, but now that the Gira were bowing down to her, Sybbyl saw the many ways she could use them.

She looked back at the warlock. Jarin was more difficult than she had bargained for. One of the reasons she wanted him for her own was because he was so powerful both magically and physically. She had miscalculated the strength of his mind, however.

That miscalculation caused her to take a step back and reevaluate. If he were going to freely give her the child she wanted, then she would have to think of another way.

It irritated her that she couldn't force him as men had forced women for countless generations. Every time she thought of all the helpless women who'd had no recourse but to submit, it infuriated her.

She had seen a man forced once before. Though, could it really be called rape when he grew hard on his own despite being tied down? Or perhaps it was because he was immobile. Sybbyl didn't know or care.

And with the way the Gira had used their magic on her, she had been sure that Jarin would have already given his seed at least twice by now.

Instead, he sat cross-legged with his eyes closed and his hands upon his knees as if he didn't have a care in the world. But Sybbyl wasn't fooled. The warlock was up to something. No one with that kind of magic sat idly.

She leaned close to the staff and put her lips to it as she asked, "What is the warlock doing?"

The smile on her face vanished in the next heartbeat. This was the second time the staff had refused to obey her. She didn't understand how it had done her bidding just by her thoughts before, and now, it acted as if it decided when and how it would do as she beckoned.

Her fingers tightened on the wood. She closed her eyes and concentrated her magic into her center. It swirled there, the light inside it beating in time with her heart.

She then focused her thoughts on the Varroki. *Where are they?* Her silent question caused the magic within the staff to vibrate.

Tell me, she demanded.

Then, to her surprise, the staff answered. In her mind, she saw herself standing before a long wall, one she knew well. Hadrian's Wall. Sybbyl opened her eyes and smiled. The Varroki were in Scotland. There were many mountains and glens to search, but she wasn't worried.

Once she was in Scotland, she would make the staff show her exactly where the Varroki hid. It was past time for them to stop killing the witches of the Coven.

But...she had an enemy closer to home. The Hunters. Edra's stance against the Coven had gone unchallenged for too long. It was time someone put an end to them once and for all.

"Show me where Edra hides," Sybbyl ordered the staff.

There was the slightest hesitation before she was shown a forest, but not just any wood. This one was different. This one was where the Hunters took cover.

With the knowledge of where both her enemies were located, Sybbyl made her way to Jarin. She sat across from him, lying the staff across her legs.

"No matter how you try, you will never get out of this Grove," she stated.

He opened his eyes, spearing her with blue irises so pale they could be mistaken for white. "You cannot keep me here forever."

"How is it that a man like you is not already bound to another?"

"What does it matter?"

She shrugged. "I know men. I have made it my business to study them. Your kind falls into three categories. Those who take what they want, those who do what they want, and those who are constantly duped."

"I suppose this is where you tell me which I am," he said wearily.

"You know which you are. You are a doer. You know what has to be done, and you see it through. You never waver from your goal. And you never quit."

He blinked slowly, utterly unimpressed by her words.

But that didn't faze her. Sybbyl held his gaze as she let the corners of her mouth lift slightly. "Every man can be manipulated. Even one such as you."

"Is that what you're attempting?" he asked with a raised brow, indicating his skepticism.

Sybbyl chuckled softly as she shook her head. "If I were manipulating you, you would never know."

"I doubt that."

"I want you. I let you know that from the beginning, but you see, my handsome warlock, you are merely a prize in all of this. With that face, body, and magic, you will create amazing babies."

As soon as the words had left her mouth, she knew Jarin's thoughts went to Helena. But she didn't care.

Sybbyl drew in a deep breath and released it. "There must be many more warlocks, but surely none as stunning as you. I offer you the chance to bear witness to a great change that will take over the entire world. It begins here. Now."

"I want no part of you," he said.

She lifted a shoulder in a shrug. "That really is too bad. Because I will find the Varroki. I already know where to look. You will be there to see me conquer them. Then, I will choose among the warlocks who will give me children. Those of the Coven will each have their choice of the warlocks, as well. The Varroki will be no more."

"Wishful thinking," Jarin replied.

Sybbyl glanced down at the staff. "Have no fear, I will

vanquish your people, but before I do that, I'll wipe out every Hunter and destroy Edra's hiding place." When he didn't immediately reply, she asked, barely hiding her glee, "What? No snappy retort?"

"What's the use? You will believe what you want."

"Perhaps. Edra and her Hunters have hidden from the Coven for many years. I give her props for having the courage and conviction to do what she's done. But her time has come to an end."

Jarin looked her over. "I suppose you want me to see that, as well?"

"Aye."

"Let me guess. We leave now?"

Sybbyl let the silence stretch before she let glee fill her face. "Not quite yet. First, I need to find Helena."

To Sybbyl's shock, Jarin smiled. It was cold, calculating. And deadly. "You cannot win against her."

"Of course, I can. I have you. She will never allow anything to happen to you."

His smile never wavered. "All this time, I've overestimated you. You are not nearly as cunning as I thought you were."

His words unsettled her. Sybbyl tried to shake them off, but she couldn't. It had been a very long time since any man had gotten under her skin. And Jarin had done the impossible —he'd made her doubt herself.

"I know what I have," she replied.

He quirked a blond brow. "The staff? It did little for you against Helena the first time. Now, she knows what she is. If you ever had a chance against her, it was before she knew she was the Living Heart."

"Nice try, but it won't work."

"Really?" Jarin jerked his chin to the staff. "You hold a bone of the First Witch. Helena has her blood, her magic."

"That has been diluted through the years," Sybbyl retorted, not bothering to hide her anger.

The warlock issued a slight shrug. "Has the magic in the bones weakened?"

"You want to make me question myself."

"I am merely pointing out facts," he said.

Sybbyl wasn't sure what to believe. He fought against the Coven, so he would say anything to put her off. And yet, Jarin's words held the ring of truth.

The bones of the First Witch were extremely powerful. A descendant would be just as strong.

If Helena had even a tenth of the First Witch's magic, then Sybbyl didn't stand a chance against her. Not in a head-to-head battle.

Then again, Sybbyl assumed that everything she knew of the First Witch—and that was very little—was fact. It was time for her to turn the tables on Jarin and manipulate him.

"Why do you so willingly fight for the First Witch?" she asked.

He gave a snort. "I fight against the Coven."

"Based on what you learned from your people. What if the Varroki are wrong?"

Jarin shook his head in disbelief. "That might have rung true, except I've seen for myself what the Coven does. I have seen them force witches to choose your path or death. I have seen the Coven kill women and children without blinking. I have seen the destruction that follows in the wake of any Coven witch."

"Not me," she said.

His flat look said he didn't believe her. "So, you have not killed innocents?"

"I did not say that. I said there was no destruction."

"Need I remind you what happened when you went after

the staff? You used magic to alter the battle in your favor. Not to mention the massacre at Bryce Castle."

She glanced up, shrugging in admission. "I'll admit, that was not my finest moment, but the staff was within reach, and I was going to have it."

"No matter who you had to kill?"

"No matter who."

He leaned forward, his eyes hard and unforgiving. "And that is why the Varroki fight the Coven. It is why we have always fought you."

"But what began it all?"

He sat back and looked away, a signal that he was tired of the conversation.

"What are you afraid of telling me?" she pressed. "That you have no idea why? That you follow this path simply because your people tell you to?"

His head snapped back to her. "I fight for the Varroki willingly, but I make my own decisions. I learned all about the Coven, aye. Then I saw for myself what you are, and I knew why there was a need for warriors like me to keep you in check."

"In check? Are you sure you did not mean to say wipe us out?"

"That is the goal, aye. We want you gone."

She studied him a moment before she smiled. "But that is not what you said. Your people believe there is a balance, that you cannot have good without evil." Sybbyl threw back her head and laughed. "Perfect."

"That was my people," he said. "I'm no longer fighting alone. There are Hunters and witches like Edra. There is Braith, Warden of the Blood Skull. And there is Helena."

As much as she hated it, Jarin had a point. Sybbyl's

laughter died, and her smile vanished. The Varroki might believe in balance, but the others wouldn't.

Especially Helena.

It was never more important than now for Sybbyl to take out Edra and her Hunters. Wiping them out would set everyone back and cement Sybbyl's rule over the Coven.

It would also remind everyone fighting her that she wouldn't hesitate to wipe out her enemies.

"This conversation has been very informative," she said and got to her feet. "But the time for talking is finished. Now, it's time for action."

29

It was strangely calm at the top of the tower. Malene and Armir stood, waiting as Helena made her way to them. There was little wind, allowing the smell of salt to hang heavy in the air.

She glanced up at the sky. It looked as if the clouds had stopped moving, as if they too were holding their breath at what was about to happen.

Helena wrapped her fingers around the edge of her cloak. The fur was soft, reminding her of Valdr. She stopped and looked over her shoulder. The wolf sat at the top of the steps. It was clear he wasn't thrilled about being left behind, but Helena wanted to keep him safe.

"I will be back," she told Valdr for the sixth time. "With Jarin."

At the mention of their master, Andi called out from overhead. It was anyone's guess if the falcon would remain behind.

Helena's gaze moved over the village until she found Jarin's family home. Bjorn was standing outside, looking in their direction. She wanted to wave to him, but he probably wouldn't see her.

She made her way to Armir and Malene. "Is there any other way of doing this?"

"Aye," Armir said with a flat tone. "You can walk there."

She shot him a look of irritation as Malene hid her grin. "I don't like being incapacitated. If there are witches near, then we will be in trouble, quick."

"We can only do what the magic allows," Malene said as she rubbed her hands together.

Armir drew in a breath as he looked at Malene then swung his gaze to Helena. "Do you remember the spell?"

"Aye." At least she hoped she did. Since she was the only one who knew where Jarin was, it was up to her to get them close to the Witch's Grove—but not too close—so they could surprise Sybbyl.

Malene turned her back to them and held out her hand. Armir held Helena's gaze for a long moment before he too put his back to her and linked his hand with Malene's before holding his other palm out to her. Helena licked her lips and turned to face Valdr as she grasped their hands. She held the wolf's gaze as the three of them stood in a triangle.

"You can do it," Armir whispered and squeezed her hand.

She could, but she wasn't looking forward to the effects such magic produced. Helena inhaled deeply and slowly released the breath. She pictured Jarin and began the spell.

The world rippled around her, then went calm. It heaved twice more, the undulations coming closer together as the spell lengthened. Then everything went silent.

No sounds of waves crashing, no gulls just...stillness.

Be brave.

She clung to the words, knowing Trea was with her.

Helena blinked. When she opened her eyes, she was in the midst of a forest with snow flurries drifting in the air.

Both Armir and Malene were bent over, sick from the magic. Helena's head felt dull, her eyesight going in and out of focus, and her hearing echoed like she was deep in a cave. Just when she thought she might not become ill, her stomach revolted.

She spun and rushed a few steps away as she emptied the pitiful contents of her stomach. It was a good thing she hadn't eaten anything in hours.

Helena braced a hand on the bark of a tree to hold herself up. She straightened, wiping her mouth with the back of her hand. She kept blinking her eyes, hoping her sight returned to normal soon.

"Here," Armir said as he handed her a waterskin.

She glanced at the commander to see his face still pale. A look at Malene showed the Lady of the Varroki still on her hands and knees.

"I'll see to her," Armir said breathlessly. He stumbled, making his way to the Lady. He fell to his knees beside her and gently pulled back her hair from her face.

Helena wished she would've thought to ask Malene if she knew that Armir was smitten with her. Though she had seen Malene gazing after the commander a few times, Helena found the Lady difficult to read.

Malene was welcoming and kind, but there was much she kept to herself. Not that Helena blamed her. If she were in Malene's position, she would probably do the same.

It was several minutes later before Helena felt well enough to stand without the assistance of the tree. She rinsed her mouth out twice with water before taking a few hesitant sips of the cool liquid. Just as before, it settled her stomach considerably.

She walked to Malene and Armir. He had managed to get Malene to sit, and the Lady was leaning heavily upon the commander, whose arm was wrapped protectively around her shoulders.

Helena looked between them and knew that each had feelings for the other. But did they know that? She suspected not, and she wondered why neither had said or done anything about it?

"It never gets any easier," Malene said.

Armir looked up at Helena and gave her a nod. "Well done, by the way."

She smiled, taking pleasure in his praise. Especially since it was her first time jumping from one place to another. Though, she would use the spell sparingly because of its effects.

While Armir helped Malene to her feet, Helena looked around the forest. The air felt heavy, oppressive. Danger was near, and that threat was Sybbyl.

"You brought us to the right place," Malene said as she adjusted her cloak and pulled up the hood.

Helena regretted leaving Jarin's staff at Blackglade, but something had told her she wouldn't need it. Besides, she wanted to make sure Sybbyl didn't get her hands on it because it was special to Jarin.

Helena's head turned to the left. The quiet of the afternoon made it feel as if they were secluded from the rest of the world. The ground was frozen, the air frigid. But neither daunted her. She blinked to dislodge a flake that had landed on her eyelash.

"This way," she told the others and began walking left.

Neither Armir or Malene questioned her. She wasn't comfortable with either of them being there. Malene was the leader of the Varroki, and Armir was just as vital to Blackglade, but neither would listen to her arguments the night before about remaining behind.

She led their little group deeper into the woods. Most Witch's Groves were known to witches, so they had a sanctuary to go to. But there were a few that were kept secret. Helena had never liked the Groves, possibly because they reminded her of the Coven.

Only twice had she been inside one. The first time to see what it held. The second when the Coven had captured her, and Leoma freed her.

"We're close," Malene said.

Helena felt it, as well. The magic. It breathed like it was alive, and in many ways, it was. Witches and warlocks brought it to life. They gave it shape, gave it purpose.

Ahead, the trees parted to form a path. She looked up at them, noting how their branches met overhead to create a canopy. Helena came to a halt.

"What is it?" Armir asked.

She turned to face them. "Seeing Blackglade made me realize a few things. Both of you are not just important to the Varroki, you two are also what holds them together. I know now why Jarin chose to be a warrior. I also understand why Trea went to such extremes to keep her power from her sisters."

Malene's brows drew together. "You're a Varroki. I think you know that. Which means, Blackglade is your home, as well."

Helena smiled, fighting back the lump of emotion. She knew that no amount of arguing would keep either of them from walking with her into the Witch's Grove.

And neither of them yet comprehended just how important they were to each other. They were one unit. One without the other simply...didn't work.

"I hope one day you can forgive me for this," she said.

Before Armir or Malene could respond, Helena lifted her

hand as purple coils shot from her palm along with a spell that suddenly came to her. The spirals wrapped around their heads, rendering both unconscious within moments.

Helena bent next to each one and placed her hand on their foreheads. She put another spell upon them that would hide them until they woke.

She straightened and turned around. Just thirty steps away was the entrance to the Witch's Grove. Every fiber of her being screamed at her to not go inside, but it was her destiny.

Straightening her shoulders and lifting her hood to cover her face, Helena started walking. She didn't slow, not even when she reached the invisible border of the Grove. She heard the whispers of the Gira before entering, but it was just a murmur compared to the booming voices once she was through the barrier.

Out of the corner of her eye, Helena spotted several Gira coming towards her. They halted after a few steps, hastily backing away.

The Gira didn't usually attack witches, but that didn't mean the nymphs feared them. They grabbed hold of anything that succumbed to their enticements. And, sometimes, they outright snatched people.

Helena's heart pounded like a deep drum with every step. More and more Gira appeared, stepping away from the trees to show themselves. Not a single one blocked her path or attempted to touch her. It looked almost as if...they were in awe of her.

Helena didn't stop to find out. If she had to fight the nymphs, she would, but her first priority was Sybbyl. The fact that there were so many Gira in the Grove made Helena uneasy. She couldn't remember ever hearing or seeing so many nymphs in one location before.

They tended to spread out since they, like many animals, were territorial. Yet that didn't seem to be an issue at present.

As Helena wound her way through the trees, she kept her head high. Unlike many Witch's Groves, this one didn't seem to have a path toward the center. It might be because it was so old, at least if the trees were any indication, but it also might mean that there were traps waiting for her.

After Helena made her way over the thick, burgeoning roots of an oak, she spotted the Grove through the limbs ahead. Helena tried not to get too near the trees, which became impossible the closer the trunks were to each other.

Her hand accidentally brushed against a Gira, who jerked back as if repelled. Helena glanced in the nymph's direction to find the Gira holding her arm as if wounded. The creature hastily fell to one knee as if in supplication.

Troubled by the sight, Helena kept walking. She breathed a sigh of relief when she reached the edge of the woods and saw Jarin sitting with his eyes closed.

Sybbyl stood not too far from him, stroking the staff. She still wore the crown and black gown, and the black paint over her eyes seemed to be a permanent addition.

Helena was surprised that the Gira hadn't alerted Sybbyl to Helena's presence, but she wasn't going to throw away such a chance. She steeled herself and stepped into the clearing.

Instantly, Sybbyl's head whipped to her. The hood of Helena's cloak hid her from the witch's view. She waited until Jarin's eyes had opened and landed on her. Then, she reached up and pushed back the hood.

Jarin's smile made her heart catch, but Helena was reminded of her conversation with Armir and kept her focus on Sybbyl. The witch's anger was palpable, which pleased Helena immensely.

"Why was I not informed?" Sybbyl bellowed to the Gira.

Helena unclasped her cloak and let it fall to her feet as she walked farther into the Grove. "You act as if you control the nymphs."

"I do. Just as I will control you." Her gaze dropped to Helena's stomach. "Or your child. I'm not choosy."

Helena grinned tightly. "It seems odd that not so long ago, I was terrified of the Coven. I dared not use my magic for food or warmth for fear of any of you locating me. I nearly died. And now, here I am."

"Oh, you still fear me," Sybbyl said as she lifted the staff and slammed it into the ground.

A shockwave of magic rolled over the ground like a wave. It knocked Jarin onto his back, and had the Gira scampering away. But Helena didn't move as she braced for the impact. Not before the magic reached her—and not after.

She recognized the feel of it. The same magic that was within her. Trea's magic.

"You're different," Sybbyl said, uncertainty in her voice.

Helena moved so that her back was to Jarin as she faced Sybbyl. "I discovered myself. I would like to thank you for that. If it weren't for you chasing me, I never would have accepted who I was."

"Do not get too attached. This freedom you think you found is about to be yanked away. By me," Sybbyl boasted.

Helena smiled as her fingers tingled with magic. "Prove it."

J arin couldn't stop smiling as he righted himself. He'd
known Helena would come. And her entrance had been
one that he would never forget. There had been no great
fanfare, no showy appearance.

Just a quiet arrival that shouted more than any flourish
ever could.

The fact that the Gira had not warned Sybbyl spoke
volumes. And not just to Jarin. There had been a moment of
shock, of utter dread that stole across Sybbyl's face, but she
quickly wiped it away.

What the witch hadn't mentioned was that she must have
put spells up so no one would get in without her knowing.
And yet, somehow, Helena had.

If there had ever been any doubt that Helena was the
Living Heart, it was now gone. Obliterated. Eradicated.

He knew that he was witnessing firsthand what would be
spoken about for years to come. Jarin wanted to help Helena,
to stand by her side against their enemy, but this wasn't his

fight. She had tried to tell him that by leaving, but he hadn't been able to accept it.

Now, he did.

There was something different about Helena. She looked more confident. As if she too had accepted who she was. That didn't bode well for Sybbyl. If Helena had gotten the upper hand before, Sybbyl didn't stand a chance now.

Helena's dare only solidified things.

Jarin leaned to the side to get a glimpse of Sybbyl. He couldn't see Helena's face, but he didn't need to. Everything he needed to know could be discerned from her stance and her voice.

She was ready for the battle. Ready and willing to end it all right then.

"Do you doubt I can?" Sybbyl asked as if the mere thought was enough to make her cringe.

Helena widened her stance. Jarin saw sparks ignite between her fingers as her magic coursed through her quickly. He had never seen such a thing, and it left him utterly awed.

"I doubt everything from you," Helena replied. "You are all words, Sybbyl."

Jarin slowly climbed to his feet and moved to the side so he could see both women. They were so focused on each other that they paid him no heed. Even the Gira didn't seem to care what he was about. The nymphs were crushed together, each vying to get a better look at the opposing witches.

He frowned as he looked at the Gira. They had recognized Helena for who she was, but would they follow her or Sybbyl if it came down to it?

He'd seen for himself what the Gira would do for Sybbyl. While he hadn't spent a lot of time in Witch's Groves, he didn't believe their capitulation was something that regularly occurred—if at all.

If it had to do with the First Witch, then surely Helena would gain their obeisance. But when it came to the Gira, no one could really know for sure.

Jarin had kept his distance from the creatures over the years, primarily because they were so unpredictable. Now, he wished he would have spent more time learning about them.

His attention returned to witches. Sybbyl had yet to reply to Helena's comment, but there was no denying the anger that contorted Sybbyl's face.

The black band across her eyes highlighted the fury in her gaze. "You made a mistake coming here. This is my territory."

Helena raised a brow as the wind lifted the ends of her fiery tresses. "Is it?"

When Sybbyl sent a gust of magic toward Helena, she calmly twisted as she leaned backward and watched it glide past her.

Helena straightened and smiled. "My turn."

She put her hands before her, one on top of the other, her gaze locked on Sybbyl. Between her palms were flashes of purple flames that grew as she pulled her hands apart.

Sybbyl took a step back, her trepidation evident in her features. Jarin didn't know if her reaction was one of fear or preparation, but he would wager it was the latter. He, himself, was impressed by the magic Helena exhibited. It was like nothing he had ever seen before.

He drank in the sight of his woman with attire that showed her beautiful body contrasted with her red hair and the purple of her magic. He'd known she was special. Now, he had proof.

"Give me the staff, now, and I will let you live," Helena offered.

Sybbyl laughed, the sound half mad. "You think I fear you?"

"I think you're smart enough to weigh your options."

"Oh, I know my options. I lead for once, and I won't give that up."

Helena pressed her lips together ruefully. "A pity."

No sooner had the words passed her lips than she loosed the flames from her hands. They twisted, spiraling and elongating as they spread out like dozens of fingers—straight at Sybbyl.

The witch dodged several before blocking them with her magic. But not before one coil wrapped around her wrist. Helena raised her hand and pulled back, tugging her magic to her.

Sybbyl was yanked forward. She gritted her teeth, her lips peeled back as she planted her feet then slammed the staff into the ground. The moment she did, Helena's magic unwrapped from her arm.

There were no more words after that. Jarin watched in fascination as the battle commenced. Only once before had he seen two sorcerers clash in such an epic way. This battle eclipsed any before it.

He could barely keep up with who used what spell because the witches were hurling them one after the other. The times Helena was unable to shield herself from the hit of magic, Jarin winced, feeling her pain as his own. Even when she didn't show it, he knew that it hurt her. The adrenaline pumped too quickly for her to feel it now, but she would later.

Jarin flexed his hand and was about to launch a spell to help shield Helena from the magic when a Gira near him turned her head to spear him with a look.

The nymph said nothing, but she didn't need to. Her silent warning was heard loud and clear. If Jarin interfered, then so would the Gira. Jarin had no choice but to remain a bystander no matter how difficult it was.

Helena got off several good jabs of magic. Then Sybbyl lunged forward with her blond hair flying around her, the staff pointed at Helena. His head whipped to Helena to find pain contorting her face before her head fell forward as she bent over.

"Block it," Jarin whispered, silently urging Helena to use her magic.

Jarin knew the agony was preventing her from thinking straight, which prolonged her pain and Sybbyl's advantage.

"Come on, Helena," Jarin murmured, his body tense with the urge to help her. "Block it."

Sybbyl walked toward Helena, keeping the magic directed at her. "I told you I'd defeat you."

Shock went through Jarin when Helena's head shifted toward him, and he glimpsed her face. Her gaze landed on him, and she gave him a quick grin. Then she flipped back her long, red locks and looked at Sybbyl.

Determination filled Helena's face. Her lips moved, forming one word. And just like that, Sybbyl's magic was blocked. Jarin was so happy, he wanted to shout, but he held it in. The battle was far from over.

Sybbyl looked Helena over as she righted the staff and braced the end against the earth. "Bravo. I honestly did not believe you would get out of that one."

"Sorry to disappoint you."

Jarin looked between the two women. Both were bloodied and bruised, but neither was admitting defeat. He had expected Helena to crush Sybbyl by now. Helena had the ability. Or he thought she did, but perhaps the Staff of the Eternal gave Sybbyl more power than he thought.

Sybbyl's chest heaved from the exertion of battle. "We could be here all day doing this."

"Your reign, the *Coven's* reign is over," Helena stated.

Sybbyl laughed and shook her head, her crown never wavering. "Not hardly, my dear. We're more powerful than ever before. Your one chance to stop me is now, and you cannot do it."

Jarin knew it was the wrong thing for Sybbyl to say the moment Helena's gaze sharpened. He sat back, a smile on his face as Helena's back straightened. In her, he saw the fearless, bold shieldmaidens of old. He saw the courageous, daring Celt females.

He saw a leader, someone who would stand against the Coven. Someone who would give others the courage to do so themselves.

Helena held out her arms to her sides, her palms facing Sybbyl as she spread her fingers. "I am light. I am darkness. I am the raven, the harbinger of all that is to pass. I hold the blood of the First. And I show the path of all who will come after me."

She blinked, pausing. "You had your chance to walk away. You should have taken my offer."

The ground erupted in purple flames around Helena. They quickly grew to lick as high as the trees. And Helena lowered her arms and stood in the midst of it all.

Every shot of magic Sybbyl used, every spell she uttered, didn't put a dent in the flames. Helena never lost her focus on the witch. No matter where Sybbyl moved, Helena's gaze was locked on her.

"You cannot win!" Sybbyl shouted and lifted the staff.

Helena didn't move, didn't even part her lips, but the flames suddenly raced toward Sybbyl. The witch tried to block them but was once more unsuccessful. She screamed in outrage as she backed into the forest.

The Gira quickly moved away from her, tripping over each other in their haste. Jarin lost sight of Sybbyl in the flames.

And just when he thought Helena had won for sure, he spotted the black smoke he knew all too well.

And then it was gone.

Jarin looked at Helena. She turned her head and met his gaze. Several heartbeats went by before she took a breath and the flames faded, disappearing back into the earth.

"She got away," Helena said.

Jarin ran a hand down his face and looked around, noticing that the Gira were also gone. "Aye, Sybbyl lives to fight another day. But you wounded her."

He glanced at the last place Sybbyl had been. The earth was scorched. He couldn't be sure if the witch was gone or not, but if Helena believed it, then he would, as well.

When he faced Helena once more, her hand was on her stomach. Jarin raced to her, gripping her by her arms. "Are you hurt?"

"I forgot about the child in the battle," she whispered, tears gathering. "Sybbyl's magic—"

Jarin pulled her close and held her tight. He closed his eyes when her arms wrapped around him. No matter how hard he tried, he couldn't think of anything that would ease her mind. Or his.

She hadn't been the only one to forget. Jarin hadn't thought once about the baby. He'd only been concerned with Helena remaining alive. What kind of father did that make him?

He pulled back and cupped her face, wiping a tear away with his thumb. "I knew you would find me."

She smiled and nodded. "Trea showed me how."

"Trea?" he asked with a frown.

"The First Witch."

"You know her name?"

Helena smiled as she sniffed. "It was Malene who told me."

"I cannot believe she or Armir would allow you to come on your own."

She wrinkled her nose and gave a little shrug. "They didn't. I just made sure they wouldn't follow me into the Grove."

"I suppose we need to find them."

"No need," Armir said as he and Malene stepped from the forest.

Helena whirled around and opened her mouth, but Malene held up a hand. "I know why you did it, and I admit, I would've done the same in your shoes."

Armir looked ready to spit. "Malene forgives more easily than I."

The Lady shot him a glare and made her way to Helena. She put her hand on Helena's belly, and a few moments later, she smiled. "Your child is fine."

Jarin thought his heart would erupt, he was so happy. For someone who'd never thought to have children of his own, he was elated to know that he would get to hold one in his arms soon.

"So," Armir said with his arms crossed over his chest. "Sybbyl managed to get away."

Helena frowned. "I should have known she would try something like that again."

Jarin shook his head as he looked at Helena. "You could not know such a thing."

"The Gira are gone, too," Helena added.

That definitely made Jarin uneasy. "I have never seen so many gathered in one place."

"How many were there?" Malene asked.

Helena said, "Hundreds."

Jarin scratched his chin as something kept nagging at the

back of his mind. "Sybbyl wanted to know where the Varroki were. She said that she would make them succumb to her."

Armir's arms dropped to his sides. "Does she know where Blackglade is?"

"I cannot be sure," Jarin admitted.

Malene set her chin. "Then we need to be ready in case she comes."

"What about the abbey?" Helena asked.

Jarin winced. "She mentioned the Hunters, as well."

They all looked at each other, fear and dread filling their gazes.

Helena held out her hands. "We have to go to them."

Jarin, Malene, and Armir took hold of each other without hesitation.

31

No matter what she did, Synne couldn't shake the unease that grew within her. There had been nothing more from the forest. It refused to offer up anything else to her. It acted as if it were either asleep or...dead.

She deftly climbed up a tree, something she had been doing since she was a small girl. For a long time, she had refused to even put on a dress, preferring pants. Edra and Radnar never forced her to wear something she didn't want.

At one time, Synne had wanted to cut her hair short, but Edra convinced her to hold off. Instead, the witch had put her hair in braids, keeping it off Synne's neck, which let her pretend she was a boy.

She grew out of that quickly, and Synne was thankful that Edra hadn't given into her whim. What Edra and Radnar—and every adult at the abbey—did was cultivate a place where each person could be whatever they wanted or needed to be. No one judged, no one criticized.

And everyone was accepted.

Witch or not, woman or not. Everyone was equal,

everyone pulled his or her own weight.

Synne hadn't understood how different the abbey was until the first time she went with Radnar and Ravyn to hunt witches. Ravyn was already a Hunter, but Synne was still in training.

She had been flabbergasted when she entered the village and saw how women were treated. Four days later, when she returned to the abbey, she was aware of the blessing it was that she had fallen into Edra's and Radnar's hands.

More and more of late, her thoughts had been about the past and the influence those at the abbey had on her. Synne knew that, out in the world, she would never be allowed to dress in breeches or learn to fight and defend herself as she did.

Her thoughts halted as the trees creaked as they swayed with the wind. It sounded loud in the quiet silence of winter. Synne removed her glove and placed her palm against the bark.

"Why have you gone quiet?" she asked. "Why are you no longer speaking to me?"

She slipped her hand into her glove once more and leaned back against the tree trunk. Her eyes hurt from lack of sleep. She blinked them several times and stifled a yawn, sleep calling to her. Feeling safe and comfortable, she gave in and decided it wouldn't hurt to rest for just a moment.

It seemed as though she had just shut her eyes when she was pulled into a vivid, horrible nightmare involving the Gira. Her eyes snapped open, but the terror of the dream lingered. Synne shuddered just thinking about the creatures. She detested them. Worse, she had a feeling that they were in the forest.

The problem was that the Gira looked like parts of the trees. A person could stand next to one, lean against one, and not know it unless and until the nymph made itself known.

She looked out over the forest. "You would tell me if the Gira were here, right? You would let me know somehow."

Synne doubted the bond Edra claimed she had with nature. The day before, she'd felt the connection, but today there was nothing. It was the first time she had felt such emptiness, and she didn't like it at all.

The black smoke dissipated, revealing the woods Sybbyl had seen in her mind. Her skin still simmered from the sting of Helena's purple fire, but the wound on her wrist bothered her the most. She would have to take care of that soon, but for now, there was something else she needed to see to.

It galled her that the witch had been so strong. Sybbyl had the Staff of the Eternal. It was supposed to give her ultimate power.

Instead, she once more had to flee Helena. If she had remained, she'd surely be dead. She needed to prove that she had the power to lead the Coven—and show Helena, Jarin, and everyone else that they should fear her.

Sybbyl might not be able to beat Helena right now, but she knew a way to ensure that she did. But the next bone of the First Witch would have to wait until after her revenge.

She smiled as her gaze roamed the trees lightly coated with snow. It was quiet and peaceful.

But not for long.

Sybbyl held out the staff and let her thoughts flow from her into the wood. She felt the magic burst from the tip of the staff and fall around her as she waited for it to reveal the direction to the Hunters' hideout.

A frown formed when nothing happened. Then she turned and saw the black dots of magic highlighting the trail. Sybbyl strode forward until the trail ended. She repeated the spell thrice more, coming ever closer to the Hunters and their witch allies.

On her fourth use of the magic, she watched as the black specks emphasized a hidden entrance. She had finally found Edra and her Hunters. And now, it was time to end it all.

Sybbyl lifted her foot to walk when she caught movement out of the corner of her eye. Her head turned to reveal a Gira. Then another and another and another.

A look showed that the nymphs had followed her from the Witch's Grove. They had chosen her over Helena. And that had to mean something. Her confidence renewed, she adjusted her grip on the staff.

"Are you ready, my beautiful nymphs?"

The chorus of whispers that answered only made her smile widen.

"Then let us wipe out all within," she stated as she walked toward the entrance.

Edra stopped mid-sentence when a chill went through her. She knew in that moment that the time she'd dreaded had finally come. She shoved at the Hunters she'd been talking with and shouted, "Prepare! We're under attack."

She lifted her skirts and ran down the corridor, ignoring the tall, arched windows that let in light, and the ornate decoration in the stones. She shouted for everyone to get into their places as she rushed to find Radnar.

So many times, they had practiced and refined this drill. And after so many years, she had begun to believe that the Coven would never find them.

She burst from the abbey and came to a stop in the courtyard. The battle was already underway. Gira flooded onto the grounds as a single figure slowly walked among them. Sybbyl.

There were shouts of battle, screams of the wounded and dying, and the hated whispers of the nymphs. Edra turned her head as she searched for her beloved. She found him with his sword out, already soiled with the blood of the Gira. Their gazes locked. Too much distance separated them for her to get to him, or he to her.

They had created something beautiful, something amazing within the walls of the abbey. And while they had never been blessed with a child of their own, they had raised so many more, watching them grow to become strong, confident adults who would continue what the two of them had begun.

Radnar smiled and placed his hand over his heart. Edra blinked through the emotion that clogged her throat and put her hand over hers, as well. And then he was fighting once more, his sword swinging at a Gira that came at him.

Edra swiped at her tears and hastily said a spell that she'd crafted years ago to protect and keep out any Hunters that weren't already at the abbey.

Then she turned her magic on Sybbyl.

A shiver ran down Synne's spine. She stilled, her hearing picking up something in the distance. She listened intently, waiting for the faint sound to come again.

When it finally did, she realized it was coming from the direction of the abbey. It could be anything. And the abbey was a fortress. It would take someone with intense magic to be able to break through the spells and wards surrounding the structure.

The sound came again, making her heart miss a beat

because she recognized the sound—a shout.

More importantly, it was a battle cry.

She hurriedly scampered down the tree so she could get to the abbey. If her people were in trouble, she was going to help. To her annoyance and frustration, her bow got hung up on a branch, something that hadn't happened in years.

"Nay," she whispered and struggled to free it.

Each time she thought it was loosened, it became caught again.

"Why?" she cried out to the trees. "I need to help my family."

Finally, her weapon was released, and she hurriedly made it to the ground. A step later, her foot slipped between two protruding roots. She yanked at her leg, trying to wedge her foot free, but it was well and truly stuck.

She slammed her hands against the ground as her leg gave out and she fell forward. "Let me go!"

There was no doubt in her mind that something or someone was holding her there. All she knew was that her family was in trouble, and she needed to do something.

The more she tried to get free, the more lodged her foot became. Her arms crumpled as she fell to her side and pressed her forehead against the frigid ground as the sounds of battle grew louder.

"Nay," she whispered.

Radnar released a war cry as he sliced off a Gira's head. He didn't think about how the beauty and peace of the abbey had been destroyed. All he focused on was killing the next thing that came at him.

He spotted Edra facing off against another witch that had

to be Sybbyl. Radnar wanted to knock the black crown from the woman's head, but no doubt Edra would beat him to it.

Radnar lifted his sword, the blade blocking magic from another Gira. It seemed that with each one he killed, a dozen more took its place. There were so many that their onslaught was overwhelming the knights and Hunters who tried to protect those who couldn't fight themselves.

Radnar peeled back his lips as he thrust his blade with both hands into the chest of the nymph before yanking his sword free and spinning to lop off the arm of another Gira.

Three other knights gathered close to him. They shifted so that their backs were to each other to form a circle as they slew nymph after nymph.

Radnar wanted to look at his wife. He needed to see that she was all right. It had been years since she had gone up against the Coven, but her magic was strong. She was strong. She would win.

She had to win.

He refused to allow himself to think of any other outcome. Edra was his life. Everything he had done had been for her.

When he and the knights still on their feet got the throng of Gira under control around them, Radnar gave a nod to the two remaining knights and glanced around. His heart clutched at the dead innocents, especially the children.

Fury swiftly rose up in him. He ran toward a Gira, who had a hold of a young boy. Radnar pulled out a dagger with his left hand and threw it, embedding the blade in the nymph's head and killing it instantly.

"Run," he bade the lad as he rushed past on his way to Edra.

There was a smile on his lips when he found that his wife was holding her own against Sybbyl. But the grin faded when Sybbyl turned the staff on Edra and sent her flying backwards.

32

The urgency, the dread that rushed through Helena made her push aside the nausea that had assaulted her upon their arrival. It was worse this time, having used the travel spell so soon after the first. Sweat beaded her skin, making it clammy, while her stomach roiled viciously.

But lives were at stake.

She wasn't the only one who stumbled, bent over, or reached to grab a tree. All of them had been to the abbey, so they knew the way. And they were all looking in the direction of the hidden entrance, waiting to hear or see either friend or enemy.

The more time that passed without a sign of either only alarmed her further.

Helena straightened and set out for the abbey. After a few steps, she began jogging, then full-out running. Something urged her to get to the abbey immediately.

Though she managed to get her group close to the abbey, it felt as if it was an eternity later before she finally reached the entrance. As soon as she went through it, she came to a halt, her hand to her mouth as she took in the horror.

"By all that's holy," Malene murmured as she came to a stop beside her.

Jarin and Armir walked around them down the steps, their faces growing grimmer by the moment. Helena didn't need to ask. She saw from the dead bodies on the stairs—both Gira and human—that the battle was long finished.

Helena looped her arm with Malene's as they slowly followed Jarin and Armir. Then they turned and got a view of the grounds and the abbey where more dead awaited them. The men were already walking among the dead, looking for survivors.

The silence was the first thing that Helena noticed. She swallowed. "It was so full of life when I was here a few days ago."

Helena released Malene and picked her way around and over the prone bodies. Tears clouded her vision when she saw the children. None of them asked who was responsible for the carnage. They knew it was Sybbyl.

As the four of them went their separate ways, searching for...anything, the hope and faith that Helena had once felt regarding being able to end Sybbyl diminished until the flame barely flickered.

Hunters, knights, and innocents were mixed with the Gira. But not one of the lifeless bodies was Sybbyl. Helena recognized the blacksmith, Berlaq, as well as a few of the Hunters and a knight that she'd met when she was there.

So far, she had yet to come across any ashes of witches or... Her thoughts halted when her gaze landed on Edra. Helena blinked, hoping that her eyes played tricks on her, but there was no denying who it was.

Helena went down on her knees beside the witch and

gently moved a thick strand of blond hair from Edra's face that was partially blackened like her clothes.

The witch was on her side, her arm reaching out. When Helena followed her hand and found it grasping Radnar's, who reached out to his wife, the tears fell unimpeded down her face. Even in death, the two were bound together.

"Why is she not ash?"

Helena looked up at the sound of Armir's voice and discovered that Jarin and Malene were also there. Jarin squatted beside her and took her hand in his.

"I held out such hope," Malene whispered, sorrow filling her voice.

Helena swallowed as Edra's cheek caved in, disintegrating. A moment later, the rest of her body became ash and floated upon the wind, leaving Radnar eternally reaching for her.

Grief and sadness gave way to rage. Helena got to her feet and looked around. "Did anyone here survive?"

"If they did, they're long gone," Jarin replied.

Armir's nostrils flared as he looked around. "There is nothing alive here other than us. The Gira even killed the animals."

Helena opened her mouth to speak when she saw movement near the entrance. She turned and spotted Synne. The Hunter let loose such a bellow of profound grief as she fell to her knees that it brought another wave of tears to Helena.

Jarin started toward the Hunter, who had an arrow notched and aimed at him in less than a heartbeat. He held up his hands and halted. "Synne. You know me."

"Why did you not stop this?" she demanded.

Helena moved around Malene and went to stand beside Jarin. She could barely look into the stricken face of the Hunter. "We just arrived."

"Why did you not stop this?" Synne yelled a second time.

"I—" Helena began.

But Malene put her hand on her arm as she walked past. "Because while we have magic, we cannot control things. Helena fought Sybbyl, and she was winning, but Sybbyl left."

"To come here," the Hunter stated as tears fell down her cheek.

Armir said, "Let us help you bury the dead."

Synne lowered the bow and returned the arrow to her quiver. Then she got to her feet and shook her head. "We burn them. Radnar once told me that was what he wanted, so he could be with Edra forever."

"Where do you want to do it?" Malene asked.

Synne sniffed and pointed to the area near the abbey itself. She then looped her bow over her arm and went to the body nearest her, but Jarin was at her side before she could lift it.

"Nay. Armir and I have this," he told her.

Synne stood numbly, looking so alone that it broke Helena's heart. She made her way to the Hunter and wrapped her arm around her. Helena blamed herself. Had she stopped Sybbyl, none of this would have happened.

The silent tears Synne cried as she watched Jarin and Armir gently gather the bodies and lay them out while Malene used magic to remove the Gira's corpses was something Helena would remember for the rest of her life.

With Armir, Jarin, and Malene's magic, it took little time for each person to have their own funeral pyre. Malene made Radnar's the tallest.

The five of them stood together as Malene held out a palm, the blue radiance shining brightly. The sun was gone, and twilight fell over the land. With one word from the Lady of the Varroki, the pyres caught flame simultaneously.

Helena was glad that she had gotten to meet Edra and

Radnar, that she had seen the incredible clan the two had created together. But she hated that they were gone.

The fires burned as night descended, and as the sparks flew into the sky, all she could think about was Radnar's ashes mingling with Edra's so the two could be together in death as they had been in life.

Jarin's fingers brushed against hers, and Helena didn't hesitate to clutch them. Her heart was heavy, the grief only outweighed by her anger.

Not one of them moved until the last of the fires had gone out just as dawn arrived. Synne was the first to walk away. She disappeared into the abbey and remained there.

"I know what you're thinking," Malene said.

Helena looked over to discover that Malene was talking to her. "What is that?"

"That it's your fault Sybbyl got away," Armir finished.

Jarin moved to stand before her. "It isn't, you know."

She forced a smile. "I appreciate what you all are trying to do, but the facts remain. Had I been able to finish Sybbyl, then everyone here would still be alive."

"Do not carry the weight of these dead," Armir cautioned. "They will grow too heavy. And everyone here knew the risks. Nobody more than Edra and Radnar."

When Jarin tugged at her hand, Helena let him lead her down the steps and across the open area where the knights used to train. They walked past the blacksmith's shop and armory, near the stable, and beyond the gardens to wander back into the woods.

He didn't stop until they reached the river. The moon reflecting off the water was a beautiful sight to behold. She looked over at Jarin's profile.

His head turned to her before he shifted to face her. Jarin

took her hands in his. "Are you thinking about going after Sybbyl?"

"Nay. Though, I will. My thoughts are centered on something—someone—much closer. You."

One side of his lips curved upward. "We have not had much of a chance to talk."

"That's true. So much has happened since the night we lay together. I know you have duties to see to, and I'm sure—"

She didn't get another word out as Jarin claimed her lips. The kiss began softly, but soon turned hungry, each trying to get closer to the other.

Helena moaned when his fingers tangled in her hair and he pulled her head back to kiss down her neck. Her body was on fire for his touch, to have him deep inside her once more.

When he lifted his head, his breathing was heavy. It took a great effort for her to open her eyes, but when she saw the hunger in his, it made her stomach flutter.

"I want you," he said. "I have craved your touch from the moment you opened those green eyes and saw me. I have no property and little coin, but I know what is in my heart. And it's you. I love you, Helena."

She put her hand on his cheek. "The only thing I want, the only thing I'll ever need is you. We will make our own home because that is what people do when they love each other."

His smile made her breath catch, but in the next instant, the hunger was back. He turned her, pressing her against a tree as their lips came together.

Their fingers fumbled with each other's clothing before Jarin let out a long curse. Helena laughed and made their clothes vanish. She didn't feel the cold, not with his hot body against hers.

His fingers caressed down her face as he searched her eyes. "Do you really want to be mine?"

"More than anything."

He carefully placed his hand on her stomach. "And we're going to have a bairn."

She blinked, the tears those of happiness this time. "Aye, my love."

"Blackglade will need us."

"Then that is where we shall go. It is where our child will be born. Then your father will be able to hold him or her."

Jarin stilled. "My father?"

"Armir took me to meet Bjorn. He is very proud of you. And...I saw the rune on the hearth. Family is everything."

A muscle tensed in his jaw, and his gaze intensified. He yanked Helena against him, kissing her deeply as he lifted her and turned. He went down on one knee, then the other before he sat back.

The feel of his arousal against her made her crazy for more. She rose up on her knees and reached between them to grasp his thick length. Then, she guided him to her body.

A low moan rumbled in his chest when she lowered herself, taking him, inch by inch, into her body. He bent her backward, causing her breasts to thrust out. His hot lips clamped around a pert nipple, causing her to cry out in pleasure as his tongue ran back and forth over it.

The horrors of the day and the chaos that awaited them were soon forgotten as they gave in to their love and desire, needing to feel alive. Needing to feel...pleasure.

Even with the bodies gone, the scar upon the abbey would never heal. Armir knew Sybbyl's next stop would be Blackglade. *If* she could find it.

Part of what had kept the Varroki safe was that they had remained out of the Coven's view. That had all changed now.

He stood in the corridor and looked out one of the broken windows to the courtyard below and the smoke still floating skyward from the pyres. So many dead. And it all could have been prevented.

Soft footsteps behind him pulled his attention. He knew without looking that it was Malene. He always knew where she was. Not from magic or because it was his responsibility, but because he was bound to her.

"You're thinking about this happening to us." She stopped just behind and to the side of him.

He turned to her. Her long, flaxen hair was in two braids, one hanging over each shoulder. She was so beautiful that it almost hurt to look at her.

His gaze lowered for a moment to the blue radiance

emanating from her palms. "Sybbyl sent everyone a message with her slaughter here. To us, that we are next. To the Hunters and all who oppose her, that they do not stand a chance against her. And to Helena, that she failed."

"But Helena did not fail. It was only because Sybbyl ran that she was not defeated," Malene argued.

"No matter how you look at it, Sybbyl still remains. Say she was fortunate in running. Say that Helena did not do enough. Either way, the outcome is the same."

Malene nodded solemnly. "Death. And it began here."

"We need to get back to Blackglade."

"Edra was a strong witch. She had more courage than others, and she opened her home to all who needed it. She knew better than most that the Coven would eventually find her."

Armir leaned his head to the side, popping his neck. "Her spells and wards were enough to keep most out, but they could not stand against the Staff of the Eternal."

Malene's gray eyes held his. "Can Blackglade?"

"Aye. We can, and we will."

Her chest rose as she drew in a deep breath. "And Jarin?"

Armir knew what she was asking. In fact, it had been on his mind ever since he realized that Jarin was in love with Helena. "You altered the laws concerning celibacy. I think you might need to change some other things, as well."

"We," she corrected. "I would like for you to help me."

The pleasure her request caused was like basking in the warm sun after a long winter. "Of course."

"Until then, I think every warrior needs to be aware of this new development, so they can take adequate precautions."

He frowned at her words. "You want to call them home?"

"Nay," she said with a quick shake of her head. "They need to remain out here. If for nothing else than to be our eyes and ears and alert us to the movements of Sybbyl and the rest of the Coven."

"And the Gira," he added.

Her lips twisted at the mention of the nymphs. "Aye. Jarin, however, is different. He will not leave Helena."

"Nor she him."

Malene walked to the window and stared out into the night. "Jarin will always be a warrior for the Varroki, but he is also the Living Heart's warrior. They are bound by their bodies, their souls, and by magic. No one can undo that."

There was something in her voice that made Armir pause. "You envy them."

"Aye, I do," she said, smiling as she looked at him over her shoulder.

"You can have that now."

Her smile faded as she lowered her gaze to the ground. After a moment, she lifted her eyes to him. "So can you."

There was nothing he could say that wouldn't reveal too much. So, Armir changed the subject. "What shall we do with Synne? She cannot remain here."

Malene turned and put her back against the wall. "She is not the only Hunter still alive. Leoma and Ravyn are still out there, and I am certain there are others, as well. We also found no sign of Asa, dead or alive."

"Someone needs to be here to tell the Hunters what happened."

Synne turned the corner, her chin held high. "I will do that."

Armir swung his head to the Hunter. He hadn't even known she was there, she'd been so quiet. "It isn't safe."

"Safe?" she asked, twisting her lips. "I did not become a Hunter to be safe. I became one to make sure others were. I will not stop now just because some witch came in and..."

Her voice trailed off. Armir watched her closely. Synne struggled with the violence that had occurred, but more because the people here had been her family. But she had steel in her backbone. She would survive.

And be tougher for it.

"Will Sybbyl go after Leoma and Braith?" Synne asked.

Armir exchanged a look with Malene before he shook his head. "She has already come up against Helena, who is the Living Heart, and barely survived. If Sybbyl hadn't run from their battle, she would be dead."

"Instead, she came here and destroyed my home and those I love," Synne growled.

"But she did not destroy you," Malene said as she took a few steps toward the Hunter. "Sybbyl will never be able to extinguish what Edra taught you and the other Hunters."

"Or what Radnar taught us," Synne added.

Armir bowed his head, sending her a soft smile. "Or Radnar."

"It's your turn to honor them," Malene said. "Take up the mantle of what Edra and Radnar began and continue it. You and every Hunter who survived."

Armir was impressed that Malene always seemed to know exactly what to say in any situation. "Every person that Edra and Radnar touched will carry on their legacy in some fashion. You get to decide what you do."

Synne squared her shoulders. "I am a Hunter."

"We can never replace anyone at the abbey, but we would be honored if you fought with the Varroki," Malene offered.

Armir wished he had thought to say that. "We all need to band together. Sybbyl wants to split us, to have us running and hiding. But that is not who we are."

"Nay," Synne replied, a ghost of a smile on her face. "It isn't." She licked her lips and looked around the abbey. "This was my home, and I shall miss it. But everyone has to leave home eventually."

Armir thought about his life. He had never left his family. They had left him. "Aye, they do."

"Then I am your Hunter," Synne told them.

Malene smiled brightly. "Do you know how many others are missing?"

Armir watched while the two walked away as they talked and planned. He could join them. He probably should. But his mind was on other things. Namely, preparing for Sybbyl's arrival at Blackglade.

It would happen. Nothing would keep Sybbyl from the Varroki. And Armir knew that Malene would be the first to go up against the witch. Malene was a force to be reckoned with, but she knew nothing about battle magic.

Everything she had done so far had come by chance or happenstance. That couldn't continue. She needed to learn more. Armir chided himself for not training her in battle magic over the past few years.

He'd known in his gut that things were changing. He'd known it and ignored it, hoping that he was wrong. The truth lay before him now in all its ghastly anguish.

Malene was the one foretold, the Lady that would change the Varroki. Of that, he was sure. But for her to continue, she had to survive. No matter what he told her, she would never agree to hide from Sybbyl.

It wasn't Malene's way. She was too resolute to do anything but what was right.

He couldn't lose her, though. The Varroki couldn't lose her.

He squeezed his eyes closed for several moments. When he opened them, he saw a form out of the corner of his eye. Malene.

"Your face is normally unreadable," she said as she came to stand before him. "You keep so much from me. I do not know if it is because you don't believe I can handle it, or if you think it is your duty. But...the emotions I just saw showed me a glimpse of the things you keep to yourself."

Armir should have known to wait until he was sure he was alone to let such things show. He'd believed that Malene was with Synne, and that had been his undoing.

Malene swallowed and glanced at his chest before meeting his gaze again. "You believe we will fail."

"I think we need to prepare for every eventuality."

"But you fear I'll fail the Varroki."

He gave a rueful shake of his head. "It is I who have failed you."

"How?" she asked with a frown of disbelief. "You are always there for me. Always."

"I could not teach you how to control the radiance," he said. "And I grew lax. All this time, I should have been teaching you battle magic. You were not born with power, so you cannot know how to fully use it."

There was defiance in her gray eyes when she said, "I learned magic." She held up her hands, showing the blue light. "This is magic."

"And it mostly controls you."

She slowly lowered her arms to her sides. "I admit, you have a point. But it's not too late. Teach me what I need to know."

"Once we are back in Blackglade."

Malene sighed. "Aye. We need to return immediately, but I wanted to talk to Jarin and Helena first."

"Then we find them."

Armir turned on his heel and strode down the hall until he came to the door. He'd seen the couple disappear somewhere near the river earlier and headed in that direction. Malene stayed by his side, lost in her own thoughts.

As they neared, Armir released a whistle that Jarin would recognize, announcing their arrival.

"Come," Jarin said a moment later.

Armir found Jarin leaning back against a tree with Helena nestled between his legs, her back to his chest as Jarin's arms held her. They were both dressed, but by their flushed faces, they had been making love.

"Sorry to disturb," Malene said.

Helena got to her feet. "Not at all. We should not have stayed out here so long."

"You are going back," Jarin guessed as he stood.

Armir nodded. "We need to prepare."

"That would be wise. What do you want me to do?" Helena asked.

Armir was surprised by the question. And by Malene's wide eyes, so was she.

Malene glanced Armir's way before she said, "You are the Living Heart. You get to decide."

"I want to end Sybbyl. Twice, she slipped through my fingers," Helena said, her voice going rough with emotion.

Jarin linked his fingers with hers, which instantly calmed her. "What she means is that Sybbyl will come for Blackglade, and we both want to be there to defend the city."

Armir ran a hand over his jaw. "We all want a piece of Sybbyl. I understand your frustration, Helena, and I think I speak for Malene when I say we would welcome your help and love for you to join us."

"Most definitely," Malene added.

One side of Jarin's mouth lifted in a grin. "Then it's settled."

Helena hesitated and looked toward the abbey. "What of Synne and the others?"

"Synne and I have spoken," Malene said. "She will leave a message for any Hunter who returns while she goes to Leoma and Braith."

Jarin flattened his lips as he shrugged. "Braith is the Warden of the Blood Skull. I doubt Sybbyl will attack him anytime soon. It makes sense for the Hunters to gather there."

"They might assemble there, but Synne has joined us," Armir said.

Helena smiled. "I'm not surprised. I think the others will, as well. They will want revenge for this attack."

"Home, then?" Malene asked and held out her hand.

Armir slid his fingers into hers. "Home."

Returning to Blackglade made Helena realize just what was at stake. For everyone. For so long, those like Edra and Radnar had stood against the Coven, not knowing about the Varroki.

Generations of Varroki had lived and died, secretly fighting against the Coven. Now, their secret was out.

The sickness from their jumping back to Blackglade lasted far longer than Helena would have liked, but she endured it. Unfortunately, she was the last one to recover. Jarin had to carry her from the top of the tower to Malene's quarters because a fierce storm raged.

Helena changed into dry clothes then hurriedly sat down because of the nausea. Malene paid her little heed as she pulled book after book from the shelves, leafing through them. Some she returned, others were placed open-faced on the table.

Helena had no idea what Malene was doing, but she also didn't ask. A short time later, the men returned and shook off the rain. Helena leaned her head against Jarin's shoulder when he sat beside her.

"Everything is done," Armir said to Malene.

The Lady set down the book she had been perusing and smiled. "Good."

"Are you sure?" Jarin asked.

Helena frowned as she looked around at the other three. "What is going on?"

"I have secured chambers for you in the tower," Malene stated.

"Only those with the highest honors live here," Jarin explained, a smile upon his lips.

Malene rolled her eyes. "I get to decide who lives in my tower."

"And who does live here?" Helena asked.

Armir nodded to Malene. "The Lady, of course. And I have a chamber."

Helena's lips parted as she swung her gaze to Malene. "I...thank you."

"You are the Living Heart, who happens to be carrying the child of our best warrior. Of course, you live in the tower," Malene replied with a smile.

Armir grinned, the corners of his pale green eyes crinkling. "I could not agree more."

"Would you like to see?" Jarin asked.

Helena sat up. "Very much."

Her hand was secure in Jarin's as they walked outside. The rain had tapered off to a light drizzle. Still, by the time they reached the lower section of the tower, her hair was soaked.

As soon as she entered, Helena smiled at the sight of Valdr reclining by a roaring fire, and Andi sitting on a perch near the window. Jarin's staff was leaning against a wall.

Helena's gaze scanned the cozy table and chairs before the fire. She hurried into another room and found it empty. The third room was the bedchamber, with a large bed waiting for her.

She looked over her shoulder at Jarin, who stood leaning against the doorframe with his arms crossed and a huge smile on his face. He dropped his arms as he pushed away from the door and made his way to her.

"What do you think?" he asked.

Helena could only shake her head in amazement. "It is magnificent."

"It is a huge honor that you are here."

Her smile died as she cocked a brow. "We."

Jarin ducked his head and shook it. "It is going to take some getting used to. I have spent too many years on my own."

"Would you rather return to that?"

His face creased with irritation as he yanked her to him, his arms holding her firmly against his hard body. "I will live anywhere as long as you are by my side. I thought I made that clear a few hours ago. Perhaps I should show you once more."

"Hmm," she said and glanced at the bed. "I think that might be wise."

They shared a smile. Then Jarin smoothed his hands down either side of her face. "I will stand with you in the most violent of storms. I will stand with you to face the deadliest of foes. I will stand with you in the calmest ocean. Because you are in my heart."

She placed her hands on his chest and gazed into his pale blue eyes. "We are bound in this life and the next. For however many times we walk this Earth, we will search for the other, never settled until we are united. Because you are in my heart."

He bent his knees and tightened his arms around her, lifting her as he straightened and walked to the bed. There were no more words. None were needed.

She had found her destiny as the Living Heart, but more importantly, she had found her reason for being—Jarin. With his love, she could do anything. And the next time she faced off against Sybbyl, she *would* defeat the witch.

But that thought was for later. Now was for the present and the man who'd saved her, the man she loved beyond all reason.

The warrior who would always stand by her side.

Sybbyl couldn't stop smiling. It had felt wonderful to find the Hunters and watch as the Gira wiped them out. But nothing compared to killing Edra and Radnar.

She had wanted to remain to await any other Hunter who might arrive. Or even Jarin and Helena. No doubt they had figured out what she planned to do. Oh, if only she could have seen their faces. But it was enough to imagine the outrage and anger. The defeat.

Despite wanting to stay at the abbey, Scotland was calling her. The next bone of the First Witch, as well as the Varroki's stronghold was there, waiting to be found.

Sybbyl used the travel spell again. She had lost track of how many times she had used it over the last couple of days. All her life, she had been warned by the elders not to use it because of the side effects if she didn't know how to properly redirect it.

Having the staff made everything easier. The bone within absorbed all the backlash of the magic, allowing her to do whatever she wanted.

Her eyes lowered to the injury on her wrist from Helena's

attack. No amount of her magic had healed it. She'd used every healing spell she knew, but it had no effect. The wound on her neck from her first encounter with Helena as the Living Heart still stung, but it wasn't nearly as deep as the one on her wrist.

Sybbyl ignored both. They would heal, eventually. She had the staff, after all, and once she had the second bone, she would be unstoppable. She would be able to heal herself if the wounds hadn't already mended by then.

She looked over her shoulder at Hadrian's Wall. Scotland was going to be a lot of fun. Sybbyl smiled as she focused her magic on the staff and asked it where the next bone was.

Synne rode through the gates of Braith's keep, her heart heavy with the news she needed to share with him and Leoma. When she reached the steps and dismounted, she looked up to find the couple at the door.

Leoma's smile faltered after she looked at Synne. "Tell us what happened?"

Braith let loose a whistle, and the gates were closed as guards took up sentry. Someone even came and took her horse. Synne inhaled a breath and took a step toward Leoma.

In a heartbeat, the Hunter was before her, her arms wrapping around Synne. Synne didn't think she had any more tears to shed, but they spilled down her cheeks.

It was several moments before Synne could speak. Finally, she leaned back and looked between Leoma and Braith. "Sybbyl attacked the abbey with hundreds of Gira. Only a few Hunters were out on a mission. The others on patrol must have rushed to the abbey when the battle began."

"Thank goodness you like to be the farthest away," Leoma

said as she wiped at her tears. "Otherwise, you'd be gone, as well. Did Edra send you?"

"E—" Synne had to swallow before she could start again. "Edra and Radnar are gone."

"Bloody hell," Braith murmured as he wrapped an arm around Leoma and dragged her against him.

Synne looked away, fighting more tears. When she had herself under control, she met Braith's eyes. "There is much I need to tell both of you involving the Varroki, Jarin, and the Living Heart."

"Living Heart?" Leoma asked, sniffing.

Synne nodded. "Helena is the Living Heart, a descendant of the First Witch. She and Sybbyl fought, and Helena was winning, but Sybbyl ran away."

"And went straight for the abbey," Braith guessed.

Synne nodded. "We've been preparing for the day when we would face off against the Coven. That day is here."

"Then we prepare," Leoma said.

Braith gave a nod, his indigo eyes flashing with revenge. "Aye."

"I was hoping this could be a new base for the Hunters. I've left a message for any who return to the abbey to make their way here," Synne explained.

"Perfect. Come," Leoma said and took her hand. "We will plan, but first, we will grieve."

COMING SOON

Look for the next Kindred book
EVERNIGHT
Summer of 2019

THIEVES BY LEXI BLAKE

Excerpt from THIEVES by Lexi Blake

I'm pleased to give you an excerpt from my friend and fellow author, Lexi Blake. Sit back and read a sample of this Urban Fantasy!

THIEVES

AN URBAN FANTASY SERIES BY
LEXI BLAKE

"Author Lexi Blake has created a supernatural world filled with surprises and a book that I couldn't put down once I started reading it."
—Maven, *The Talent Cave Reviews*

"I truly love that Lexi took vampires and made them her own."
—KC Lu, *Guilty Pleasures Book Reviews*

Stealing mystical and arcane artifacts is a dangerous business, especially for a human, but Zoey Wharton is an exceptional thief. The trick to staying alive is having friends in all the wrong places. With a vampire, a werewolf, and a witch on the payroll, Zoey takes the sorts of jobs no one else can perform—tracking down ancient artifacts filled with unthinkable magic power, while trying to stay one step ahead of monsters, demons, angels, and a Vampire Council with her in their crosshairs.

If only her love life could be as simple. Zoey and Daniel Donovan were childhood sweethearts until a violent car crash took his life. When Daniel returned from the grave as a vampire, his only interest in Zoey was in keeping her safely apart from the secrets of his dark world. Five years later, Zoey encounters Devinshea Quinn, an earthbound Faery prince who sweeps her off her feet. He could show her everything the supernatural world has to offer, but Daniel is still in her heart.

As their adventures in acquisition continue, Zoey will have to find a way to bring together the two men she loves or else none of them may survive the forces that have aligned against her.

Books in the Thieves series:
Steal the Light
Steal the Day
Steal the Moon
Steal the Sun
Steal the Night
Ripper
Addict
Sleeper
Outcast, *Coming 2018*

"Vampires and faeries and werewolves, oh my!" the demon said with a smile of great pleasure spreading across his face.

He was in human form. He appeared to be a tall gentleman with lanky grace and a designer wardrobe. He wore an immaculately cut three-piece suit and the vibrant blue tie stood out.

"You run with interesting company, little human." The demon's accent was crisp and British. I wondered briefly if demons had nationalities. Halfer had a bland Midwestern accent.

"Did Halfer send you?" I tried to sound more blasé than I felt. I felt like screaming and running away, but I knew it wouldn't do me any good. The backpack I was carrying suddenly seemed heavier than before.

"Are you talking about Brix? He's going by Halfer? That's so obvious." The demon rolled his eyes. "Not at all. He would be perfectly perplexed to discover I showed up, which is, of course, the point. Did you enjoy the trio I sent to you at the club? Brix was pissed that I tried to take you. I wasn't going to hurt you.

Much. I only wanted to ask a few questions. Luckily, he's easily led. He thinks he caught the culprit. For a doubt demon, he is really sure of himself. I like to think of it as his tragic flaw."

"Why would you fight another demon?" Dev asked. "Shouldn't you be on the same side?"

The demon laughed. "Oh, yes, the Hell plane is a magical place of demonic harmony where we all hold hands and shit rainbows. We're at war. Always. As for Brix and myself, you could say we're auditioning for the same part, and I've decided to play a little rough."

"What exactly are you looking for?" Don't say the box, don't say the box, was the mantra going through my head.

"Dear child, I'm looking for the box." He dashed my every hope. "Please call me...well, I'm certainly not going to give you my real name. I don't want to get summoned. Let's go with Stewart. It fits this meat I'm walking about in."

There was a moment of silence as my stomach churned at the thought.

"You're in a human being?" Dev's voice shook ever so slightly.

I looked at Daniel in the hopes that he would tell me this Stewart thing was lying. The only demon we'd dealt with up until now had been able to change form at will. Daniel frowned and nodded, indicating that everything he sensed was indeed human.

Stewart rolled someone else's brown eyes and sighed. "You don't have to sound so disappointed. Not all of us can do that thing Brix does. It's impressive, but do you understand the kind of will it takes to completely dominate a human? Even now I can hear this miserable piece of meat screaming in our head. It's distracting, but I persevere. And I can do things Brix can't even think about."

Neil growled at the demon.

"Now that's just rude." The demon gave him a coquettish frown. "And here I've tried to be so pleasant. Vampire, call off your dog if you want him to live. Don't think I won't do it because the truth of the matter is I'm really more of a cat person."

"Neil, you should change now," Daniel ordered.

There was that rush of power that always filled the room when Neil changed forms and then he was back to his human body and in all his glory. One minute he was a beautiful wolf, and the next he was a gorgeous man. Neil was utterly lovely. He was smaller than Daniel and Dev, but perfectly formed. His hair had changed back to his normal blond and it curled over his ears.

The demon stopped, his eyes widening, and I would have sworn there was a hint of drool. "Goodness, and by goodness I mean badness. I take back what I said about cats. You look scrumptious, puppy."

Neil shrugged but gave no obvious emotion. "I get that a lot." He picked up his clothes from the floor as I turned my head, trying not to blush. I was never going to get used to random nakedness.

"Please don't. Not on my account." The demon practically purred like the cats he purported to love.

Neil laughed, though it held no humor, and I turned again as he was pulling his white dress shirt on. He left it and the top button of his pants open for effect, showing off his perfectly cut chest. He smiled his best male model smile. "It's not on your account, Stewart. It's totally on hers."

The demon gave me a *tsk tsk* sound. "Humans and their odd morality. Here you are, little girl, stealing an important thing from these seemingly pleasant faery creatures, but god forbid you see a very lovely penis. I have no comprehension of your people."

"Right back at ya, buddy." I started to slowly shuffle my way backward as the demon seemed to be closing in on me.

Stewart stopped his stalking of me long enough to look at Daniel and Dev. "And the two of you are panting after her? Someone is going to have to explain that to me. At least I can somewhat understand the vampire. She has that special blood you crave. She can make you strong. But you, faery, explain the fascination the human girl holds. I can see she's vaguely attractive, but she's certainly not in your league. Yet you fear for her. Even now I can feel your anxiety for her. You hope that I don't break her. You and the vampire would exchange your lives for her pathetic human one. It doesn't seem like a fair trade to me." He looked between the men and then suddenly turned to Neil, frowning. "Not you, too, puppy. I thought better of you."

"In a heartbeat." Neil crossed his arms over his muscled chest. "She's my friend. I'll do what I need to do."

Stewart looked back at Dev as though waiting for an answer.

"I haven't slept with her yet," Dev said bluntly.

I shot Dev the dirtiest look I had in my repertoire. He shrugged and smiled sheepishly. I forgave him because I knew what he was doing. He was trying not to give the demon any emotion. It was already apparent this Stewart was an empath. He thrived on emotion, the nasty kind. We needed to stay as unemotional as possible, or he could use it against us. The menace was heavy in the air. All it would take was for one of us to panic and he would have us.

And my panic was only inches from the surface.

"And she's the vampire's whole world," the demon said quietly as though he truly pitied Daniel. He studied Daniel for a moment. "But she doesn't give you what you need, does she? You're Vampire. She is obviously a companion. I can barely look at her, she's so bright. It should be easy, but nothing is easy for you, is it? Everyone on the Hell plane is concerned with you, Mr. Donovan. You're different, and different in the vampire world is bad. You could say you're the talk of the town. So when I found out you happened to be involved with Brix, well, you understand I had to learn what was going on. And I had to find out why he wanted that box."

"Do you know what it does?" The longer I could keep him talking, the more time Daniel had to recover from being shot forty times. I glanced at him, waiting for some sign of what he wanted me to do. I planned the heists. Daniel got us out of hot water.

Stewart never took his eyes off Neil. "Not a clue. I only know that if he wants it, I have to keep it from him. That really won't do."

Dev raised his pistol and tried to fire. Stewart turned to him, and with a simple flick of his wrist, the pistol flew across the room. Dev looked down at his empty hand dumbly and then back to the demon. The demon smiled before flicking his wrist a second, more decisive time. This time it was Dev who flew across the room. He hit the far wall face first and slid down.

I tried to run. I tried to get to him. I needed to make sure he was all right, but Stewart was standing before me with one hand held out, and I found that movement was impossible. I couldn't get a single muscle to comply. My feet felt nailed to the floor, my hands at my sides. I had to concentrate in order to breathe.

"Oh, are you stuck, dear? How much farther should I go? I could stop your lungs or your heart." He turned to Daniel, a smug smile on his face. "You see, vampire. I am strong. I do what it takes to be strong. I don't let insignificant things like a conscience keep me weak. You should have taken her whether she wanted to be taken or not. You are Vampire. She is chattel."

I glanced at Daniel, who stood staring at the demon with no emotion at all in his eyes. He was relaxed and still in a way only a vampire can be. If I hadn't known better, I would have thought he was ignoring all that went on around him.

Neil helped Dev up. He stood on shaky limbs, a smear of blood on his face. I'd led everyone into this. They all depended on me, and I couldn't move my feet.

"Now, I will have that object on your back, bitch," the demon said with a snarl that went against his gentlemanly persona. "After that, I will kill you, and there is nothing your weak-ass vampire can do about it."

My heart seized, and I worried he'd decided to stop it. He started to come toward me when Daniel moved. I didn't so much see him move as felt the effect after he was done. One moment Stewart was coming toward me with a look of inexplicable evil on his face, and the next Daniel was behind him, turning his neck in a way the human neck doesn't turn. There was a horrific crack, and the demon slid to the tile, his borrowed body limp.

"Even weak ass, I'm still faster than you."

THANK YOU!

Thank you for reading **EVERBOUND**. I hope you enjoyed it!

If you liked this book — or any of my other releases — please consider rating the book at the online retailer of your choice. Your ratings and reviews help other readers find new favorites, and of course there is no better or more appreciated support for an author than word of mouth recommendations from happy readers. Thanks again for your interest in my books!

Donna Grant
www.DonnaGrant.com
www.MotherofDragonsBooks.com

NEVER MISS A NEW BOOK

FROM DONNA GRANT!

Sign up for Donna's newsletter!
http://eepurl.com/bRI9nL

Be the first to get notified of new releases and be eligible for special subscribers-only exclusive content and giveaways.
Sign up today!

ABOUT THE AUTHOR

New York Times and *USA Today* bestselling author Donna Grant has been praised for her "totally addictive" and "unique and sensual" stories. She's written more than eighty novels spanning multiple genres of romance including the bestselling Dark King stories, *Dark Craving*, *Night's Awakening*, and *Dawn's Desire*. Her acclaimed series, Dark Warriors, feature a thrilling combination of Druids, primeval gods, and immortal Highlanders who are dark, dangerous, and irresistible. She lives with two children, a dog, and three cats in Texas.

Connect with Donna online:
www.DonnaGrant.com
www.MotherofDragonsBooks.com

www.facebook.com/AuthorDonnaGrant
www.twitter.com/donna_grant
www.goodreads.com/donna_grant
www.instagram.com/dgauthor
www.pinterest.com/donnagrant1

CPSIA information can be obtained
at www.ICGtesting.com
Printed in the USA
BVHW071955181118
533069BV00001B/1/P